Dirty Linen

Also by Nicholas Kilmer

Poetry (Verse Translation)
Poems of Pierre de Ronsard
Francis Petrarch: Songs and Sonnets from Laura's Lifetime
Dante's Comedy: The Inferno

Fiction (Art Mystery)
Harmony in Flesh and Black
Man with a Squirrel
O Sacred Head
Lazarus, Arise

Art (Biography/Art History)
Thomas Buford Meteyard
Intimate Light: The Paintings of Frederick Frieseke

Travel Memoir
A Place in Normandy

Dirty Linen

Nicholas Kilmer

Poisoned Pen Press

Poisoned Pen Press
6962 E. First Ave. Ste 103
Scottsdale, AZ 85251
www.poisonedpenpress.com
info@poisonedpenpress.com

Printed in the United States of America

For Julia
(from a secret admirer)

Acknowledgments

In the following story, fictional people, who the author pretends are alive, speculate on the lives and actions of real people who are dead. The story is fiction, but the author (like his characters) has relied on the advice, and on the research, of many. Footnotes would confuse the tale and twist it away from its fictional nature, as well as further complicate matters by seeming (falsely) to authenticate the story's central thesis, that a crime committed in 1858 did not, in fact, take place. Unfortunately, my story cannot correct the crime.

This book could not have been imagined, or written, without the assistance of Mathias Spiegel, Robert Humphreville, David Robertson, Alexander Finberg, Walter Thornbury, John Walker, Jack Lindsay, Andrew Wilton, Martin Butlin, Mollie Luther, Ian Warrell, Mary Lutyens, Marion Lochhead, Frederick Kirchhoff, William R. Crout, J. N. P. Watson, Wolfgang Kemp, Kenelm Foss, C. J. Holmes, Gerald Wilkinson, Dinah Birch, Diana Hirsh, and others.

Direct quotations from historical personages are presented in italics in the text.

Chapter 1

Fred's scalp blazed between the bristles of dark hair. There was no shade where he stood to the rear of the audience seated on wooden folding chairs. Because of last-minute trouble with the tent, the closest cover was three hundred feet away, under the row of maples that marked the edge of the field. The field itself throbbed, with heat, and with the impending conflict. They'd attracted a good crowd on short notice, pulling in this mix of professional dealers, wealthy locals, and gawkers from as far away as Boston and Providence, and making it feel like a party. Many in the audience wore straw hats against the gorgeous weather. Now and again the ocean breeze got under the rim of a hat, and everyone grabbed, making a wave of festive motion.

Heckie White, who'd been prospecting the crockery, slid to a stop beside Fred and muttered in his ear, "Jesus, Fred, what's here for you? What masterpieces haven't I noticed?" Heckie was mostly glass, though he'd also pick up a rug or the odd piece of furniture sometimes.

"I'm here for the porno. Meanwhile, what's wrong with the view?" Fred said, gesturing across the field of battle. It had been mown right to the edge of the bluff, beyond which a bright sea winked against the annoyance of hundreds of thousands of dollars' worth of skidding sailboats making tracks for Cuttyhunk or the Elizabeth Islands or, beyond them, Martha's Vineyard. Runnymede House, three fields and a small woods away, was invisible from here. They were less than two hours south of Boston, an easy pleasure cruise from Newport and the islands, and within spitting distance of the lotuslands of Nonquitt and Little Compton.

A young flunky made his way from the auctioneer's vans, passing through ganged furniture and the folding tables that displayed the objects destined to go under the hammer. He coughed a flunky cough into the mike until the crowd got quiet, then remarked lamely, "Testing one, two, and like that."

Fred glanced toward the vans, where Alphonse Bird was separating his linebacker's worth of bulk from the huddle of his runners, next to the folding table where a line of women waited to man the telephones, and to record sales. Heckie White scratched his armpits through the straps of his yellow tanktop. Below that he wore khaki shorts. "They're all dressed up! Have you noticed, Fred, as soon as New Englanders get rich, they think they're English?" Heckie asked, running his eyes across the crowd.

A number of pros were here, but the majority of the audience was civilians, drawn in by the scent of wealth and scandal, because the sale was associated with Runnymede House, on exclusive Cobb Point Preserve. There'd be dancing later, and drinking, and a picnic for the social set. As Heckie noted, most of the civilians had dressed for an afternoon wedding, or the races at Ascot. The crowd plunged into a lurid hush when a gray Daimler drove onto the field and stopped at the head of the audience. Its uniformed driver came around to open the rear door for a woman whose startling athletic youth, beauty, and blondness were not at all concealed, as she emerged, by the chic short-skirted black suit she wore, and the black veil.

"The grieving widow—not!" Heckie said. "Imagine, Fred! I can't. I'm too much of a gentleman. The old boy died in the saddle, it is said. Humped himself to death. Oh, Lordy, Lordy, and who wouldn't!" A sigh of lustful sympathy rippled the crowd as the widow sat. Things should get started now.

Fred had been catching furtive glances from persons in the trade. There was no way he could not stick out. Anyone who cared knew that he was here to act for Clayton Reed, and anyone who knew that much understood that whatever Reed wanted in this sale, it was good. Therefore, whatever he was after, it was also very well concealed.

He'd stayed out of sight until, among the pros remaining for the sale, nobody was left who was exclusively interested in works of art. Those folks had come, looked, and departed. But eight of the furniture and antiques dealers knew paintings well and could risk big money on them. And those who had left, if they'd spotted what Clayton had, might still be planning to operate from deep cover, by phone.

Bird, the auctioneer, was aware of Fred's continuing presence in the back row. He also must wonder what he had for sale that was worth Clay Reed's attention. Wherever Fred showed interest, Bird would find a way to tip off one of his claque. Bird, a small-timer from the South Shore, based in Scituate, knew how to milk a sale. He had been known to handle objects of significance, and he understood the business well enough to get good value even from an object he failed to understand. Although their collusion kept his hammer prices down, he did both open and undercover business with a fast cash crowd, the South Shore pool of runners and dealers, whose members, Bird's drinking buddies, had followed him down for this day's sale, some distance from their normal stamping grounds.

Aside from a wild card on the telephone, or a civilian gone berserk, Fred had to expect his opposition from the South Shore pool. They were tough and knowledgeable, and dangerous competitors. He had watched them as they looked through the lots, loafing through the display like sharks, before they schooled to discuss their tactics for this sale. Their existence as independents depended on their willingness to collude, up to a point.

As far as the art went, there were very few original paintings of any quality or virginity. For the most part it was an uninspiring selection, ranging from copies to shopworn retreads that the auctioneer's crony dealers were attempting to pass off as "estate" items despite their tawdry new frames and slick masking varnish. Since there was not much to account for Fred's continuing to stand watch at the rear of the crowd, wasting an afternoon, half of what the members of the South Shore pool were discussing among themselves had to be, therefore, "What does Fred Taylor want? If he's here, there's big money to be made. What are we missing?"

The pool's members, hearing the microphone squeal, looked up as Alphonse Bird made his way to the lectern at the front of the crowd. They finished their deliberations hastily, nominated their representatives, and fanned out.

Alphonse Bird was casual in jeans and a white knit shirt below whose arms bulged biceps the size of his head. He tapped his papers and surveyed the crowd. A lazy smile flowed onto his face as he made a tentative noise of vocal commitment.

"That asshole," Heckie White complained as the auctioneer began his warm-up. "I've told him a hundred times he isn't Jerry Seinfeld."

"You know, folks, have you ever noticed...," Bird started—and then took ten minutes of stand-up time to tell everyone that they were in Westport, Massachusetts; that they were honored to be attending a Sunday charity auction for the benefit of the Runnymede House Museum, established under the bequest of the late Lord Hanford; that on account of time pressure and the number of items being offered, the auctioneer had had insufficient time to do meticulous background research; that all items were believed to be as described in the printed list, but after that, buyers were on their own. "Which means, folks, and I want you to understand this. Some of you may be attending your first auction sale. I don't want anyone to come back later and say, 'This isn't what I thought it was.' We've done our best to describe what is here. Beyond that, the only guarantee is: You buy it, you own it. You are the expert. Look carefully and don't raise your paddle unless you are sure. If you want to bid, get a paddle with a bidding number on it from Linda, over there next to that escritoire we've had a lot of interest in, folks, which George the Third of England could have used himself. It, like most of what's coming before you today, is from Lord Hanford's estate. It stood in the master-bedroom suite in Runnymede House."

At mention of the master-bedroom suite in Runnymede House the crowd responded with a communal held breath, as if it had been caught the moment before accidental orgasm. Heckie stage-whispered into Fred's ear, drowning out Bird's spiel, "And, folks, now you've seen her, imagine Lady Hanford bent right over that escritoire. Can't you see it? Her pink Brit butt? Correction: the Brits call it a bottom. A *bawtomme*. It's all they think about. You seen any of that English TV? They want a laugh, they pull out the old British bawtomme. They will not shut up about it."

"It's American," Fred said. "She's from Toledo."

Heckie flicked a suggestive gesture with his green bidding paddle. "Great bawtomme anyway. I'm not prejudiced," Heckie said.

While Bird went on, running through the usual gamut of presale business, Heckie warned Fred, "The trustees of this museum they're going to build are salted through the crowd, the way Bird likes to slip three genuine Hummels into a run of fakes. He's told them how to bid things up, especially what they donated themselves, to make the tax deduction better. That's, next to the widow, Spar Ballard, the chairman of the board. He's also chairman of Friends of the Dartmouth-Westport Heritage and Cobb Point Preserve Society. You got their brochure? No? You'll find it under your wiper. Spar Ballard—the only reason he ever left the womb is, he dropped his cigar."

Alphonse Bird flashed the boyish grin that had gotten him into the pants and attics of so many widows. "And now a few words about the charity in whose behalf we are gathered: the Runnymede House Museum!"

Bird gave a toenail sketch of the "retired financier-philanthropist-gourmand and aesthete, Lord Hanford," who, late in life, had, as Bird put it, "fallen in love with Westport, Massachusetts."

"The truth is Westport, Massachusetts, got him by the balls," Heckie muttered, "and his heart, his mind, and his money followed. What was he, eighty when he married her?"

Lord Hanford, Bird pushed on, had made a generous bequest to the Friends of the Dartmouth-Westport Heritage, comprising Cobb Point, where they all sat and stood, including his lovely home, Runnymede House, which Lady Hanford would continue to enjoy during her natural life; much of his fine collection of English eighteenth- and nineteenth-century art; and seed money for the new museum that was to be erected on this very spot. Lady Hanford had also made available to this sale much of the financier's collection that had not previously been earmarked for the museum.

Next Bird introduced the "lovely widow, Lady Hanford. Lady Hanford, would you let the people see you?" The woman in black stood, to subdued applause (her husband was, after all, only five months in the ground).

"Do we know why Westport wants a museum of British art?" Heckie asked. "Because normally I'd say that was a contradiction in terms, like English gourmet cooking."

"Never mind that Yale's got the biggest collection of British art outside of London," Fred agreed, "just ninety miles away."

Heckie said, "These people would not be comfortable in New Haven. It reminds them they're Americans. I'm going to take a leak." He glanced at the lines already pressing toward the pair of tottering Port-O-Lets. "Fuck that!" Heckie muttered. "Let's be a trend-setter." He made off in the direction of the line of trees.

Fred scratched his arms and sweated while Chairman of the Board Spar Ballard, a vertical dumpling dressed for drinks on the deck, and Isabel Cooney, the decorative director-designate of the new museum, took their bows and said something. Finally the sale began, with a pair of silver-plated candlesticks.

"What say we buy it together and knock it out?" a suggestion of sweat and nicotine drawled into Fred's left ear. "It's the Hoesslin you're staying here for, obviously. Not everybody's heard of Hoesslin. It's a sleeper." The whispered voice went all too well with John Columbo, a South Shore picker who spent most of his research time collecting rumors in or near the men's room at the Boston Public Library. Fred hadn't seen him, so Columbo had also been keeping out of sight. Columbo, even on this sweltering day, had pried his skinny legs into yellow leather pants that were set off by a black T-shirt. His rat's face twisted with ingratiation. Fred shook his head.

The candlesticks sold for $150, a price it took Bird forty-five seconds to reach. "Jesus, this is going to take forever," Columbo complained.

Fred looked over toward the line of trees from whose shade Heckie White, zipping ostentatiously, was emerging. John Columbo went on arguing as the auctioneer commenced drawing in bids on a cast-iron doorstop. "Why hurt each other, Fred? Is Clayton Reed too pure to indulge in a little illegal restriction of free trade?" Columbo demanded. "Fred, you know and I know there's only the one decent painting here. Unless—shit! I can't imagine Clayton Reed's falling for the Constable. You're not talking, huh? Maybe I'll take a second look at the Constable. I'm around if you want to talk, Fred. If you have second thoughts. Why waste our money sending Fonzie's kids to college?"

Columbo darted toward the tables where the prints and paintings were laid out.

Chapter 2

Heckie took up his position again, next to Fred, a pair of hot dogs in one fist, along with his paddle. He carried a can of Black Label in the other. When he began buying glass, he bid by waving with his diminishing lunch. "Good of them to start with the glass," he said. "It's fucking hot!" He shook his head and let a cut-glass vase go to a pair of recreational buyers. Fred settled in to wait, conscious that he was being watched. He responded as appropriate to Heckie's occasional observations, but for the most part occupied himself in a stupor of vigilance while he waited for the art, two hundred lots down the line.

An auction sale is choreographed like any other concert. It is business, but it must be entertaining also, so that the audience will enjoy wasting its time and money. After the glass and china, and the silver, and then a couple of dozen lots of the less interesting contemporary furniture were sold came the interval of levity, the moment Alphonse Bird, stand-up comedian manqué, had been waiting for: a section of the sale entitled "Curiosa."

The presence of the widow in the front row prevented Bird from delivering all the juicy lines God and his own native instinct were simply handing him, but he did what he could. "The next group of items," Bird intoned, "is unusual in my experience of auction sales. Unusual and—I know this is New England, but even so, please, folks, let's not be prudes! Our cause is just. We've come a long way, baby!"

"Lie back and think of England," Heckie whispered.

Alphonse Bird went on, "Not meaning to be mysterious about the next twenty-seven lots, folks, but you have examined them. They may not be what we'd call, today, politically correct. But tastes change. Who knows about tomorrow?"

He was rewarded by Westport, Massachusetts's idea of a guffaw—a strained silence. Someone in the audience complained, "Let's get this done!"

Lot 127 was described in Fred's catalog as "Group. Stone. 19th century? Inuit?" It represented a pair of husky dogs, one humping a second, the second humping a stooping woman, and all carved from a single block of black stone. The bidding flickered hesitantly against the embarrassed silence of the audience. It didn't help when Bird encouraged, "It is an ethnographic work." The thing finally went for eight hundred bucks plus the auctioneer's vig, to Marek Hricsó, an antiques dealer who was new on Boston's Charles Street.

The next item, mislabeled as a chastity belt, sold by mistake for $130 to the booster efforts of the chairman of the board, Spar Ballard, who strapped the apparatus around his waist and announced that he would use it to open beer. Marek Hricsó was the underbidder. Next came a soiled canvas packet the size of an overnight bag.

"Folks," Alphonse Bird said, "I hope you have looked at this lot carefully, because it represents a great deal of work. Marcelle, honey, help the people."

Throughout the course of the sale, the lots under bid had been brought forward and displayed by the flunkies in their shorts and red knit shirts. Marcelle, the small and curly person whose turn it was to carry this item, turned as red as her shirt.

"Give the folks a peek, Marcelle," Bird teased. "In case somebody came in late." The girl put the package on the display table next to the lectern and started to flip it open. The inner flaps of its canvas cover glanced color that, when added to her blushing, made it appear that the package was done up in a Sicilian wedding sheet—the bottom one—used for the first-night ritual over many generations. Marcelle selected and held up an indistinct smudge on faded blue paper.

"They're old, and somebody put lots of attention into them," Bird pleaded. "And there's a lot of them. What'll we start at? A thousand dollars? Five hundred? No? What's your pleasure?"

The chairman of the board held up his hand at $250. "I mean, they have to be worth something," Bird prodded. Hricsó held up his paddle and the price rose by fifty dollars. A flurry of interest started then, and the bidding moved up to fifteen hundred.

"What's in the bag?" Heckie asked Fred.

"Dirty pictures," Fred said, and shrugged. "As long as Bird wants to take his time, why doesn't he sell them one by one?"

"Oh, Jesus, don't even *think* it," Heckie said as Marek Hricsó scooped the lot in at $1,750. "I didn't know the Hungarian liked porno kitsch," Heckie added as they watched Marek get involved in the next lot, another "group," this one of bronze, an explicit Italian door knocker. "I've got some copulating Japanese china he might like. I'll take it by next week. If they ever get to the art, Fred, good luck. I'm out of here."

Bird didn't reach the paintings until four o'clock. From the South Shore pool, Cy Fiske had been nominated to place bids on the art glass, and it was soon apparent that Chris Lappin was to front on the paintings. Lappin was a competitor on the Hoesslin up to twenty-five hundred dollars, so it was a two-way confrontation until then, between Fred and Lappin. Once Lappin had dropped out, signifying that the South Shore pool had officially lost interest, Columbo raised his paddle, and he and Fred went head-to-head until, at Columbo's bid of five thousand dollars, Fred figured the man had learned his lesson. Fred's feint, and Columbo's greedy counterattack, would stick the runner with a picture that Fred was certain would not clean. In a month it would turn up again, in Ipswich or Litchfield, before it started on the southern leg of a long, long journey to Detroit and points west. Having finessed the Hoesslin into Columbo's hands, Fred waited for lot 259.

Bird had been careful, listing the painting only as "Landscape study. School of Constable. Oil on wood, 15 x 18 inches. Inits. illeg." What looked like laziness or ignorance was in fact self-protection. He'd given the thing enough publicity to draw in a wide range of people who were just barely expert enough to draw their own conclusions. Others in the audience, if seduced by the scent of blood in the water, could drive the price up to whatever plateau their hope and credulity might fancy. Since the sellers had not actually stated that the picture was by the famed British landscape painter, no one could later demand his money back on the grounds that it had been falsely represented. If the John Constable experts were later to declare that it did not fit within the canon of the artist's work, tough luck! Nobody had outright *claimed* that Constable was the painter. At the same time, the printed description made it impossible for anyone to miss the attribution to John Constable at his most breezy and atmospheric. And who could fail to decipher the "illegible" initials in the lower right, below the hay wain, J.C.?

Action stirred at the telephones. The members of the South Shore pool glanced in Fred's direction, from their vantage points in and around the audience. The crowd rippled as a boy named Larry, in the uniform shorts and red shirt, held the wood panel up next to Alphonse Bird, who reeled off the catalog description deadpan: "School of Constable. A landscape sketch." He looked the audience over and added, "Lots of interest in this one, folks. It could be the sleeper of the sale." Then he asked for a thousand-dollar opening bid, and was stonewalled only until he dropped to $750, at which point a man in the audience raised his paddle, knocking his straw hat awry, and they were off.

Fred watched the seagulls sail and squabble overhead, and did not get into it until someone up front bid five thousand against Chris Lappin. The opening bidding had been desultory, the competitors unsure whether the bone of contention was an overpriced decorative picture of no distinction, or—it *does* happen—the real McCoy: a plein-air sketch by England's foremost interpreter of English landscape, and predecessor of, trailblazer for, the French impressionists. As soon as Fred raised his paddle, ten more shot up at once, including Columbo's.

A scramble ensued—Bird knew how to tap in on the adrenaline of a good fight—among Chris Lappin, Columbo, Fred, the bidder in the front, and two women at the phones who waved, pleading to be recognized on behalf of their clients. The price climbed fast and kept moving up to twenty-five thousand, at which point Columbo abruptly dropped out, glaring at Fred. Lappin stayed in long enough to make one last bid of thirty-two thousand, after which—the telephones' operators having both relaxed without ever being given the chance to bid—the duel was between Fred and the bidder up front. It was the first good fight of the afternoon.

The spectators craned their necks to follow the action, front to back, as if they were at a tennis match, until the bidder up front folded at Fred's bid of thirty-nine thousand. The telephone ladies cajoled their clients but finally had to shake their heads toward the auctioneer and hang up. Fred's was the lucky number. Bird hammered the picture down to him as the audience applauded.

Alphonse Bird took a drink of water, fondled his hammer in his ham of a hand, and started in on a foxed and sun-bleached seascape watercolor by George Howell Gay. Fred consulted his list, scratched his face, and wandered toward the tables near the Port-O-Lets, where perspiring women were exchanging bills of sale for money. Chris Lappin let the Gay go to a recreational buyer who needed something inoffensive to go over her couch, and followed Fred at a short distance until Fred had turned Clay's check over to the harassed woman whose name tag identified her as Linda. Lappin stuck to him as, with his bill of sale stamped PAID, Fred moved on to the line at the cordoned-off area where, in the trampled grass, the sold goods awaited their purchasers. He watched the kid named Larry trot his suddenly valuable School of Constable through the gap in the ropes, and prop it against a pair of andirons.

Lappin, small, and hot, and stymied, was wearing white overalls and no shirt, and was burning. He moved in now. His confidential whisper smelled of Black Label. "I was prepared to go as high as fifty grand in the knockout," he said, not caring who might hear him. "Just between you and me. What about it, Fred? The thing cost you thirty-nine K plus ten percent. That's forty-two nine. You want to make a fast profit of seven grand? Not bad for a day's pay. And you can have it in cash. Come to Slimmy's in Fairhaven once we get finished here. That's where we're getting together."

Fred said, "I'll keep it." He handed his stamped bill over and took the painting.

Chris Lappin stayed with him. "I'll go two thousand more," he offered. "After that there's nothing left in it for me."

Fred repeated, "I'll keep it." He started slowly toward the line of trees, the painting under his arm.

"You son of a bitch, how much will you take, then?" Lappin persisted.

Fred stopped and turned, facing the dealer until it dawned on Lappin that Fred could be dangerous. "I am not for sale," Fred said.

"Well, shit, then," Lappin said, and turned back in time to place a bid of seventeen hundred dollars on a print by Rowlandson. Fred moved on toward the line of trees.

Marek Hricsó waited in the cool dampness under the maples. Hricsó was lean, lithe, and beautiful, an aging boy who belonged—but for his gnarled hands—in a misty movie about sexual ambivalence, which ends badly for someone.

"I make it seventy-six hundred dollars for all this dirt you wanted," Marek said. He wore slim white jeans with a black knit shirt, and heavy gold chains at his neck. The jeans sported a pronounced matinee-belt bulge that promised another kind of opulence.

While Marek fidgeted, Fred began counting out bills from the stash in his money belt. "Anything in the sale you liked?" he asked.

"It's all junk," Marek said. "A waste of time for me. As for these terrible junk of fucking that you wanted—now all those men who work out of their car, who see me buying vulgar ugly things, they begin to come to me saying, 'I have a bronze girl with six penises, better than the one you bought, beautiful, that I sell you cheap.' They come like flies, to embarrass me and my customers, all because of you, Fred Taylor, and how you are a puritan prude."

"Let's find somewhere private for the transfer. There's another thousand for you," Fred said, handing the money over. "A little over ten percent. And a thousand extra beyond that, so this long hot afternoon won't be a complete waste of time for you. That all right?"

"You owe me nothing," Marek said, taking the money smoothly. "Still I am in your debt, mysterious Fred, for times before; and so I wish that you and Mr. Reed will in good health enjoy these disgusting things I have bought for you."

Fred dropped the School of Constable into his trunk and followed Marek's car down the long dirt road and on into the lovely countryside until Hricsó found a suitable turn-in behind a gas station where, unobserved, they could shift Marek's purchases from his trunk to Fred's backseat.

"Thanks. I'll be off," Fred said.

"Now that I know your taste," Marek started, "I can soon have as much of this horrible garbage as you want."

"This'll do us," Fred assured him.

Chapter 3

Fred listened to the muffled conversation behind the brown veneer door to room 413 of Fall River's Silver Spur Motel. He was puzzled until he recognized the newsreader's voice, proceeding oblivious to the snorts of contemptuous disbelief that came in reply.

The motel's hallway was dark and beige and flocked with tangible despair. BORN LONESOME, the blinking neon light over the office door did not need to say. The Silver Spur had been the choice of the room's occupant. Working hastily through the Yellow Pages the previous evening, he had exclaimed, "Silver Spur! Aha! Sounds like the Golden West—Puccini!"

Fred, coming through the lobby with the School of Constable, as well as one of the three filled cardboard boxes Marek had turned over, had noticed permanent-looking OUT OF ORDER notices pasted up to obscure the signs for SWIMMING POOL, COCKTAIL BAR, and MEN.

Fred knocked and the door opened a chained crack, within which Clayton Reed's blue right eye appeared, blinking under its festoon of naturalized white hair. "Are you alone?" Clay asked. Fred nodded and Clay eased the crack tighter so as to loose the chain and open the door to Fred and his burden. "What's all that? Didn't you get…"

"I have it," Fred said. The motel room was an exhausted orange flavor, its twin beds shrouded in rust, with sailboat art on the wall and Jim Lehrer, disoriented by the unaccustomed Sunday evening, giving way to a preview of a similar program about muskrats. Clay had appropriated the bed farthest from the door, closest to a window offering an unobstructed view of closed blinds smeared with body dirt and Fall River's dust. Fred put the School of Constable landscape on the dressing table next to the TV and the big box on the floor near the other bed.

"Not to complain about the place you chose," Fred started.

Clay, in white linen suit and golden tie, was trembling in anticipation, struggling against his instinctive courtesy. "It had become so late," he said. "I feared…"

"Alphonse Bird takes his time. I'll shower, then we'll take a look," Fred said. "I feel as if I'd spent the day in old New Delhi."

"By all means, yes. As long as—you are positive there's no mistake? I am surprised to see the painting. I respect your judgment, Fred, but as you know—"

Fred said, peeling the wet blue shirt over his head and making for the bathroom, "What you want is in the box. Give me five minutes."

When Fred came into the room again, dressed in the motel's anorexic towel, Clay was standing exactly as he'd left him, electric with anguish, like a well-trained dog who had been ordered to "stay" three feet away from a lubricious roast. Behind him, serious people in liberal attire were discussing something on the TV screen, about which they were pretending not to be in complete agreement.

"You're suffering, Clay. But it's your fault. If you won't even tell me what we're hunting—"

Clay snapped, "I wanted you to enjoy deniability. Therefore I kept you in the dark." Fred began taking Marek's purchases from the box, setting them on the rug. Clay tapped his foot, glancing without interest as Fred set aside the Indian couple in acrobatic red sandstone, the baroque hermaphrodites in bronze, and the rest of it.

"My theory was," Fred explained, "buy the whole haystack, and they won't know there's a needle in it. The only thing we missed out of the entire run of curiosa was mislabeled anyway. What they claimed was a chastity belt is a cornshucker, as I know all too well from long, hot evenings in the Midwest. If anything, its effect is the opposite."

Clay interlaced his fingers. "And in due course you will explain the…'Constable'?"

"I had to be there for something," Fred said, taking out the folded canvas parcel. "It's all there was we could even pretend we wanted. And we were well within your budget. Also, though it was expensive, it might one day serve for other purposes. For everything but the painting, Marek Hricsó is the buyer of record."

Clay smirked. "Well done, Fred." He was staring at the package, shaking so hard that Fred glanced around the room for other signs of the earthquake. The foursome on the TV screen was interrupted by a sound from next door, a confused jangle of businesslike giggles.

"What have we got?" Fred asked, laying the package on the bed. Clay gawked at the makeshift canvas satchel as if it might contain a bomb, then reached his long, inquisitive fingers toward it and began, with excruciating care, to stroke the cloth. The canvas was very brown, stiff, and so stained it might have been used in the past to line a coffin. When Clay turned the package over, Fred saw that the rough cloth was marked with a cursive scrawl in black ink, which, when he corrected his vision to see that it was upside down, became words drawn with a fine brush: *dangerous rubbish.*

"'Dangerous rubbish'?" Fred said.

"Indeed," Clay said, and started. "Who's that talking?"

"People in the next room," Fred said. "We've got walls as thin as the towels at this place."

"No, it's the television talking," Clay said. "It does go on and on. Make it stop, Fred, if you know how. The young woman who turned it on for me expected so large a tip I did not like to ask her back."

Fred found the remote and ended the discussion on the TV. "Are you aware you've booked yourself into a chicken ranch?" he asked.

"I should not touch anything without Roberto here to guide me," Clay said, his right hand resting on the canvas pack as if he hoped to read it in braille.

"Everyone and his monkey has been fooling with the thing for two days," Fred said. "One more monkey won't hurt. But Roberto won't work with paper, will he?"

"Paper?" Clay asked.

"We bought paper," Fred pointed out. "Drawings on paper, right? Approximately three hundred sketches of a variety of erotic subjects, possibly French, possibly nineteenth century, according to the auction list. Since you instructed me not to be seen looking at them, I did not look at them. So I am interested, having spent the whole day landing the thing. Your goddamned package was out there on the table in the weather, with the wind and the seagulls and people drinking beer. It had more folks messing with it during the presale viewing than the shroud of Turin."

"You have eaten?" Clay asked, turning away from the bed and his wrapped purchase. He could leave it unopened for days. What he claimed was self-discipline was in fact pure cussedness. Fred flipped the canvas open, the first flap, and—with Clay turning back to stand shivering next to him in an agony of defeated indecision—the next flap, and the next, and on, opening the thing out slowly onto the orange bedspread until the stack of paper it contained, about four inches high, lay exposed on its wrapping, a vertiginous riot of dirty, brutal color.

"A Sicilian wedding sheet, I thought it looked like," Fred said, "seeing it from the back end of the crowd. I'd have to say that the bride's brothers took exception to the groom at the moment of truth. Let's see these drawings I fried for all afternoon."

"Careful," Clay commanded, catching Fred's arm. "Fred, what's the matter with you?"

"God help us, it's a painting," Fred said. The room shivered as he walked around the dingy bed and looked down from the other side. Squeaking thumps from next door were instantaneously magnified and swept away as the room reeled. The gouts of dangerous color on this unfolded canvas were specific and intentional, suddenly correcting themselves as Fred adjusted his vision to comprehend the painting on the horizontal plane. He'd been bemused, like everyone else in the crowd, and like the auctioneer, by the false description that made the painting into packaging.

The cloth was mournfully dirty, and the crust of paint on it was stained, cracked, and abused. An almost four-by-five-foot expanse, the canvas presented a white vortex of rushing snow or water, thrusting in a tormented spiral through the center of the rectangle and shoving brutally, toward either side, what looked like heavy veils of flame, or blood, or wrath. In the midst of the vortex, pinioned beneath its active integument, someone was drowning—no, not someone: *two* someones. Even their despairing yelps could be heard. No, that was next door.

"They are copulating," Clay observed. "I am sorry to indulge in an expression so grossly Latinate, Fred. But there is no help for it. None other is adequate to the moment." He had come around to stand next to Fred. "Having come thus far, let us enjoy the rest." He reached out reverently to touch the top drawing, or painting—it was both—with its dust of red and white paint; then he lifted the pile of paper with both hands. The top drawing was on blue paper, a gouache impression of a disembodied vagina troubled by high wind. The drawing had a real presence. It pulsed with friendly menace. A luminous purpose worked here that was more than mere prurience, if no stranger to it. It was honest, observed, as fair a job of work in its own way as a brick staircase. Its quality burned with a similar but lesser light to that evident in the much-folded and -unfolded painting, the entirety of which could be seen now. Clay carried the drawings to the desk, where he set them next to the Gideon Society's Bible.

The door to the room on the other side of this one opened and closed firmly, and hushed voices started a discussion about zippers.

"You are certain you were not followed?" Clay asked. Fred shook the question off.

"Security is of paramount importance. Shall we hang the Do Not Disturb sign on the door, or would that rather alert them?" Clay mused. He came back to the bed, stood looking down at his painting and smiled, a broad and open smile that took years off him. "Confess it, Fred," he crowed. "When I told you I would allow up to three hundred thousand dollars, you feared I had lost my mind."

"No, keep the light on," came a gruff male voice from the other side of the plasterboard. "Also your shoes; I like shoes."

Fred said, "I respect your judgment, Clay. And you respect your money."

"Gracious, this is a noisy place," Clay said. "I take it for granted that you did not tell Marek Hricsó he could go that high?"

"Of course not. He was buying pornography as a favor for a friend, is all. We got it for seventeen-fifty plus the vig. I told Marek he could go up to ten thousand. I'd have taken over after that. All Marek knows is that it was worth ten thousand to us. Nobody else saw what you did, Clay, and I congratulate you. It's—whatever it is—an amazing thing to touch, this painting. So abstract and expressionistic for its age. Can it be French? It has some of the feel of Delacroix, the aftermath of a massacre. You're right about the subject of the painting: they're indistinct, but there's no doubt what that couple's up to. Who's the painter?"

"I shall be interested to hear your thoughts as they develop," Clayton said. He was going to be cute.

The room to Fred's right, which had been silent for a time, began to produce first chatter and then dramatic groaning and the responding encouragement of the insincere. Clay chuckled. "Fred, I have made a coup. It is a coup of astonishing magnitude if I am right, and all my instincts tell me I *am* right.

"It's early," Fred said. "We can get this to Boston inside two hours."

"No," Clay countered. "The painting is too large and too fragile to be moved except by a conservator. We should not have unfolded it."

"I'm uneasy about leaving you in this place alone," Fred interrupted. "But I'd planned on driving back to catch up on Molly and the kids."

"My intention is," Clayton went on evenly, carrying the drawings back to his bed and beginning to look through them, "to stay with my purchase here tonight. We will deliver the painting tomorrow to Roberto Smith, who must drive over from New Bedford. I shall telephone him shortly. Look, there is writing on some of the drawings. I could not examine them closely last night because I could not risk seeming to take an interest.

"Concerning another matter, Fred, I cannot take even you into my confidence. While you were making your ablutions, I was visited by a wild surmise. A golden opportunity opens before me. But if I am to take advantage of it, we must make haste."

Cavorting barnyard sounds developed in the hall outside room 413. Clay did not hear them. He was transfigured.

"Suddenly, and unexpectedly, I am placed upon the threshold of opportunity. There is a tide in the affairs of men, which…We have less than a week at our disposal," Clay said, "to do work that would properly take months, nay, even years; and we must labor in absolute secrecy if we are not to lose the prize. I must be able to demonstrate the full history and nature of my extraordinary find. Questions abound. We do not even know that the material is in this country legally. And how do we explain Lord Hanford's ignorance of its true nature? How to proceed? My prevailing instinct is, as always, to maintain a low profile."

"You're doing fine so far," Fred said, "especially if you refuse to tell me what the devil we have picked up."

Clay rolled on, staring at his new painting as if it contained the secret of the origin of life. "I must know everything. Simply put, what are they? How to prove their authorship? What is their provenance? Did I say a week? Indeed, we have five days! We start first thing tomorrow morning. How early can you telephone me here?"

"If you stay, I stay also," Fred said. "I'm not sure it's a house requirement, but I'll put on pants before I bring in the rest of the stuff."

Chapter 4

Mom's ecstatic with the Royal Hunt Tour so far," Molly said on her end of the telephone. "She saw the Princess Royal going into Claridge's."

"Which one's the Princess Royal?"

"Search me. I have a tin eye for royalty. The important thing is that Mom's happy, and she's forgiven Sam for breaking Elizabeth's coronation mug, since she has two more."

Clay having volunteered to venture into the world and find them dinner, Fred was taking the opportunity to put his feet up and call Molly. He had been living with her now for so long that the domestic business of keeping in touch this way had become a friendly habit. Being lovers, they must be conscious of each other's lives. Molly and her two children, Sam and Terry, were at the moment staying in Cambridge, house-sitting for her mother in a place that, Fred tended to agree with Terry—though with far less delight—was "exactly like a Cracker Jack box, Fred!"

True, if the Cracker Jacks were made of porcelain and glass.

Terry was wild with joy because she had wheedled for herself principal responsibility for Prince Charles, the Welsh Corgi Molly's mother loved too much to board out while she was touring England's royal haunts. The dog could barely move in the small house near the river, though he managed to exist there without breaking china, which was more than could be said for Sam. Sam didn't know where his limbs were at the best of times, and at Molly's mother's all the surfaces had doilies on them that slid like magic carpets toward you until the commemorative assignation-of-Prince Andrew-and-Koo Stark ashtray got under your elbow.

Given where Molly was, Fred didn't know *where* he was living. He still had the room in his place in Charlestown if he wanted it; or he could find space in Clayton's; or in Molly's empty house in Arlington—or, for that matter, under a bridge. Nothing seemed much less comfortable than Molly's mother's bedroom. When he'd stepped into Molly's mother's house the week before, to help them move in, the furniture had tottered and all the loving years of precious knickknacks chattered with alarm in their wall sconces and étagères. There was nowhere, ever, any more than two and a half feet of open space.

"She's keeping you informed, then," Fred prompted.

"She faxes me each day's complete itinerary, which the coordinators can't make up until the last moment, when they find out what the Royals are up to," Molly said. "The Royal Hunt Tour promises Royals, and it sounds like Mom's getting them. The Royal Hunt bus dumps her group on the sidewalk in time to catch the quarry making their appointments. When Princess Alexandra, the Honorable Lady Ogilvy, attends a garden party for the League for the Exchange of Commonwealth Teachers at Saint Mary's University College, Strawberry Hill, Twickenham, Middlesex, Mom's going to be right there with her umbrella, watching the princess back out of her car. With poor Di gone, all the other princesses secrete the sudden glow of lucky understudies. She's having so much fun, Mom says, she may never come home. Tomorrow night she and the gang are going to stalk the Tower of London for a reception that's to be visited by the Duke and Duchess of Gloucester. Then, the high point—"

"Is Sam holding up all right?" Fred asked.

"I took him to Arlington to pick up his bike and his fishing rod. He's fishing now, in the Charles, though he understands that anything he catches has to be thrown back. Terry and Prince Charles went down there with him. Where are you holed up? It sounds…"

The noises on either side of room 413 were becoming so familiar that Fred no longer paid them much attention. "In case you need me, here's a number," Fred said. "Clay wants to play it close to his chest for mysterious reasons only he can understand, so it's not for general broadcast. We're in Fall River, room four-thirteen, the Silver Spur Motel."

"Sounds like a 'spo'tin' house," Molly observed.

"Clay's choice."

Fred had pulled one of the stained, plush-covered armchairs over to the window and opened the blind to look down into the parking lot, where his scuffed brown car seemed too at home, and Clay's golden Lexus too outlandish, in the shadow of the abandoned mill buildings. Up the highway, on the far side, Fred could just make out the sign for Hop Sam's Chinese Eats, where Clay was buying dinner. Although dressed like a prince, he should be all right from here to there and back—but even so, Fred was keeping watch out the window while he talked to Molly. Clay looked as rich as he was: a prime target for muggers.

"And the auction went OK?" Molly asked.

"You bet," Fred told her.

"You want to tell me about it?"

A hot, fast, scarlet Moray squealed into the lot, failed to sideswipe Fred's car, and jerked to a stop. Three big young men in their twenties climbed out laughing, in baggy shorts and aggressively untucked pastel shirts. Each carried a pair of six-packs. They urged each other toward the entrance of the Silver Spur, just under Fred's window.

"I guess we landed something big," Fred said. "Clay won't tell me what it is, but it'll come. I'm bad with names. Does the name *Admiral Booth* mean anything to you?"

"No."

"We bought a huge stack of drawings wrapped up in a painting that I'd recognize in a minute if I saw it in a different context."

Fred glanced across the room at the painting spread across the second bed. He'd shoved the boxes containing Marek's other purchases underneath so there'd be room to move around. The painting's manner was familiar, the paint laid on thickly, but with a brush, not a knife. For all the weight of the material and the medium, the effect was of transparencies broadly executed in watercolor. The outlines of the figures were tentative, almost clumsy, as if they had been inscribed and then buried many times, under successive layers of paint.

"English?" Molly asked.

"Must be, since the auctioneer said French. I haven't studied the drawings yet. Wanted to let you know I won't be back tonight. What are you up to?"

"I'm in Mom's all-white, don't-tread-on-me bedroom, with the air conditioner on, talking on the telephone to my ugly friend Fred and leafing through a complimentary catalog of junk she has, 'British Royalty Commemoratives,' a unique selection for the advanced and beginning collector, from the coauthor of the popular book by the same title."

Outside in the hallway came the unmistakable sounds of three young men with six six-packs and four women. In the distance Fred saw the door of Hop Sam's Chinese Eats open and close behind Clayton in his white suit, carrying paper bags, moving gracefully, like a lighted baptismal candle through a naughty world.

"My supper's coming," Fred said.

"Noisy supper."

"That's someone else's. I see Clay walking down the highway with Chinese. Tonight I'm a bawdyguard. I'll stop by at your work, or call, tomorrow."

The three men from the Moray and their party set up shop next door on the right. They were well established by the time Clay knocked and entered with his bags.

"You are keeping a weather eye on my vehicle," Clay observed. "That is wise. I had not been familiar with Fall River. Wishing to be fair, let me merely suggest that if there is a more salubrious portion of Fall River than this, this is not it."

The sounds that accompanied them as they ate accentuated this observation. Fred tossed their trash in the receptacle next to the ice machine in the corridor, scrubbed his hands, and began searching through the piles of drawings that Clay had begun to sort on the broad shelf that served as a windowsill. Clayton, in the meantime, had managed to reach Roberto Smith by phone, and was engaged in persuading the restorer to make a house call. From where he sat Fred could keep track of the goings and comings in the parking lot, as well as of most of what went on in the corridor and the adjoining rooms.

The drawings were enough to study for six months. It seemed to be true of all of them, at least on brief inspection, that whether more or less complex, they fit well within the boundaries defined by the word *curiosa*. They were in pencil, gouache, watercolor, or ink, or a mixture of these media; some were hasty and others quite studied and meticulous. Often they boasted splashes and shattered arguments of racing color, laid on more as if applied by wind, or lust, than by a disciplined hand. Fred did not usually care much about subject or story line. The image of a man's head between a woman's legs meant neither more nor less than its inverse: what mattered was the method, the desperate vigor of the artist—Fred did not doubt it was a man's work—sometimes intently observing, often in an impassioned state of reverie. The burden of the increasingly frantic cumulative cry issuing from the works was somehow, like the prophet's tragic message, "Folks, all flesh is grass."

That all the drawings were the work of a single person, Fred felt sure—but they had been done over many years. As Clay continued sorting them by type and by style, medium, and make of paper, a chronological pattern might emerge as well. A number of them had words or phrases on them. In all, the group presented the kind of puzzle both Clay and Fred loved to get lost in.

As Clay finished his call, Fred noticed that two of the hefty young men who had been next door were making their way across the parking lot to meet a taxi that had pulled in off the highway. "Ten-thirty," Fred said, leaving the drawings to Clay, who gathered them gingerly together and stowed them in a suitcase. "I'll leave that painting on my bed. I've slept on worse floors than this one."

"It is a shame you did not bring your nightclothes," Clay said. He had two suitcases with him, and a fresh suit hanging in the closet space.

"I'll make out," Fred promised, lying on the orange carpet in his clothes, across the doorway.

The sound that brought him to full alert came at three-thirty: a thin whine. Fred stared at the poisonous gloom of the dark room. The night had been filled with noises, but this one stood out. It was a whistle of pain and panic forced through tormented vocal cords. It signified mortal agony. Fred trotted across the room, nudged Clay into wakefulness, and told him, "Don't move unless I call you."

The corridor was dimly lighted and quiet except for the cruel whistle, which came from the room where the large party had been. Fred tried the knob before shouldering the door open in a rush of easy splinters. Inside the dark room a naked man gasped, standing to lean the weight of his upper body onto both his straightened arms and pressing them into the humping bed-clothes. The air throbbed with a silence stinking of sweat, fear, and mankind.

Fred tripped on cans and skidded in their slick as he raced toward the group. He hacked the man's arms upward, breaking their hold, before he kicked his legs out from under him. He whispered, "Move and I'll break your neck," as he leaned over the bed to tug the heap of covers back.

Enough light crept in from the open doorway to show the woman. She sprawled naked on her front, writhing, her skin ocher with welts of startled purple. She gaped to breathe but could not. If her windpipe was broken, she was gone, however close the nearest medics were. Fred fumbled for the phone, found it next to the bed, and informed the desk, "Trouble in room—I don't know, four-eleven or four-fifteen. The door is open. Get an ambulance."

The woman kicked. Fred held her by the shoulders, telling her, "Be still, we're getting help." He wept with helpless worry until she breathed in, shuddering, and out again, and in.

Fred turned his attention to the man at his feet as two long shadows crossed the room from the open doorway. One of the men looked Asian in origin; the other was some version of the mixture Americans insist on calling "black." Both shadows were black.

"You want to stand by that window with your arms extended nice and wide so we can see your hands at all times?" the Asian suggested.

"I called the desk," Fred said, stepping back smoothly to the window. Both men carried guns in their waistbands, but they weren't about to shoot up their own place. "The boy on the floor is the one you want," Fred finished. "The female needs help."

"Keep your hands where they are and don't tell us our business," the other man said. "I see what I see." He kicked the door shut and flipped the switch, bringing them muted light from the lamp between the pair of ragged beds. The floor was littered with empty cans and a scurry of tossed clothes. The woman moaned and moved her limbs. "Take care of Joe College, Pig Lee," the man instructed.

The naked young man, an unhealthy shade of pink—he'd been taking the sun unwisely the day before, evidently—his eyes staring, still lay curled where Fred had put him. Pig Lee, the Asian, crossed to stand behind him, grabbed him by both ears, and lifted, twisting. When the kid gulped to scream, Lee closed the bottom of his face off with one huge hand, telling his partner, "Check the whore, Sammy, if you would be so kind. Who is that, Neetha?"

Sammy was already bending over the young woman, listening to the whisper of her first complaint. "Shut up a minute, honey," he said. "It's the one from Atlanta, calls herself Daiquiri. What did you do to the man, honey?" He leaned close and listened to her whisper.

"I'll get back to my room, as long as the cavalry has arrived," Fred said.

"Why don't you, pretty please, stand where you are for one more minute?" Pig Lee advised, giving the naked man at his feet a hard kick in the kidney. Sammy held out his hand for peace and silence and listened again to the whispered words of Daiquiri. She turned over and struggled to sit up. The welts of heavy fingers showed big and raw on her neck.

"Seems Joe College was killing her, which is against our house rules," Sammy told Fred as he stood up. "I reckon you saved this whore's life. We thank you. Daiquiri thanks you too. Don't you, honey?" The woman fluttered her hands. She looked beaten, around shoulders and narrow breasts that bobbed with her gulping breaths.

"We take care of the denouement from here," Pig Lee said, smiling and showing teeth made of steel. "You free to go back to whatever you were doing, buddy. You in four-thirteen?" Fred nodded. "We'll take care of this former client."

"Wanted a few things that were not on the program," Sammy explained. "Which he had not paid for. And then could not execute same. We service what we sell. Therefore our code of ethics is, we fix his ass. Thank you kindly, mister."

Fred said, "I can't let you kill him."

"You what?" Pig Lee and Sammy exclaimed together. "Honey, the day you let us or don't let us do this or do that..." Sammy trailed off.

"Gentlemen, you and I are in business," Fred said, lowering his arms. "It will mess up all of our business if you kill this man."

The young man, gripped into silence, stared and thrashed, and tried to plead through Pig Lee's huge hand. He'd been high on something when Fred came in, but pain first, and now anticipation, had brought him back to this earthly paradise.

"You see the red Moray out there?" Fred asked. Pig Lee and Sammy nodded. Daiquiri swung her feet around in order to start rising slowly from the bed. She was about Molly's height, and older than she had first appeared. "That's his car, the Moray," Fred went on. "My counsel, from the point of view of business, is that you fix it so this boy goes back to his friends and has to explain what happened to about sixty-five thousand dollars' worth of car he used to drive, which can't be insured against vandalism that might occur."

Sammy found the man's pants on the floor and shook the wallet out of them, opened it, and looked through the contents. "Glaswicz. Anthony Emil Glaswicz. Anthony Emil? You listening? We keep this wallet, with your cards and name and address. We'll start with the car. Something unforeseen in the way of a tragedy could still eventuate upon you in the future, Anthony Emil."

"We might mess Anthony Emil up a little before he goes back to college," Pig Lee offered Fred. "Don't have to be fatal. That meet with your approval?"

"I'd say that was a risk he ran," Fred said. "But I'll be watching from my window. I want to see Anthony Emil walk out the front door."

"This guy's in four-thirteen with the Lexus, the Prince of Denmark who paid cash for a double and went out for Chinese food," Pig Lee said. "Buddy, be cool. Go back to Prince Hamlet. Daiquiri, round up a couple girls to help us straighten Anthony Emil out on some of the facts of life."

⸺⊷⊶⸺

When Fred let himself back into the room, Clay was asleep. He sat at the window and looked across the parking lot—silent and without life—toward the dark highway, empty of cars. Forty minutes later Anthony Emil Glaswicz hobbled out from the entrance of the Silver Spur, four floors below, still naked, flanked by two women wearing bathrobes, one on either side of him. Each of these held a string that was attached to his privates. Sammy and Pig Lee followed behind them, swinging crowbars. The women jerked their captive to a halt ten feet from his car and made him stand there while Pig Lee and Sammy began working the Moray over with their iron. When the men signaled that they were finished, the women dropped their leashes, and all four watched their client stumble toward the highway, the strings dragging on the ground.

A wash of blood, nostalgia, pity, and terror crossed Fred's eyes. "Turner," he said aloud. "Our boy is Joseph Mallord William Turner."

Clay muttered but did not waken, enjoying the sleep of the innocent. Fred did not normally pay attention to English painting, but Turner was the exception. Turner's late work, from the 1830s on, had been a crucial stepping-stone in the culture's progress through impressionism to abstract expressionism. Everyone knew Turner's rainbows, fogs, sunsets, and mountain gorges; his ships and steam engines. His atmospheric canvases, suffused with blood, and light, and weather, had pioneered an emotional reading of the landscape that proclaimed the artist as a visionary. In his late career, as his paintings became more exalted and introspective, most critics, riding the Victorian wave of sentiment and illustration, had dismissed his work with ridicule. He'd almost disappeared. Had it not been for the critic John Ruskin, Turner's junior by a generation, the artist's greatest works would simply have rotted in obscurity. Ruskin had made Turner the subject of a crusade. He had, almost single-handedly, rescued the painter's reputation and brought it to the prominence it still enjoyed.

As best he could, Fred brought back images he had spent time with in New York, London, Boston, Washington. He'd hit it, he was confident. Just in Boston's MFA, the *Slave Ship* and the *Falls of the Rhine* were painted in a similar manner to Clayton's canvas; and at Harvard's Fogg Museum, the unfinished *Juliet and Her Nurse* could almost be the twin of what lay on Clay's spare bed. All three canvases fit the swirling, turgid agony embedded in the discarded painting Clay had rescued. Turner was a monumental figure, a grand old man. No wonder Clay was nervous, proud, and more paranoid than usual.

But what about the subject of the painting? Did that fit? Could there be anything so off-color in the Turner story? And, creeping naked out of the cold blue marble halls of Victoria's England, could those be Turner's drawings too?

"Clayton, you clever bastard," Fred chuckled. If this was Turner's work, and this much of it, it was a staggering find.

Chapter 5

I'll get us breakfast," Fred told Clay as his companion opened his eyes to a dirty dawn. Fog had rolled in at about five-thirty, with a dreary, whimpering rain to back it up. Clayton Reed slept in green pajamas that looked tailored. Fred was still sitting at the window, staring out into the corner of some foreign field that is forever Fall River. He'd been wakened at five by clankings below, in time to watch the tow truck hitch up to and drag off the remains of the Moray. After that he had visited again with Turner's ghost.

"Coffee and the papers, and orange juice for you, Clay," Fred said. "I know your drill. No stimulants." He opened the door and leapt the obstacle in his path, his rubbed nerves firing toward action before he recognized and discounted the pyramid of fruit in cellophane. He carried the basket into the room and put it on the TV. "Who knows you're here?" he asked, tearing the blank envelope off the ribbon it had been taped to. He handed it to Clayton.

"No one." Clay read the card. "It says 'We owe you.' *Who* owes me? For what am I owed? Is it a joke? A threat?"

"I helped the management with a problem in the room next door," Fred told him. "While you were asleep. They're saying thanks." He looked at the other side of the card, on which a penciled "Get well soon, love Poppy" had been crossed out.

"A lavish gift, however inedible," Clay approved. "Roberto, as I told you, will arrive at nine. Then we return to Boston with my drawings. I shall outline our research program after breakfast."

"How do so many Turners escape captivity?" Fred asked.

"Ah, you agree, then," Clay said. "Yes, Turner was my thought also."

Fred took the stairs down. The building was for the most part quiet as he moved from one floor to the next, though here and there a shower or toilet ran. With the Moray gone, eight cars remained in the lot this morning, besides his and Clayton's. Sammy lay dozing at the foot of the stairs in such a way that his legs would also block any attempted exit from the elevator. He rose to attention when Fred was six stairs above him, turning the final corner.

"I got the tribute," Fred told him. "The fruit."

"I wanted Daiquiri to bring it, but we had to leave her the fuck in the hospital, they said, for observation. If she takes off—well, hell, that's not your business. Joe College messed her up inside. Regard the fruit as a gesture from the management. They said, send a girl on the house, but I told them, look, a man signed for the room, OK? He's got another man in there with him drives a car looks like it could use a thousand dollars' worth of spare parts, except they don't make those parts anymore? What do they want with a girl?"

"Where's the nearest place I can get coffee?" Fred broke in. No one else was in the cramped and shabby lobby area. A bell sat on the desk, of the kind that asks to be struck with the heel of a hand. Sammy would have wakened if anyone had opened the glass doors from the parking lot.

"The management says there's no charge for the room. Anything he wants, it's on the house, in case he swings both ways. He wants to give the girl a tip, that's up to him. I'll send a girl up to tell him. Here, this is for you." Sammy peeled a hundred-dollar bill from the outside of a small roll he took from the back pocket of his jeans.

"Breakfast," Fred repeated, tucking the bill into his shirt pocket. Sammy pointed down the highway toward the left, where the view of rain was cut off by clapped-out mill buildings. "I'm coming back. I'll give the guy your message."

Sammy shrugged. "He can stop at the desk for his refund," he said. "Give us both a break. Don't offer to pick it up yourself." He scratched, yawned, and drifted to the desk to sit behind it.

"Molly asks you to telephone. She says it is urgent," Clay said as Fred pushed into 413 with their breakfast. Clay, standing at the desk in front of the School of Constable, had peeled an orange, tried it, and set its naked sections aside.

"One of the kids?" Fred asked, alarmed. The Charles was a small river, but it had taken lives.

"She did not say."

Fred checked his watch as he poked numbers on the phone: eight forty-five. Clay had put on a suit, a light-gray one, to complement the weather. The orange peel set it off.

"Home of Prince Charles," came Terry's voice.

"Terry, put your mom on," Fred demanded. "Is everyone all right?"

"She's gone. To work. Sam's asleep. He's a pigface. How come you never come to see our camp, Fred? Sam said Prince Charles smelled like an ashtray. He couldn't help it; he was wet. Mom said you have to talk to a man that called, called Mark Crisco. It's really, really important. So call him up right now."

"Did she leave me a telephone number?"

Terry objected, "You want me to read it all? There's two. It's a lot of numbers."

"Go slow, then."

Clay glanced warily over while Fred wrote down the numbers. He poured canned orange juice into a glass from the bathroom of the Silver Spur, and made a face as he unwrapped what passed for a croissant at Bee's Beehive.

"Marek," Fred informed Clay, punching in the first phone number, which should reach the dealer in his living quarters above the shop. One ring brought Marek's voice.

"It's Fred," Fred told him.

"I am watched. We must talk," Marek answered. "Also, we must not talk on the telephone."

"Yes?" Fred prompted.

"Where can we safely meet? No, this is better. Come to me at Marek's. Everyone comes to Marek's. Why should not you?"

"Trouble?"

"Maybe for someone."

"From yesterday? Your trip?"

"Say nothing."

"Expect me," Fred promised. He hung up and opened his coffee. Clay had wandered to the window and was looking alternately out into the rain, then at the landscape painting on the desk, and then at the many millions of dollars' worth of painting he had purchased the day before for a song. A smile of triumphant expectation played over his face. Napoleon had worn one like it the evening before Waterloo.

The huge painting, sprawled in all its lurid, frank display, cast pheromones of risk into the room. Fred said, "Clay, are these things hot? Stolen? What's the story? What's the secrecy? What's the risk? According to Marek, there's trouble for someone."

"What trouble?" Clay asked.

"Marek wouldn't say. What trouble do you expect?"

Clay deferred. "Simplicity is always an illusion. I cannot answer your questions, Fred, before we do our research, and now Marek's call threatens further complication. I must think. But I see Roberto Smith descending from his van."

"At least tell me if you suspect the things are stolen," Fred pressed.

"It is unclear, since we know nothing," Clay scolded. "Let us prove what they are, as well as where they come from. Once you have talked with Marek Hricsó, get him, as the purchaser of record, to confer with Alphonse Bird, the auctioneer. Marek understands that it is imperative that he not reveal for whom he acted?" Fred nodded. "He cannot have guessed what he bought for us. And you trust him?"

"I trust as many people as I understand. I'll drive to Boston and see what's brewing."

"It may be nothing. There's Roberto." Clay grabbed the landscape and faced it toward the wall.

Fred opened the door to Roberto's tap. The conservator came in tall, stooped, bald, and dressed for lawn tennis in a different country in another century. The light rain had splattered his long white pants and sweater. He dropped a black leather bag on the floor. His walrus mustache responded to the wind of his brief greeting, which he himself interrupted when he saw the painting spread out on the bed.

"Good God," Roberto exclaimed. "I thought they were extinct! You found one in the wild?" As if there were no one else in the room, he focused every atom of his attention on the painting. If the young woman next door, Daiquiri, had been killed the night before, she could not have received better service from the medical examiner. Roberto walked slowly around the two sides of the bed and its foot, occasionally leaning down to poke or pry, to brush his fingertips across a suspicious scab of color. He paused to tut and grieve where paint had been lost. Both Fred and Clay stood back. Male voices developed in the hallway, and a clatter of work commenced on what had been the door to room 415.

After five minutes Roberto opened his bag, took out a headband equipped with both a light and a magnifying bar, put it on his head, and started the slow circuit again. Finally, "You want it lined?" he asked accusingly.

"Only as an absolute last resort," Clay said. "With those terrible folds I don't know what else you can do, but I have seen you work miracles, Roberto."

"Flattery," Roberto said. "I like that. We will see what we can do short of lining it. The canvas is sturdy, a good Belgian linen, and I see no tears. I shall do what I can here, now, to stabilize it so that no further damage will be done between here and New Bedford. You did right, Mr. Reed, to have me come. I am particularly concerned about these areas—here, here, and here— where it is heavily worked, and where I see incipient separation of paint from the support. In such places I may wish to inject wax from behind and use heat to adhere the paint again. We shall see. It may be that after all it will be necessary to line it."

"I place myself in your good hands, as always," Clay assured him.

Roberto went out to his van and returned with four four-by- eight-foot sheets of waxed corrugated cardboard, two of which he and Fred eased under the canvas until the painting rested on a flat surface.

"There's so much dirt," Roberto cautioned. "I cannot anticipate what I will find when I get this onto my table, under proper lights, and clean it. An oil painting, as you know, never really dries; at best the paint is only somewhat less wet than it was." He took a jar of white powder from his bag, along with a soft brush and a handful of cut squares of rice paper. He carried the jar into the bathroom and came back mixing water into it with a tongue depressor. "Rice paste," he explained. "Everything I use is neutral. I trust the water is all right. If not, we are protected by dirt and old varnish. 'First do no harm' has always been my motto; with such a painting, we shall do better to err on the side of prudence."

One by one he saturated the squares of paper, eight inches to a side, with the paste, and then laid them onto the face of the painting, starting at a corner and overlapping the margins of one sheet with the next. "We may truly need this treatment only in a few areas," he assured himself. "Still, just to be certain…" He used the brush to smooth out areas where the paper bubbled or creased. As it began to dry, it cleaved to the contours of the impasto.

When the glued sheets were initially laid down, they were almost transparent, but as they dried to a protective skin they became cloudy, and then milky, until, dry, they were opaque white paper again, with whiter margins where the layers overlapped. Clay watched in misery as his new acquisition was gradually concealed under the rice-paper bandages.

"As I told you last night, I am presently occupied with sixteen other projects," Roberto warned Clay when he had finished and was standing back to let the last of the patches dry completely. "I will not rush or be rushed."

"You have responded to the emergency," Clay replied. "After this there is no need for intemperate speed. The painting now is safe, Roberto. Tell me, in your experience does Turner present particular difficulties for the conservator?"

"In my experience, no," Roberto answered. He allowed his mustache to twitch. They all three understood that Clayton was trying tactfully to ascertain whether Roberto had ever worked on a Turner in the past—understood, too, that Roberto would not tell him.

When the conservator's touch confirmed that the paper patches were dry, he made a sandwich of the canvas between cardboard sheets and taped the cardboard together to keep it rigid. Then he and Fred, one at either end, walked the cardboard package along the hall, past the new door to 415, and down the stairs.

The rain had let up. Roberto remarked, as they laid the cardboard on the floor of the van, "An odd place to encounter Mr. Reed."

"Yes, isn't it? I can't tell whether he realizes that."

"He tends to breast his cards," Roberto approved. "If it were my business, I would wonder what Mr. Clayton Reed was doing with a Turner in a whorehouse in Fall River. But as it is not my business, I do not wonder."

—⟨⟨⟨⟩⟩⟩—

"Shall I take the drawings with me to Boston?" Fred asked, finding Clay seated at the motel room's window, reading Simon Schama's *Citizens*. "Aren't you coming home? You made it sound as if time…"

"Yes. Time is one of many pressures. However, your conversation with Marek Hricsó makes me uneasy," Clay confided. "I shall wait where I am until I hear from you."

Chapter 6

Molly looked up from her place behind the Cambridge Public Library's reference desk. She saw it was Fred, and stood to kiss him, making him lean across the monitor. Her dark-brown curls brushed his face. She'd found a yellow summer dress with no sleeves. Her arms were delicious. "Tired of the good life at the Silver Spur?" she asked.

"Join me for lunch?"

"I took mine early. Had to interrupt my day to drive Sam's swimming suit to camp so he wouldn't get a demerit and miss the Aquarium trip. You in town for a spell, stranger?"

"I'm on my way to Boston. Don't mean to be a stranger, but after that I don't know."

Molly was working alone in back of the desk. Fred had to step aside to make way for a woman who had a question about Russian grammar. Molly knew everything, and what she didn't know, she could find out. Next came a boy wanting guidance on antitank missiles. When the coast was clear again Fred said, "I also have a research topic."

"That's what I'm here for," Molly told him.

"The English painter, Joseph Mallord William Turner. Died maybe in the mid-eighteen hundreds. England's greatest painter, many would say, at least in that century."

"Flaming soup," Molly agreed. "Big, atmospheric canvases. *Rain, Steam and Speed.*"

"That's him. What do you know about him and dirty pictures?"

"*That's* what you've been fooling with in Fall River? It isn't what Turner's known for, is it? Isn't he big landscapes and ships in tormented oceans? Seems to me, though," Molly said, "didn't I hear somewhere that after he died his wife burned a lot of pornography he'd made? That sticks in my mind. Terry gave you my message? It'd easy enough to check. Why don't you—"

"Your story sounds familiar," Fred said. "But I have to get to Charles Street, to see Marek. Pressing errand. I just couldn't be this close and not lay eyes on you. The kids are going to survive your mother's house? White on white on white?"

"The kids will. I don't know about the house, though. First Terry tracked in mulberries. Then after you called last night they brought that dratted dog back soaking wet. Don't smile like that. It's no joke cleaning up after Prince Charles."

The sun had burned off the ground fog during Fred's drive north on 24 from Fall River. Now it was hot again. Before he left the library's parking area, Fred cranked the windows open so as to catch the breeze of his own motion. In the backseat the purchases Marek had made for Clayton the day before responded to the road by tinkling against each other. The drawings had stayed with Clay, but Fred had the rest, including the School of Constable. Clay had directed briskly, "Give it six months, then dump it at Butterfield or Du Mouchelle. Or burn it. I don't care what it cost. I shall never live it down."

The public schools had let out for the summer, so the streets of Cambridge displayed samples from all the generations of its population, with no more than two people in ten representing the same national origin. Except for those required to compel respect in their professions, who wore too much, everyone in the streets looked like a summer tourist.

Choosing a route that would let him enjoy the river, Fred swung down Western Avenue and crossed the Charles, whose dirty water glared metallic-blue reflections at the sky. The white motorboats shoving through it were too large for this waterway. He turned left to get onto Storrow Drive and, keeping the brown city on his right, headed for the circle at the Salt-and-Pepper-Shaker Bridge, where he could hook a right onto Charles Street.

This portion of Boston was built on fill, a plateau of flat dirt dumped into the old Back Bay to provide foundations for buildings so that the residents of Beacon Hill could have someone to look down on. None of the pedestrians milling about on Charles Street was less than eighteen years old. There were plenty of them, browsing the antique shops and gift stores, where they could purchase soaps and coffees with exotic additives and, later, sniff at the packaging and wonder which was which.

Marek's, to Fred's brief glance as he drove past it searching for a parking spot, was no more or less busy than was normal for this time and day of the week. A scattering of people was visible through the big front window, behind the gilt bamboo and pyramids of jardinieres. Even double parking was out of the question, so Fred turned left at the light on Mountjoy and climbed Beacon Hill as far as the bib of pink-brick parking area next to Clay's house. The narrow building, of brick covered with ivy, projected stately British coolness. Fred dragged the boxes and the painting in through the downstairs entrance. The whole floor was either his work space or storage. Books and old sales catalogs lined the walls, with pictures leaning against them while they were being studied. In back of the office, a second room was filled with storage racks to hold the paintings that were not on Clay's walls upstairs or in what he called cold storage—meaning in a place with guards.

Fred checked the mail before rooting for the telephone on his desk, under auction catalogs and fliers.

"Marek's," announced the most beautiful human female legs in the known world.

"Lakshmi? Fred. Don't say my name. Put Marek on. Something's up. I'll come by if he's there, and if he's free."

"I first have something to read you. I have been saving it for Molly, but for the moment you will do." Lakshmi's voice was Gujarati and Welsh: cream laced with curry and spikenard. She'd done wonders for Marek's. That voice, when coupled with the legs, brought gouts of money, in joyful spurts, out of the pockets of surprised old men. "It is Ruskin, a wisdom gurgled from the font of John Ruskin, the English critic of art. Of course you know him," Lakshmi said.

"Marek wants—"

"In a moment. Until I said to myself this morning, Are you crazy? I was thinking I had to write my thesis on John Ruskin. Because that boy had his foot in everything—literature, art, art criticism, sociology, philanthropy—you name it. He knew everybody. If any one man did more to set the tone of Victorian England, I don't know who it was. But I can't stand him. He's so smug, and pure, and, though he's real polite about it, he's a man after all. I don't trust him. Here's the last straw, which I ran into yesterday: according to John Ruskin, a woman's work is fivefold. *One: To please her fellow human beings.* (Meaning men.) *Two: To feed them appetizingly. Three: To clothe them. Four: To keep them clean and tidy. Five: To teach them.* Now I shall fetch Marek while you dwell on all this wisdom."

"I am busy, Mr. England," came Marek's voice after a pause. For reasons of his own, he was speaking in code. "I shall come with you to look at ormolu. But I warn you, I give no more than ten minutes. Also I am not wanting ormolu. I love it, but no one buys. I do not care if Marie Antoinette has sat on it, and Catherine the Great and all her saints."

"Be there in five," Fred said.

———

Fred had known the shop better when it was Oona's, before Marek was unkindly ripped away from Liszt and Chopin to sell antiques, after Oona herself had been horribly translated into the hereafter. Fred still put his head in from time to time, but the young man's taste was infected by the urge to flabbergast, and he catered to a crowd that set Fred's teeth on edge. Oona had enjoyed variety. When Marek took over, he purged from her inventory anything funny, or odd, or on which you could strike a match. He also sprayed around that gift-shop scent. Walking in, Fred looked, as Molly's mother might put it, like a bull in a candy shop.

Lakshmi was dressed to sell. Her tight little plaid skirt just cleared the lower hemispheres of her buttocks. Miles of rich skin below the hem, on her right ankle rode a gold chain with bells, set above sandals with heels so high the woman's head was lifted almost to Fred's eyebrows. She stood in the doorway of the cool showroom, available to any of the three customers in the shop who might ask for assistance. Her perfect head and coloring would have let her pass for the Indian daughter of Alexander the Great; her breasts, under a simple shirt of thin white cotton, suggested temple sculpture done in material far more yielding than red sandstone. A Japanese man in a blue suit that screamed *tourist* beckoned from where he stood before a locked cabinet filled with china and silver.

"Something to show Mr. Hricsó," Fred announced, shaking his head slightly to let Lakshmi understand that they did not know each other. "Did he go out?"

"I'll ring," Lakshmi said. Maneuvering herself with long strides along the twisting aisles of precious furniture and objets d'art, she pressed the buzzer under Oona's desk, now Marek's. Then she turned her attention to the Japanese tourist. The young-urban-professional-looking pair who were discussing maps and prints in a bin as they flipped slowly through them—a man and a woman—looked up. Were they husband and wife or brother and sister? They had the same milky coloring and dark hair cut short. The man wore a tan suit, the woman a blue skirt and gray blazer over a white shirt that would go fine with the uniform.

Marek came through the door from the back room, allowing a quick glimpse of the gold and jewels behind him. The back room was where he kept the things he loved. He was dressed, as always, in black and white with gold trim. On entering his shop, visitors inevitably looked first at the bulge in the front of Marek's pants, then at Lakshmi, then guiltily away, back at the inorganic baubles they would have to settle for instead.

Marek told Fred, "Ten minutes only, Mr. England. I am busy." He strode through the shop, holding the front door open for Fred to follow him. Once outside, he turned immediately toward the river, walking fast. "Those two, did you see them, Fred? What do you think?"

"I am in the dark," Fred said. The sun burned on them whenever they stepped out of a pocket of shade. Ahead, the river thrust back the hot sunlight, dotted with sailing students busy tipping and overturning their small craft. Marek walked across the parkway until, at the water's edge, he stopped at a bench under a maple tree and motioned Fred to sit where the joggers and cyclists could threaten their feet.

"I cannot tell if we are followed," Marek whispered.

"I can," Fred told him. "We are not."

"Then we shall talk. I am alarmed and upset and maybe pissed off, Fred Taylor."

Fred said, "I wonder if it is possible to capsize repeatedly into the Charles River and not drink any of it."

"Last night at midnight a voice telephoned me. The voice will not say who it is. Those two, pretending to look at maps in my store, they are English. I do not trust the English. It is why, to warn you, I called you Mr. England."

"And the voice wanted?" Fred prompted. "The midnight caller? He was English?"

"The voice wanted to buy from me those drawings and paintings of pubic regions and pubic behaviors which I bought for *you*. I tell the voice they are not for sale. The voice offers me five thousand dollars, and then ten thousand dollars, which is what you told me Mr. Reed would pay. I say no, I shall keep them, I like these filthy things for myself. The voice asks will I take twenty thousand dollars? Twenty-five?"

"Jeekers," Fred cut in. "That's a lot of money for dirty pictures. I don't care how old they are."

"So I thought." A fat white Chris-Craft scattered the sailboats, and several of them toppled. "I warn the voice that now I hang up. It tells me, 'I am not finished. I will come to see you.' I do not like this voice." Marek paused and stared at the traffic on the river and at Cambridge shimmering on the far side.

"What's the problem?" Fred asked.

Marek gazed across the water. "The voice says, 'I will come. Think about what you will accept.' It hangs up, and I do not sleep. I am afraid. Also I think you have lied to me, Fred Taylor."

Fred said, "I won't insult you by asking if you think you should have more money from Mr. Reed."

Marek worried with his teeth at his full bottom lip. "My word is my word. But also I am in business. Should Mr. Reed wish to sell, I have, perhaps, a buyer. Thus and then, considering the amounts of money we are talking, I might feel better. Tell him I have a buyer. He may name his price."

"Sounds like an eager beaver," Fred agreed. "I'll tell Clay Reed, but I warn you, he always thinks he's going to figure out who did any unsigned picture he finds. We've got a whole binful, and they're all still as anonymous as when he started. He won't sell. But sure, I'll tell him."

Fred stood up. The big sale and its instant profit drained from Marek's large black eyes. "I'm going to stretch my legs," Fred said.

"You will call me after you speak to Mr. Reed?"

"If there's positive movement," Fred promised.

"The offer is much more than he intended to spend, Fred Taylor," Marek insisted, rising. "I am not happy, I think. Maybe someone is being cheated. Tell him this voice sounds very interested. But who knows when it may decide suddenly to buy something else instead? Such persons are like this."

Marek went back to his shop and Fred turned to walk upriver. He kept on for four blocks before cutting over to make for Mountjoy Street again, uphill.

"Saw your car," John Columbo said, separating himself from the shadow of a magnolia on the far side of Mountjoy Street. "But your doorbell didn't raise anyone." He was still dressed in the yellow leather pants from the day before. He always was. He still smelled, as he always did, of yesterday's sweat, though the shirt he wore was different—a red T this time. He still looked like a rat. His whiskers twitched.

Fred said, "I was not in."

"Clay Reed not home?"

"No wedding is complete without him."

Fred stood at the top of the steps that led down to his office level. Columbo stood next to him. Fred raised his eyebrows. "May I come in?" Columbo asked.

"I'm leaving shortly. What's on your mind?"

"I got to thinking. On the Hoesslin. Jesus, you faked us all out on the Constable. Nobody thought it was right. But on that Hoesslin, the *Grotto at Capri*? Somebody told me later—we got together after at Slimmy's, in Fairhaven—that Reed won't let you go in with other dealers. Won't join the pools or look out for his interest that way. So if that's the way it is, OK. It's hot out here."

"It is," Fred agreed.

"So maybe," Columbo continued, dodging in the sunlight, "I figured, you got on the wrong leg in the bidding, Reed's limit on the Hoesslin was five K, you got cut off. Am I right?"

Fred scratched his arms.

"Anyway," Columbo went on, "if Reed wants the picture for five thousand plus the percentage, plus let's say a hundred for my trouble, he can have it, and no hard feelings."

"My final bid was forty-five hundred," Fred said.

"Then, hell, take it for that," Columbo offered. "No hard feelings. I did good on a couple other things. You want to stop someplace for a drink?"

Fred said, "Clay won't be interested in your offer. You know, after the hunt is over, who wants a dead fox the dogs have been chewing?"

"What did you think of that Hungarian buying all the porno?" Columbo asked.

"I saw that," Fred admitted.

"Did you happen to notice—had you looked at that bunch of drawings?"

"Can't say I had," Fred said.

"Somebody said later, at Slimmy's, maybe they were good, those drawings," Columbo said.

Fred shrugged.

"Maybe we all missed the bus on that one," Columbo persisted. "Maybe we all got fooled."

Chapter 7

The phone was ringing when Fred reached his desk, after abruptly leaving John Columbo gaping in the hot afternoon.

"Mr. Clayton Reed?"

"This is his telephone," Fred said.

"We've been calling all day. There's something wrong with your answering machine."

The problem was not with the machine—because there *was* no machine. Clayton would not have one in the building, being convinced that somehow it would "let them know what we are doing."

"How may I help you?" Fred asked.

"This is Linda. From the offices of Alphonse Bird? Alphonse Bird Galleries?"

"Yes?"

"Mr. Bird had to go out. Can he reach you here in about…" Linda's voice was breathless and harassed. "I need—that is, he needs—you have to bring it back."

"What's the problem?" Fred asked. "You lose the check?"

"We have to hold it, maybe return it. Mr. Bird will explain when he speaks to you."

"Fill me in," Fred suggested. "I'm moving around today, so I'll be on the road most of the time."

"I don't know…."

"We bought lot two fifty-nine, the School of Constable landscape. I paid with a check drawn on the Perkins Stillton Bank in Pride's Crossing. The check is good. The transaction is complete. People don't bring things back. Tell me, what is Mr. Bird's problem?"

"There's going to be a challenge to the will, and to the executors. Maybe *by* the executors also, since the chairman of the board…the widow…it's a terrible, terrible mess. They're claiming that the whole sale is null and void. We have to notify all the buyers and ask you—meanwhile, all the money from the sale has to be held in escrow—and ask you to return your purchase. We'll keep it on our premises until the legal formalities…you will get something in tomorrow's mail, but Mr. Bird wants me to notify everyone today by telephone—the important buyers, like yourself. It's a nightmare."

"Spar Ballard didn't like his chastity belt? Linda, good luck," Fred said, putting down the receiver. "Good luck especially with the rug dealers," he added to himself. He glared at the telephone a moment before telling it, "Jeekers!" Then he picked up the mail and the School of Constable, set the alarm, and headed for his car. His engine was turning over, adding its little gesture of support to the heat of the afternoon, and Fred was looking over his shoulder into Mountjoy Street, before he remembered: There's all that garbage Marek bought as well. Let's be consistent.

The cardboard boxes went into the trunk, next to the painting, which Fred had wrapped in one of the unmarked towels provided by the Silver Spur Motel.

—◆—

Molly's mother's house was one of a line of little clapboard buildings, facing another, similar row of clapboard buildings, on Rush Street, which ran between Brattle and Mount Auburn, a championship spit's distance from the river. There was never a place to park on Rush Street, and if there was, Molly's red Colt was in it, with her mother's lone visitor's parking permit on the dashboard. Since the city of Cambridge allowed each of its residents to have only one friend who drove, Fred could either find an open meter or be an outlaw in a resident-parking-only spot, risking a tag-and-tow whose combined cost would be more than his car was worth. He blocked Rush Street long enough to unload the boxes into the house, then parked six blocks away in a spot good for two hours' worth of quarters. That would bring him almost up to six o'clock, after which he'd be golden till morning.

This part of Cambridge gave a hint of the village it had been in the early eighteenth and nineteenth centuries. The houses on this flat land next to the water were small and unpretentious because they had been built for people of modest income at a time when it was regarded as unhealthy to live within reach of the river vapors. In the end it was the taxes, not the vapors, that did for the modest people, once the rich discovered there was pleasure to be had in living near the water—so long as they could do so without rubbing elbows with the poor.

Fred walked back from his car, keeping to the shade of the big oaks, maples, and ash trees that spread out over the houses. The landmark for Molly's mother's was a purple mulberry tree that towered above a neighbor's yard. It filled the street and sidewalk with cast fruit and the droppings of sated birds.

The house of Molly's mother also stood out for the fact that it alone had a sign in front, Wombswell Croft. The proud owner had picked it up on a previous trip to England. The sign hung from a scaffold next to the ten-foot walkway between sidewalk and front porch.

If there was anything in the way of a Royal Commemorative souvenir that Molly's mother did not own, it was only because she hadn't yet had an opportunity to buy it. The house that Fred now eased into could serve as the Cambridge annex to the Tower of London gift shop. Prince Charles came trotting down the white-carpeted stairs and set up a loud greeting. Fred took the boxes to the basement and stashed them behind the water heater. He propped the School of Constable on the mantelpiece in front of a framed replica of Gainsborough's *Blue Boy*, then found a place in the living room where he could sit without smashing china. He telephoned room 413 at the Silver Spur.

Fred told Clayton, "Marek's been offered twenty-five thousand dollars for the drawings, by a voice he hasn't seen. He's not happy. Feels cheated. He could make trouble. He wants the drawings back, to sell them. I told him fat chance. He won't even tell me whether the voice is male or female. John Columbo—I happened to run into him because he was hiding under the magnolia across from your house—tells me that after the sale, there was talk in the trade that possibly Marek had scored...."

"Can you not tell me this in person?" Clay protested. "The telephone is no place—"

"But more seriously, and perhaps more interesting," Fred pushed on, "Alphonse Bird's office says there's a court order in force, or coming, that will nullify all of yesterday's transactions."

"What!" Clay screeched.

"Something is in the mail, according to Linda," Fred said. Prince Charles, disappointed in the large man's company, trotted upstairs to watch for Terry from the landing. "They're demanding the return of that School of Constable we bought," Fred continued. "Which we don't care about. My big worry is Marek, and whether he'll hold out against legal paper—"

"This spells disaster," Clay interrupted, fuming. A frenzied tapping sounded from his end of the phone. His habit, in his own house, was to strike with a pencil on a Wedgwood plate when so moved. What substitute for Wedgwood had he found at the Silver Spur?

Fred marched on to the next logical plateau. "Already Marek was looking slippery on his own account, and threatened to take action because of the other interested party. I don't trust him to keep our confidence when his opponent has the power to deport him. I do not know what his status as an immigrant may be. Even if that's on the up-and-up, he has to fear the IRS, like anyone else who does a cash business. As far as the auctioneers are concerned, he's small stuff; they'll start with the big-ticket items, like our School of Constable. They must be climbing the walls. There goes eight thousand of their take, on that picture alone, when you put together the vig paid by both sides."

"One moment," Clay said. "That will be my tea." Vague sounds came through the receiver before Clay's voice continued, "Very well. In ten minutes I shall be free. Fred, I am with you. I hate it, yes, but on principle I would not dream of returning the painting you purchased. As to the rest, what is the nature of the legal challenge? Is it serious?"

"I don't know. Shall I call Marek again, warn him about what's coming, and instruct him to say—if he agrees—that he sold the whole batch to a man he didn't know, for cash, for an instant profit? It's almost true. The problem is, he's got this other idea too, that there's still money to be made. He'd defend the story better if there was something in it for him. Perhaps another five thousand."

Clay sputtered, "I hate for another man to know my business. This is intolerable. The provenance must stand up to public scrutiny. We cannot now put a single relevant direct question to anyone connected with the sale! At a time when the need for subtlety and speed is paramount!"

"If Marek stands fast, nobody will know what you have," Fred reminded him. "We can both keep our mouths shut, you and I. But for God's sake, Clay, what's the rush?"

Clay said, "My reasons for haste are as private as they are compelling. Bear with me, I implore you. Tea is a social art, do you not agree?"

"What do I say to Marek?"

"Do not offer him a bribe. Any compulsion that is offered to him by Alphonse Bird will ruffle his feathers and keep him in our camp. His instincts are on the side of our interest. Wait before you talk to him again."

"It's risky."

"My decision is made. You and I will both stay clear of my house now. We will not be seen. We will not receive this demand. Telephone me later. I must go. A young lady is to join me for tea. Civilization shall continue its advance, however dark the interruptions. Drat! This is ghastly. We have five days, and...talk to me later. Devil take me, I am upset! I shall lose my opportunity. I am in trouble."

Terry and Sam arrived with a whoop and a clatter, whacking the front door knocker of Wombswell Croft-upon-Charles. "I told you, nobody's gonna be here," Terry's voice shrieked over Prince Charles's welcome, as the dog leapt against the inside of the door. Fred eased himself out of the chair where he had been dozing and let them in.

"He always says to let *him* carry the key, and then he lost it," Terry complained in triumph. "He has to be the *man* and the *oldest* and the *boss* and *have* everything and *lose* it."

"We'll go to Dickson's and get a couple of copies of my key," Fred said. "Maybe get some ice cream in the Square someplace. Then each person will have a key."

"And bring Prince Charles with us," Terry said, throwing her arms around the dog. "Oh, don't you hope he gets to live long enough to turn into *King* Charles?"

"It's in the pocket of my swimming suit," Sam said, negotiating the difficult passage down the hall toward the kitchen and cold Kool-Aid, with Terry and Fred behind him. "I didn't lose it. Ha! It's in my locker, in my swimming suit, so tomorrow I *can't* forget my swimming suit. So don't make such a big deal about it, Terry. You want some, Fred?"

They drank Raspberry Ranch Kool-Aid together, hovering over the white linoleum in front of the sink, each watching for the others' drips. Fred's mug was emblazoned with Prince Philip in a polo helmet. Terry had someone called Princess Michael of Kent, and Sam, the Queen Mother's Seventy-fifth.

"I hope we don't run into that dog Pearl again," Terry said. "Yesterday Prince Charles kept trying to climb up on him."

"That was mating," Sam informed her scornfully. "Or trying to." He put his mug in the sink.

"Well, anyhow, let's take a different street," Terry said. "I hardly could hold his leash, he got so jumpy. It's like you were going crazy, you bad dog. Yes you are. You have to be a good Prince Charles."

They walked together all the way to Molly's library, where they persuaded Molly to let Fred buy them early dinner at a place where Prince Charles could mourn outdoors while everyone else ate hamburgers inside.

Once the sun had lowered in the sky, the remaining heat of the day turned pleasant. Molly and Fred and Molly's kids strolled through Harvard Square almost like a family. The crowd was less than it would be once Harvard's summer session kicked in. Still, there were jugglers, fire eaters, puppeteers, and skate-boarders, with acres of uncovered tattoos tracing homegrown runes reminiscent of the symbols for elements in medieval alchemy. Molly and Fred lagged behind the children and the eager dog.

"He wasn't married," Molly announced. "Wait a minute." She balanced, holding Fred's left arm as she did something to one shoe. The yellow of her dress was evening primrose.

"*Who* wasn't married?" Fred asked.

"Turner. You were asking about the painter Turner? I had a couple of minutes and checked. He never married." Her shoe adjusted, Molly rebalanced herself on her own feet and dropped Fred's arm. Together they looked at a bank-window display of photographs of solitary flowers and wistful cats. "So that story we both heard is an old wives' tale," Molly said. "I never thought of Turner as doing people anyway, beyond little stiff figures in silhouette in front of broad vistas, or those frightening scribbles of drowning people in the wake of *The Slave Ship* at the MFA. That's the Turner painting Ruskin said was the absolute best. It's on the label. Ruskin was Turner's sublime interpreter, you know."

They started walking again, keeping an eye on the kids, who'd slowed to criticize a juggler. "No, he could draw a human when he had to," Fred said. "Or when he wanted to. By the way, Lakshmi gave me a quotation for you from John Ruskin, but I fail to remember it. It was for you to nail up in your hall of infamy. She's still rooting among the dead white males hoping to find underneath them all a thesis topic she can stand. Meanwhile, she's as happy as a you-know-what in you-know-what, at Marek's."

"He fired her," Molly blurted. "I wasn't going to bring it up until later, we were having such a nice time. But she—"

"Fired her!?" Fred exclaimed. He stopped and let the traffic of pedestrians sweep past, bearing their ice cream cones and Walkmans. "I was there just this afternoon. She and Marek were getting along like Scylla and Charybdis—between the two of them, the customer doesn't stand a chance."

"Let's keep up with the kids," Molly said, dragging him into motion. "She called me, very upset, half an hour before you all showed up at the library. She wants you to call her, but she'll be out until ten. Marek fired her because he claims she's your spy."

"Jeekers! I may have got her the job, but so what? What does Marek have, or know, that *I'd* be after?"

"Anyway, call her. I have her number. She's very upset. She's also mad enough to tear Marek to pieces with her teeth. He gave her three minutes to get out and watched her as she packed up her things. Two hundred dollars cash he shoved into her handbag, and told her never to darken his door again."

Chapter 8

A man named Small is staying at the Royal Court Hotel," Lakshmi Thomas said at the end of a brief and bitter speech. "That son of a bitch Marek says I'm your spy? OK, I'll be your spy. If any money changed hands, Small will be looking for you and Clayton Reed."

"Can you describe him?"

"A little English twit in a twit brown suit that's a size too large, wearing a straw twit hat."

"How much money, do you know?"

"Search me. Anyway, it's just my guess as to what happened, from the fact that that bastard fired me before he went into the back room with Small. In front of Small he fired me, and then the two of them watched me gather up my things. So what do you think, Fred?"

"I think Marek made at least one mistake."

"He has that video monitor in the back room, so he must have seen me telling you that stupid Ruskin quote about the five pillars of womanhood. No, that was on the phone. He knows we're friendly, though. I liked that job. I even liked that crazy Marek! He thinks you made a fool of him. He was stomping around and swearing in that back room of his."

The kids had been sent to bed, with Prince Charles pattering anxiously up the stairs behind them in order to sleep with Terry. Lakshmi was talking from her apartment five miles away, in Watertown, wondering how she was going to pay for it. Molly and Fred had retired to the air-conditioned master bedroom, which resembled a wedding cake turned inside out. The bed was too small for the two of them and the telephone. "Lakshmi, I'm sorry. And thank you for the tip," Fred said. "I knew that Marek was a jerk, but not that he was a fool. If I hear of something else..."

Molly turned off her bedside light as Fred broke off the connection. "I should fill Clayton in," Fred told her. "You want me to use the phone downstairs?"

"It sounds interesting. I'll snooze while you talk. Unless—is it dangerous?"

"Our opponent is an English twit named Small," Fred said. He telephoned Clay and let room 413's extension ring until it woke him. "Reading between the lines, and making educated guesses, here's the situation," Fred began. "A man named Small is apparently interested enough in learning who purchased the package you care about to buy the information."

Fred waited for Clayton to digest this. Molly snored. She could move into sleep as quickly as if she controlled it with a switch. "Does Small know what we have?" Clay asked. "This is an infuriating complication. Just when the two of us should be giving our full attention to those drawings—"

"There's a nice little painting too," Fred reminded him. "Remember? The one that was wrapped around them?"

"I can enjoy the painting without provenance. That is for my enjoyment alone. The drawings are a different matter. I have a deadline. We must concentrate on our research, and we cannot. Will you come in the morning?"

"Ten o'clock," Fred said. "And I have an idea about the research. See you shortly."

"You going to join me?" Molly murmured in her sleep.

"In a minute. One more call. A quick one."

Clay stared when he opened the door of 413 to Fred and Lakshmi Thomas. Fred had advised Lakshmi to dress for the Silver Spur. She had chosen baggy bib overalls and a denim shirt, so her effect was muted though not concealed. For that she would have needed a fright wig and a rubber Richard Nixon mask.

Lakshmi waited in the hall as Fred explained her presence to Clay. "Lakshmi is an old friend who's working toward her Ph.D. in English literature at Tufts University. Research is second nature to her, and she's discreet. She's also available. She worked for Marek Hricsó until yesterday, when they parted company—Marek's idea."

Clay said, "I do not want outsiders knowing my business."

"She knows how we bought what we bought, and what it is," Fred said. "She knows we need to prove it and defend it. She knows the story up to now. She can be trusted. We are cornered. You claim time pressure? We need her. Come in, Lakshmi."

Clay moved backward, making space, as Fred ushered Lakshmi into the room and closed the door behind her. The beds were neatly made. Clayton had closed the blinds again; he might as well be living underground. Schama's *Citizens* lay open on the windowsill. Following Lakshmi's gaze to the book, Clay remarked, "French furniture was worse after their revolution. Unspeakable, much of it. Nothing was gained."

Lakshmi sat in one of the armchairs, Clay in the other. Clay stared at Lakshmi, daring her to speak up in favor of the furniture of the Empire or the Directoire period. "Your field?" he finally asked.

"Nineteenth-century English literature. My orals are completed. I am casting about for a thesis topic."

"Very well," Clay said, reaching a decision. "Our situation can hardly be worse. Fred, I must either trust your judgment or do without you. Miss Thomas, shall we acknowledge that in the fullness of time, we will agree on an appropriate wage?"

Lakshmi nodded. Clay gave her a moment to say something unnecessary before continuing, "Very well. Because my hands are tied; because there is a time consideration; and because the hounds of law and of avarice are upon our traces...Miss Thomas, you recognize the allusion?"

"Swinburne," Lakshmi said. "*Atalanta in Corydon.* In your opinion, does the word *traces* in the poem refer to tracks, or to the leash?"

"Very well," Clay said. He breathed in a great sigh. "Swinburne." He had dressed for this day in his white linen suit, set off by a green necktie. His stack of white hair was brushed into a rough puzzle. He laced his fingers together while he organized his mind.

"I will give you a bit more of the story up to now. Five months ago," Clay said, "Lord Hanford died. He was an old man, but his death was not expected. It was sudden. It does not concern us. Fred, you may wish to sit? This will take time."

Fred leaned against the door.

"Lord Hanford had spent the last several years of his life in Westport, returning only occasionally to London to vote or to make a tedious announcement in the House of Lords. That also does not concern us." Clay tapped a pencil in a glass ashtray perched on the windowsill next to his book.

"Six weeks ago," Clay said, "a distant relative of my wife—my wife is deceased, Miss Thomas—who spends his summers in Westport and hobnobs with his neighbors, telephoned and asked me to join the board of the Runnymede House Museum, which was being assembled under the authority of Lord Hanford's executors.

"I demurred, especially once I discovered that there was to be a fee involved. I am not one to purchase honor. Each trustee was expected to make a substantial contribution, either in cash or in kind. I had not taken to Lord Hanford on the two occasions when I met him. Also, I did not approve of what I had seen of his collection. It celebrates the most vapid and soporific aspects of British art. Are there questions?"

Lakshmi was listening, her hands folded in her lap. She shook her head.

"In the course of the conversation with my relative," Clayton went on, "I learned of the prospective auction, which, it seemed to me, was being organized with undue haste. 'The funeral baked meats did coldly furnish forth,' and so on. I was given to understand that the bulk of the sale would be made up of Lord Hanford's estate, whatever was not earmarked for the museum. But also to be sold were items to be donated by new board members. At this news I became intrigued. There are excellent things still left in some of these houses.

"I was encouraged, too, to hear that the museum's director was to be Isabel Cooney, who had been Lord Hanford's curator. She is a fool, a decorator, and a decoration. Hanford was headstrong and heedless and could not retain the services of any curator worthy of the title. Ms. Cooney has no reputation and even less learning.

"I expressed my regrets. Nevertheless, I made a contribution to the enterprise, which earned me the invitation to preview, quietly, along with a few other friends and benefactors, at a cocktail party the night before the sale, the objects that were to go under the hammer. Again that evening I was asked if I might not reconsider. But it was now out of the question: had I undertaken to act in the best interest of this redundant, backwater, and wholly unnecessary little museum, I would have placed my own best interest in jeopardy.

"Miss Thomas, as you now understand, two days ago I purchased, with Marek Hricsó acting as intermediary, an important collection of erotic drawings by Joseph Mallord William Turner. Although they were not identified, I knew them as soon as I touched them. Their value, both aesthetically and from the point of view of scholarship...is beyond calculation.

"There is a problem, however. Their provenance must be proved, and on unimpeachable authority."

"There is no unimpeachable authority," Lakshmi declared.

Clay stared at her in awe, followed by an expression of sudden, interested relief. "Miss Thomas, we may do very well together. Will you take refreshment? Coffee? Perrier?"

"No. Your story is refreshment enough even for this warm day."

Clay melted into still more willing narrative. "Turner died in the mid-eighteen hundreds."

"Eighteen fifty-one," Lakshmi interjected. "I am familiar with this, since John Ruskin wrote about him. I have spent time reading Ruskin. Ruskin was Turner's great champion, as you know. In fact—forgive me—I am reminded of an entry in the young Ruskin's journal, written after his first meeting with his idol Turner, in eighteen forty. With your permission?"

Clay nodded, taken aback.

Lakshmi recited, "*Introduced today to the man who beyond all doubt is the greatest of the age; greatest in every faculty of the imagination, in every branch of scenic knowledge; at once the painter and poet of the day, J. M. W. Turner. Everybody had described him to me as coarse, boorish, unintellectual, vulgar. This I knew to be impossible. I found in him a somewhat eccentric, keen-mannered, matter of fact, English-minded gentleman; good natured evidently; bad natured evidently, hating humbug of all sorts, shrewd, perhaps a little selfish, highly intellectual, the powers of the mind not brought out with any delight in their manifestation or intention of display, but flashing out in a word or a look....*"

"I am impressed," Clay said with a grimace.

"Me too," said Fred, giving Lakshmi a wink.

"'Truth to nature'" Clay said. "Was that not Ruskin's doctrine? Yes, I had known of young Ruskin's devotion to the cause of Turner."

Lakshmi asked, "May I see the drawings?"

"In the fullness of time, perhaps," Clay said. "As you are your-self a scholar, Miss Thomas, you may imagine my present frustration. Just three evenings ago I recognized Turner's hand and screwed my courage to the hazard. I spent the night in agony at the indifferent carelessness of the ignorant many who were fon-dling the collection; ogling it; laughing at it, even; dismissing it as worthless. I raced to this vantage point to be nearby, and organized my attack...." Clay gestured toward Fred.

"The next afternoon we made the purchase, expecting there-after to justify my risk by meticulous research. Due to circumstances I need not go into now, it must be undertaken in haste, and with great care. While I prefer to do my research *before* buying, this would not be the first time my connoisseurship had to await justification after the fact. A small Dutch painting of the seventeenth century, one of the stars of my collection, about which Fred will not have told you—and about which he *will* not tell you—is a case in point.

"Given complications that have developed since the sale, I cannot act. Neither Fred nor I can afford to be seen in our usual haunts. I am almost frantic with my impatience to work myself, as well as to release Fred to initiate the direct inquiries that are now impeded."

Lakshmi took an orange notebook from the bib pocket of her overalls and unclipped a pen from the same pocket.

Clay continued smoothly, "I must—we must, Miss Thomas, if you will—without my being discovered to be the drawings' owner, demonstrate that they are in fact by Turner, and show how I come to have them. What trace can you find of this collection? *Trace*, in this case, meaning '*track*,' Miss Thomas. 'Spoor.'"

"Surely the drawings themselves are eloquent of their author-ship?" Lakshmi objected.

"Indeed. But we must also demonstrate a line, a succession, of title—what is called provenance. Here are some observations. We assume that Lord Hanford brought the drawings from England.

In business he was a daring and ruthless man; as a collector he must have exercised the same qualities. He was also a dolt, as witness his ownership of a collection of this kind, which neither he nor his curator could identify as the work of England's best-known artist."

Fred put in, "It's not impossible that the drawings were the contribution of one of the trustees. If we could afford to show our hand as the purchaser, we could ask the auctioneer for the name of the previous owner—and maybe even find it out, if the owner agreed. Unfortunately, we can't do that now, but nevertheless we need to know for certain who owned them last. From there we can work back."

"Or why not work forward?" Lakshmi proposed. "Knowing where our end point is, what is our beginning? Why not start where the drawings were last seen? Or start with the artist. You said it was about three hundred pieces? Aside from the artist himself, who might have owned so many of his works? Where were they made? If they are erotic, who…?"

"Clay, you've spent hours looking at the drawings," Fred said. "Do they themselves in some way hint at where they've been? Or those marks and words and phrases I noticed on a few of them, do any of *them* suggest a person or a place? I noticed, for example, the name *Admiral Booth* on one. Who's that?"

"I've not recorded the words. That should be done. But I have completed sorting the drawings by the paper they were made on. That in itself, given the number of them, was an enormous labor." Clay stared searchingly at Lakshmi a final time. She sat quiet, attentive, her pen poised at the notebook on which she had as yet written nothing.

"I will show a few of them to you," Clay said. "But first we must all wash our hands."

Chapter 9

"No. If time is a factor," Lakshmi interjected, "I'll begin right away. Given its commitment to this field, I should work at Yale. Mr. Reed, can you get me quick access to its libraries and collections?"

Clay hesitated, tapping on his ashtray, which bore the crest of the Best Western. He said, "I'm an alumnus of Yale, and I agree with you entirely, Miss Thomas—nevertheless, in this instance, I prefer that we settle for second best, and fall back upon Harvard. We have no time for London. Steer clear of Yale, please: 'pitchers have ears.' Shakespeare. I shall telephone a friend. Harvard will open to you."

"There'll be a bus from Fall River?" Lakshmi asked, standing to tuck the notebook into her bib pocket. "I'll telephone you each evening. Shall we say at nine? To keep you informed of my progress."

"Marek can't give us away, since he does not know where we are. Nevertheless, I'm going to have a look at Small," Fred said. "When something sniffs my tail, I like to see what kind of teeth it has. I'll drive you back, Lakshmi. Clay, let's put those drawings in a safe-deposit box. If I make copies of them all at Kinko's, you can work from those."

"Great God!" Clay exclaimed. "Fred, this is not a joking matter. We are all on edge, but that is no excuse for levity. I am protected at the Silver Spur. Our enemies—but perhaps I over-simplify— would never think to look for Turner's drawings in Fall River. They are safer here than they would be in a bank. Before you go, Fred, one word about the Royal Court Hotel. As putative rival to the Ritz, you will find that it still falls short, in many ways, due to an endemic managerial confusion between nobility and class. However I may cavil, the sad fact is that the chain is making money. It is, therefore, hard to precipitate significant change. You may agree with me that the hotel is at this juncture, even in its choice of name, more reminiscent of a highway motel in Mississippi from the 1930s than a major Boston hotel with pretensions of being first class. In many ways it is as vulgar as Windsor Castle."

Fred interrupted, "Will your relative give you the names of the new museum's board members? We need those. And someone should talk to the widow."

Clay announced flatly, "My priority shall be to determine our legal status. What is this challenge to the will? How can a purchase made in good faith be nullified? By what right can my prize be snatched back from me? I await a return call from Myron, Fred. I shall put these questions to him. Miss Thomas, Fred, good hunting."

—⁂—

Fred searched the lobby of the Royal Court Hotel for a small twit in a straw hat. There were too many who fitted the description. He'd dropped Lakshmi in Cambridge, ditched his car in a parking garage, and taken the subway into Boston. Although the city was hot, its air was moving on the surface. The Boston Common and the Public Garden were antic with tourists. Newbury Street, where people strove to look as if they were prepared to spend far more than they should for clothes, sported its normal complement of pedestrians, who passed between small groups of almost naked men engaged in noisy street repair. All this was overlooked by the Royal Court Hotel. It was shortly after one o'clock, according to Fred's Timex. Fred sat at the Royal Court Hotel bar for a while, discouraging a draft beer while he kept his eyes open and listened for the tang of a British tongue. Again, there were too many, three quarters of them American-born. After half an hour more he left the flat brown liquid at the bar, told the bartender, "Be right back," and went to the desk to ask if Mr. Small was in his room. The concierge, a long-faced West Indian branded with a name tag identifying him as Mr. Sanhedrin, shielded the keyboard from Fred's gaze, punched the tones for 611, and listened at the receiver to the ring.

"There is no answer," Mr. Sanhedrin advised.

Fred shrugged and went back to the bar. He was almost alone there. Despite its being dark and cool, it was not a place that people were fighting to be in this afternoon. Fred sat on his stool and took two more consultative sips of his beer before once again telling the bartender, "Be right back," and making off in the direction of the room whose polished brazen sign suggested that Gentlemen were to be had inside.

—⁓⁓—

The plastic sign hanging on the knob of the door to 611 told anyone who could read five languages, DO NOT DISTURB. Fred thumped the door and waited. Two minutes later he thumped the door again, demanding, "Open up." The sixth-floor corridor offered a luscious field of roses, pink and yellow, after the pattern vouchsafed in a vision to Laura Ashley. The field of roses did not limit itself to the horizontal but climbed the walls as well. Fred thumped again.

"What do you want?" a male voice asked from the other side.

"Open up," Fred repeated.

The door opened against its ornamental chain. A couple stepped out of the elevator down the corridor to Fred's right and started moving in his direction. They hung on each other's arms and waists and lips, like honeymooners who had known each other intimately for years. Within the crack of the door to room 611 stood a balding young man on the skinny side, with a towel around his waist. In the voice of an English twit he asked testily, "Can you read, man?" Beyond him, inside, a heaving form attempted to become one with the bedclothes. The honeymooners passed behind Fred in their aura of pink pollen, saying, either one or both of them, "Snookum ookum poochums?"

Fred snapped his wallet open and shut against the crack of the door, at the level of its visible tenant's face. He waited.

"I shall join you in the vestibule in an hour," the man said. "This is not convenient."

Fred told him, "You don't want me bringing in more security, Small. Give me five minutes of your time now, unless you want us to shoot for an overnight gig downtown."

Small hesitated for half a minute before taking the chain off and standing belligerently back. A squeak came from the hump under the tousled bedclothes. The room was painted a pink that echoed an element in the color scheme of the corridor, whose wallpaper pattern was also repeated in the curtains overlooking the green and pleasant land of the Public Garden. Fred strode in and sat down in one of the armchairs placed in the roomy window. The handmade original-antique oil paintings decorating the room were shocking schlock, disgracefully nondenominational: roses or cows or landscapes or maidens. No one could say what they really represented. No one could look at them long enough to care.

Small stood like an Englishman without pants who is in a foreign hotel room from whose bed are coming sounds he does not care to explain, and in whose chair a sudden large American male is seated, glowering. Fred said, "We want an explanation of your visit yesterday to the alien Marek Hricsó."

Small's mouth fell open.

"We will check your story against his," Fred continued. "Take your time."

Small sought to splutter and bluster, but he had missed his cue if that was to be his response. He had to settle instead for injured innocence. "Everything about me is in order," he stated.

"Congratulations," Fred told him. "You are unique. Your business with Marek Hricsó?"

"It was business. *My* business," Small said, and looked belligerent still, if not pugnacious. His face resembled one of the starchier vegetables. Fred crossed his legs and let a foot swing. "Still, it is only business," Small added. "A client of mine—I maintain a gallery in London, off the Burlington Arcade. My card." He reached for his wallet and learned that he was dressed in a towel.

"Alexander Small," Fred said, nodding. "Yes, yes, we know. Go on."

"I am undertaking a confidential purchase through Mr. Hricsó. We are in negotiation."

Fred said, slowly and skeptically, "And your other business in Boston?"

"This has been interesting," Small said, intelligence joining his roster of responses late in the game. "May I see your identification again?"

"I have what I need," Fred said. No other questions would be answered now. He stood. The bed had gone still, though its arrangement eloquently showed the presence of burrowing limbs. The woman's Louis Vuitton bag was with her clothes, a blue suit in two parts and pedigreed underwear, all laid carefully across the second bed, next to the man's. Fred had lost the jump he'd lucked into when he caught Small in the sack with someone.

"I'll keep in touch," Fred promised.

Fred found John Columbo lounging in the narrow shade on the top step of the Boston Public Library's new building, the extension Sargent had not lived long enough to decorate with murals celebrating the war in Vietnam. "Oh, John," Fred said. "How's tricks? Can I buy you something cold?"

Columbo stood slowly, looking around with exaggerated surprise. He picked up a black canvas bag and slung its strap over his shoulder. "Fred," he said. "Second thoughts?"

"Why don't we sit in the shade somewhere and bend an elbow?" Fred offered, leading the way across and down Boylston Street to Clarendon, toward a grove of umbrellas shading tables on the sidewalk. This part of Boston offered two shops for every church. Columbo stayed next to and slightly behind Fred. Today's T-shirt was yellow, but it smelled just like yesterday's red one; unlike the pants, it seemed yellow on purpose, rather than by default.

They sat among a crowd of refreshment seekers, at a table watched over by the fussy front window of an almost vacant bookstore. Columbo ordered a beer that cost more than the imports because it was a local microbrew. Fred's iced tea justified its price with a floating leaf of mint and a lemon seed.

"Hot day," Columbo told Fred. Fred drank his weak tea. "About the Hoesslin," Columbo continued. "You reconsidered my offer. Talked with his majesty, and now he's changed his price limit. Do you have a smoke? I'm trying to quit." His small black eyes looked around him, into the seated crowd, then out at the sidewalks, for a friend who smoked. A long block away, someone else had taken his place on the step of the BPL.

"I'll tell you, Fred, I was ready to do the deal yesterday, in all good faith. You know I was. Even offered to take a loss. Am I right?"

Fred nodded. Columbo took a last swig from his glass, considered the fit of the liquid in his mouth, and swallowed. "I no longer have the picture," he said. His narrow lips cornered into a smirk. He waited and watched for Fred to feed him a straight line. A tour bus stopped and farted a black cloud into their faces.

"You get a call from Bird?" Fred asked.

"Are you kidding me? I sold them back their fucking picture. It's like the first and only time I ever had those bastards over a barrel. 'Bring the picture back,' they say, 'and we'll hold it *and* your check.' Who do they think they fucking are? The Federal Reserve Board? You bet I took that picture back. I hung on to it until I had my check, which I told them I had a right to see to make sure they hadn't deposited it. I grabbed it, tore it up, and put it in my pocket."

The tour bus farted again and moved away. Columbo arched back in his garden chair, reached into the front pocket of his leather pants, and pulled out some fragments of light-blue paper. The wind scattered a few of them into Clarendon Street. Fred beckoned the waitress to bring another beer.

"Fucking picture wouldn't clean, I found out," Columbo said, nodding his thanks as the empty bottle was cleared away, then pouring anew. "I mean to say, *after* I talked to you yesterday, I took it to my guy in Charlestown. He tested it, and the fucking thing wouldn't clean. He tried everything there is. You got lucky on that one, Freddy boy. But what's the story on the Constable? You taking it back? I can't imagine Clayton Reed...who do they think they are, those fucking lords and lordettes, selling you something and then telling you they'll sue you to get it back?"

At the next table two elderly women were deciding that the snack they were having now would do for dinner. Each seemed to be wearing a hat designed for the other.

Fred said, "Our position is that we own the Constable. We paid for it. We have it. Let them come and get it if they want.

Due to some snafu, we never received our formal notice in the mail. I only talked to Linda. What is their legal rationale?"

"Restraining order. Notice of impending action. Gobbledygook. I signed for the notice at nine-thirty—the courier woke me up. Nine-forty-five I'm reading it to my lawyer. Eleven-thirty I am down there at Bird's, in Scituate, doing exactly what I told you." Columbo took a deep drink and wiped his mouth on the hem of his yellow shirt. "What their rationale is, I could not give a shit. But the scuttlebutt, if you care, sounds like a good story. If you like stories."

Columbo collected his thoughts and signaled the waitress. That done, he continued, "The son, I guess that's the new Lord Hanford, is making a big stink from England, wants the old man's body dug up, claims he was bumped off. Heckie White's ripshit. He pretended to leave the sale, then sneaked back later and bought that Chippendale tea chest for seventy-five grand. He goes in today with the bank check to pick it up and finds out they're going to hold it. He already had it sold. He can't do a thing with the bank check, with Bird's name on it. There was a bunch of not-too-happy dealers down there who'd bought over the phone and all— and others—like a real lynch mob. I was the only happy camper within ten miles of the Alphonse Bird Galleries. Fonzie Bird was not smiling for once, and I wish you could have seen him when I grabbed my check and started ripping it up." Columbo blew the last of the pieces into the foot traffic.

Fred put in, "There's a son, huh? The word I had was that Lord Hanford died in the saddle."

"If you want to believe everything a naked woman screams into the phone on a Sunday afternoon, about the rich old man dead with his pants down? If she stands to win maybe three hundred million on the deal? And according to what I heard, the guy's backside is scarred and blistered till it looks like he sat on a grill? If you're the son of the first wife, and cut off with a lousy half million bucks, are you just gonna sit there?"

"I guess it would depend on the state of my backside," Fred said.

Chapter 10

Lemme tell you about the English," John Columbo started in as he accepted his third beer from the waitress. He hunched his chair closer to Fred's and glanced ostentatiously around. The crowd at the café, and on the sidewalk, was being plumped by rush hour.

"Lord Hanford had a son?" Fred prompted.

"First lemme tell you about the English," Columbo insisted. He rubbed the sweating bottle with both hands before he poured. He flicked the filled glass with an index finger and made it ring. He leaned closer to Fred and confided hoarsely, "Like Heckie White says—you know Heckie?—for the Brits, the be-all and end-all is the blessed butt. You ever been to England? All they do, all they can think about, is spanking. It is the Anglo-Saxon thing. *Flagellatio*. The birch, the cane, the rod."

Columbo twitched, drank a sip, and looked around. "This thing gets out, the press is gonna have a field day. Lord Hanford's heinie. And I quote: *What a treat in this seminary for the idolators of the posterior shrine! To see [the old boy's buttocks] blushing under the rod, exercised by a woman of supereminent charms! It must be the sublime of felicity indeed, to taste chastisement from the hand of [Lady Teasel]. Her ladyship is charming in the extreme with a rod in hand. Her bust shrouded by her sable locks, from forth which her eyes, fierce as a panther's, glare—*"

"They didn't arrest the widow!" Fred interrupted.

"Woman like that? She's got friends. Shit, the D.A. of Bristol County's in their club. Everyone down there's trying to hush it up, but naturally there's talk. You didn't hear the talk when you were at the sale? Did you see that chauffeur? See, with the English, it all goes back to public school—what *they* call public, which really means private. Eton and Harrow and the rest, where the snobs go, the class boys. All those schools have a long tradition of flogging." Columbo fondled his narrow lower lip.

"Tell me about the son," Fred said.

"I'm getting to him. One trick they have over there, see, is the boy that's to be beaten gets hoisted up on the strong back of a buxom servant wench, and he's got to hang on there while the master warms his butt."

At the next table an older man wearing a striped jersey and a Greek fisherman's cap, despite the heat, coughed and recited, "*Here, kiss the rod, you wicked Elf./The next time on my maid herself;/A strong-back'd wench, who takes delight/In horsing naughty boys and girls!/I whipt upon her back last night/A French Duke, and two English Earls;/The first of which, with frock and sash,/I drest just like a full-grown miss;/Then gave him many a vig'rous lash./I've thrown your Breeches now aside;/Your half-whipt bum, tho' seeming sore,/With all the glowing prospect wide,/Pants for a vigorous encore!*"

"Pants seem like a good idea," Fred remarked. He tucked money under his tea glass and left them to it.

———◈———

"Clayton's got something in mind for those drawings," Fred told Molly. "I've never seen him so close and nervous. It's not enough he's made the biggest score of his life. He's looking for something bigger still." He'd arrived at her mother's house too late to have supper with the family, so he was eating a sub on the front stoop of Wombswell Croft. Molly, beside him, took a sip from his iced tea now and then. Something was on at Harvard's theater tonight. Suburban cars nosed down Rush Street hunting open spaces they'd regret if they found them. They'd be towed.

"What are they worth?" Molly asked.

"In the real world, and if we can keep them clear of the scandal that looks like it's brewing…not that I've really checked into it, but my guess is you could match a dozen of the best ones against your mother's house."

"You're kidding!" Molly exclaimed. "Fred, once a week Mom gets a call from a Realtor. Maybe you don't know it, but these single-families are gold! Three quarters of the neighbors are in *Who's Who*, and the others just didn't want the notoriety. That's why they all hate Mom. It ain't Brattle Street, but still..."

"I know we're surrounded by gentry," Fred said. "That is why I put my tea in a glass rather than drinking it straight from the pitcher. I'm amazed your mom's neighbors don't burn garden gnomes on her lawn. They're trying to be so much subtler about the whole class-English thing than she is."

Molly slapped a mosquito and dropped its body between two boards of the porch floor.

Fred went on, "Before my informant got sidetracked, he intimated that there's a juicy murder-and-sex story that might interfere with the whole collection, whatever Clayton is planning. For polite company, a bunch of erotic drawings, even by Turner, was already pushing the envelope. Add to that flagellation and murder and a mysterious chauffeur and a jealous son who's as good as disowned and bent on revenge—unless there's a truly good clambake of a train wreck to keep the front pages occupied, Clay's discovery is going to be so drowned in muck he'll never be able to clear it, even if it turns out his title is secure. The son wants the body exhumed. If he makes the case that the old boy was bumped off—and especially if he can lay suspicion off onto the widow—the least he can hope for is that she'll settle a big chunk of the estate on him."

Under the shade of the big trees on Rush Street, the evening was more pronounced than in the open air above the river. If the city were less polluted, fireflies might be flickering their sexual semaphores between the shrubs and grasses on either side of the macadam. "I don't understand Clay's rush," Fred mused. "He's normally the prototype of what the Justices had in mind when they coined that term for stalling, 'all deliberate speed.'"

"Clay ain't a hasty fellow," Molly agreed. "Lakshmi thinks he's the neatest thing since rhubarb."

"The thing that bothers me most," Fred said, "is that Marek's being pursued by a London dealer. He's small-time, but I think he's here especially for the Turners. That means the news is out. He wasn't at the sale. He advertises in *Apollo*. Tiny ad. Evidently he doesn't specialize in anything, just has a gallery space and takes what comes. I have to talk to Clay. So Lakshmi called? Is she looking for me? I should talk to Marek. Later. First let's stroll by the river and see if we bump into Prince Charles and the kids."

"Mom saw the royal Charles," Molly said. "She's in heaven. They got her group around to a side entrance at Saint James's Palace, and they caught Charles trying to sneak in that way. He had to host the launch of something called 'Roots of the Future,' a publication and exhibition that portray ethnic diversity in the making of Britain. Fascinating lives these people lead. Mom's seen the Duke of Gloucester and the Countess of Snowdon. What time is it?"

"Seven-thirtyish," Fred told her. "I left my watch next to the shower." He crumpled the paper wrapping from his sandwich, tossed and caught it.

"Lakshmi said she'd stop by and call Clayton from here, so you'll know what she's got so far. But we could stroll for an hour or so till then."

"I'll call Clay first and tell him about the London dealer. And since I'm buffaloed about Marek's role, I'll invite Clayton to put in his two cents. Let's bring the phone outside."

Clay listened with prolonged disquiet to Fred's news. Small might be no serious player on his own, but there was no telling whom or what he might represent. His presence, and his interest in Marek, argued that he knew or at least suspected what the drawings were: millions of dollars' worth of Turners. Marek's silence might mean he was trying to organize a bid that would bring the drawings back from Clay. Or, as Lakshmi had guessed, Marek might simply have taken a payment from Small in exchange for revealing the identity of the actual buyer. If that was the case, Small was no doubt sitting impatiently in his room at the Royal Court and trying Clay's number every half hour. Though none of this posed a real threat, it was a nuisance. The true threat was the legal question. "What did Myron tell you?" Fred asked. "Did he call back?"

Clay huffed. "Myron was circumspect and not completely reassuring. We do not understand the nature or the seriousness of the challenge. Speaking theoretically and with no knowledge of the particulars involved, my attorney says the following. If the challenge has merit—for instance, if the widow had no right to sell—a reputable auctioneer, or one who wished to pass for reputable, should do as Bird is doing with those items that have not already been delivered. He should hold them, since he retains some fiduciary responsibility. As to the matter of lots that were paid for and carried away, that becomes more complex from the point of view of the challenger. Myron was astounded by the suggestion that we were obliged to return the Constable—I call it that as a matter of convenience only, Fred."

"Point taken." The evening was lovely. Molly was ready to roll, sitting next to him on the porch in her blue shorts and one of his own white shirts, whose tails were tied up so as to let her tummy have some breeze.

"All they can do is sue me," Clay said. "Let them sue me for the Constable." He chuckled. "As far as the Turners go, the worst they can do is sue Marek Hricsó. And good luck to them. He wrote you a receipt?"

"Not much of one," Fred admitted. "Such as it is, I have it in the office. I paid cash. Even if he's talking, we can simply stonewall. But then…"

"About Miss Thomas," Clay put in. "She seems an intelligent person, and I do rely on your instincts about people, Fred. But those plumber's overalls! Is this the fashion of the day?"

The Charles had gone gray under the slow dusk. On its grassy banks couples and small family groups were sitting. Runners and cyclists tore along in both directions under the sycamores. Harvard fisted as large a grab as it could take from both banks, though the river itself continued to run through its fingers.

They'd walked in silence for a time until Molly said, "If I didn't know better, I'd say you were distracted and morose."

Fred said, "I like the way that when a boat's screw churns the water, it makes a mixture of milk and light. If I didn't know better, I'd say something was on your mind."

"There's no way to guess which direction the kids went," Molly complained. "Or even if they decided to cross a bridge and let the dog go after ducks on the far side. I'm thinking of looking into real estate."

"Move out of Arlington?" Fred asked. Molly's house in Arlington, with its small yard and on its quiet street, had always seemed a fixed thing.

"No, *selling* real estate. I can learn whatever it takes and do whatever it is you do to get a license." Fred walked more slowly, or Molly did.

"And drop the library?" Fred asked. It wasn't a huge income, but it was an income, and Molly was good at her job. She let Fred pitch in too, though whether she'd ever allow him to do anything big, like help the kids through college, neither of them had dared discuss.

"I suppose it would depend," Molly said. "I believe I could sell. The library's feeling safe and regular. Maybe I'm feeling safe and regular."

"It's not the money?" Fred asked carefully.

"No. Power, probably. Power and romance." She grinned up at him.

Terry leapt out of a clump of bushes in front of them, shrieking with triumph.

"Terry, where's Sam?" Fred demanded. "You shouldn't be alone out here. It's getting dark."

"He's in the bushes, keeping Prince Charles quiet. You have to kind of sit on his head. Dogs are always so happy to see you, and bark, and ruin it. Don't yell at me, Fred! Mom, tell Fred not to yell at me."

"Fred's right to worry about your being alone," Molly said. "Come out now, Sam," she called. "You scared us."

Sam and the dog came out, boasting and barking, respectively, at their stealth and skill and patience. "You gave me a heart attack," Molly promised Terry. "The two of you run that dog now. I want him really tired when we get home. And Fred's right! Stay together. Go!"

"Power and romance," Fred reminded her after the kids had raced off, Terry now holding Prince Charles's leash.

"Distracted and morose," Molly reminded him.

"Mankind makes me dismal sometimes," Fred admitted. "I'd love to work on this puzzle of Clay's, but instead I'm reduced to sitting with John Columbo in an outdoor café, listening to dirty stories. I haven't even told you about the fabulous Turner painting

Clay landed. It's a crusty, violent, wild thing, filled with eerie passion. An old man's painting. But an old man like Titian—it's a plateau not every good painter reaches just by aging. It strikes you first as being clumsy, like an old person on the stairs. But there's a mind or spirit working independent of the feet or the hands. Was Turner crippled with arthritis? I don't know. I don't know a thing about him, though I've seen a hundred of his pictures. He's one of the big guns. I just never happened to look into his story—never even wondered how he lived."

"What's the painting about?" Molly asked.

"The image is of a couple on a bed. They're coupling. What he shows you is big red curtains, and sheets, and the people's legs. A man and a woman, I reckon. But the painting's about...I'd say it's about loneliness and old age. It's sweet and defiant and terribly, terribly sad. Its sadness would make sense if Turner had no mate. Earlier today, in the course of business, I had to interrupt a different coupling, and it didn't bother me then. But now...I don't know anything about women, but I always think of a single woman as complete somehow, whereas, it was occurring to me, walking along, the sexual sadness of a man alone..."

Chapter 11

The porch light at the front of Wombswell Croft held the attention of the few insects hardy enough to withstand the miasmic vapors of Rush Street. Lakshmi had ditched the overalls in favor of red shorts and a white T-shirt. The ensemble looked like the uniform from Camp Wayward Winds, and Lakshmi like a counselor who should be watched. She opened the briefcase she'd unstrapped from the back of her bicycle when she rode up. The steed itself was chained to the signpost next to the sidewalk. Fred and Molly had coffee, which Lakshmi refused until her business on the telephone was completed. She was five minutes late.

Courteous greetings at the other end of the line betrayed the attention of Clayton Reed.

"Let's start with the big picture," Lakshmi began briskly. Like a good trial lawyer, she spoke off the cuff, but with her hand resting on stacks of notes and papers, signaling that if challenged, she could take days of your time cross-referencing facts and figures.

"Turner died on December nineteenth, 1851, at the age of seventy-six. He was baptized May fourteenth, 1775, at Saint Paul's, Covent Garden, London. His father, a barber, died in his son's house in 1830; his mother, insane, had died long since. There were no siblings. My first assumption is—and we'll get to this— that what you bought, there being so much of it, was in Turner's estate. What I'm looking for at the start, Mr. Reed, is blood relations who might complicate the inheritance. That is what blood relations do, in my experience."

A sound from Clay's end encouraged her, and she continued, "Now, when Turner died, the contents of his studio on Queen Anne Street were left to the National Gallery. With strings. It was not until five years after he died that the material was actually accessioned. But listen to what was in his studio and reported to be included in the Turner Bequest, as it was called: about three hundred paintings, some unfinished, and upwards of nineteen *thousand* works on paper, comprising drawings and watercolors, some in sketchbooks. His will was contested. That contributed to the delay. The will is what I will look into tomorrow."

Lakshmi listened to an interjection from Clayton. Molly took a sip of her coffee, which she had allowed to reach the temperature of the night air. All three of them were sitting on the stoop, the telephone pulled outside from the front hall, the screen door resting barely ajar on its white cord.

"Right," Lakshmi said. "Suppose your collection was originally part of what was in his studio. There's so much of it. And suppose somebody took it, or stole it. Our problem is, we want to find the published history of stuff nobody could admit they had—whether they had a right to it or not—because of its subject matter. Am I right? We're talking Victorians, and we're talking contraband, yes? We're talking a period in the history of our civilization when a person caught peddling smut, or even owning it, could be stood in the stocks overnight in a public square, his head or hers, and hands, clamped—and left to the mercy of the public whim. If they wanted to beat the prisoner to death, they would."

"If it was that dangerous to do pornography, or have it, how did old Turner get away with it?" Fred mused.

"Because then, as now, everyone's a hypocrite," Molly said. "Everyone. Including the law."

Lakshmi was listening to Clay, fanning bugs away from her face and chest and legs with her free hand.

"Exactly," she said. "So how did they get to Westport? Who took them? If they started out in Turner's studio, the subliminal question must be, *Quis custodiet ipsos custodes?* Who in a position of trust could have spirited the drawings away? Of course I'm just beginning, but I have to tell you, one name keeps cropping up: Charles Locke Eastlake. Remember, I'm new to all this, and I don't know how to weigh the information as I start to assemble it, but if we begin with the question of who had access and power back in those days, Sir Charles Eastlake stands out. He was a painter, collector, and man in the middle of the London art world for years—most notably the very years that interest us."

She shuffled among her notes until she found a list that she then read from. "Eastlake was president of the Royal Academy from 1850 to 1865. Of course, Turner was R.A. himself; for an artist, it was the only game in town, and he'd been elected a member quite young. Eastlake was also secretary of the Fine Arts Commission from 1841 to 1865, the year he died. My method is to gather too much information, on the theory that you never know what may turn out to be useful. Eastlake, anyway, was keeper, whatever that is—" She stopped to allow another interruption from Clay's end. Fred looked with envy at the sheaf of papers, notes, and Xerox copies she had assembled.

"Keeper—curator, then—of the National Gallery from 1843 to 1847, and then finally the National's first director, from 1855 until his death a decade later in Pisa, Italy. His wife, Lady East-lake—who looks to have been a hot ticket, by the way—I'll just mention while I have the notes in front of me that *she* didn't die until 1893....

"My point is, Eastlake was pretty much the C.E.O. in charge of the gallery; curator at the time of Turner's death, and then director while his will was being hashed out, and after the bequest came through. So he was there the whole time. I'll focus on the will tomorrow, as I said. Also, John Ruskin made a lot of notes on the material that was in the bequest, and I want to see if there's anything helpful there."

"Get Lakshmi to tell you the five jobs of being a human female," Fred whispered to Molly. "Not one of them is selling real estate. You may be on to something. To disagree with Ruskin gives you a leg up, according to Lakshmi. She hates Ruskin."

"I always think, start with the boys—excuse me, the *men*—in power," Lakshmi said into the phone. "There'd been an adminis-trative crisis at the National Gallery for about five years, starting in 1850. It's why I say Eastlake was really in charge the whole time. Eastlake was appointed a trustee that year. Given that trus-tees are human—which is just one way of being above the law—what if there was a deal of some kind among them? One of them might have stolen, or skimmed, or whatever, the pornography after Turner's death. So I dug up the names of all the other trustees besides Eastlake, which I'll read you now, to save time, in case one stands out. There was William Bingham Baring, the second Baron Ashburton; and Thomas Baring; and Samuel Jones Lloyd, who the same year was made Baron Overstone; and William Russell. Russell and Overstone were still on the board in 1856, when the Turner Bequest finally came through. So was Thomas Baring, nephew of the first Lord Ashburton and brother of the first Lord Northbrook. Thank you—thank you, Mr. Reed. I can't tell at the start what may prove to be important. I appreciate your encouragement. Now I'll read you the names of the other trustees who were sitting in 1856. One of them may mean something to you: the Duke of Sutherland, the Marquess of Lansdown, the Marquess of Northampton, the Earl of Aberdeen, the Earl of Ripon, Lord Ashburton, Lord Monteagle, Lord Overstone—no, I already mentioned him, he'd been Samuel Jones Lloyd, you remember? And finally Sir James Baring, a baronet."

Lakshmi listened to Clay's voice working the invisible end of the line. Bugs beat against the light. Sounds came from an upstairs window: Terry singing to Prince Charles. Molly whispered to Fred, "Did you notice how as soon as a perfectly good Sam Lloyd is given the alias of an honorable title, he sounds like a hobbit? 'Lord Overstone'! Who are they kidding?"

Lakshmi began jotting down notes on a sheet of paper in response to directions issuing from the Silver Spur. Molly put down her cup between herself and Fred and remarked, "Following Lakshmi's line of reasoning, suppose one of the dozen or so trustees had a taste for scurrilous stuff, filched it, and passed it on to a son or daughter? It wouldn't be mentioned in a will since the law wouldn't even have allowed anyone to *have* such contraband in 1856. So it gets passed down secretly. My point is, over a hundred and fifty years, one spawning male trustee—female trustee? in those days? dream on!—might be responsible for, let's say for the sake of argument, an average of four surviving offspring to a person, and twenty years to a generation—that's sixty-five thousand, five hundred people who might be alive today, any of whom could be the inheritor from just one of those trustees. Multiply that by twelve—we're pretending twelve trustees—and you're up to almost eight hundred thousand souls. Even if one of them is it, that still leaves an awful lot of McGuffins. Lakshmi, I hope your calendar is clear for the next three hundred years."

Lakshmi said into the phone, "Yes, yes, all right, then, Mr. Reed. We'll concentrate on the will tomorrow. Thank you. It's fun. Good night." She stood and brushed particles of flooring from the seat of her shorts.

"I'm going to pay a call on Marek," Fred announced.

"That son of a bitch," Lakshmi reminded him. "Give him my best regards if you can think of a way to do it that'll draw blood. But listen, Fred? I'm grateful to you for putting me on to Mr. Reed. Molly, I'm in love."

"What!" Molly and Fred yawped simultaneously. The voice of Terry above them stopped singing and was replaced by an intense silence.

"With Lady Eastlake," Lakshmi explained. She pulled a stalk of grass from the ornamental clump next to the porch and chewed on its blunt end. "I can't wait to finish this project for Mr. Reed so I can begin spending all my time with her. She hates John Ruskin even more than I do. Listen to this." She took a folded paper out of the pocket of her T-shirt and read from it: "*Mr. Ruskin's intellectual powers are of the most brilliant description but there is not one single moral quality in their application....*And here's another good one: *His writings had all the qualities of premature old age—its coldness, callousness and contraction....*Don't you love her?"

"She must have known Turner, no?" Fred asked. "As the wife of the director of the National Gallery, and part of a small world..."

"Yeah, sure," Lakshmi said. She rooted around in her bag and pulled out a small book bristling with yellow Post-It notes. "My bedtime reading for tonight," Lakshmi announced. "I may be onto a thesis topic if I can trust love at first sight. Yes, here's Elizabeth Rigby's journal entry for March fourth of 1844. (I like her better under her maiden name, before she married Sir Charles Eastlake.) *Mr. Lokhart and Charlotte to dinner—also Turner, the artist, a queer little being, very knowing about all the castles he has drawn—a cynical kind of body, who seems to love his art for no other reason than because it is his own. Lokhart grew black as thunder when Turner was pertinacious and stupid, and looked as if he could have willingly said, 'You blockhead!'"*

"I'll be off," Fred told Molly.

"There's somewhere else she describes Turner as well," Lakshmi said. "*Like an old hen in a fury,* she says. Don't you love her?" She strapped her briefcase onto the bike's rack and unlocked the chain.

Fred, who had started down the sidewalk, turned. "Lakshmi, don't forget we have to go at this like commerce. Real estate. All information is fun, but only one piece of it is going to make the sale. I don't need to tell you how…anyway, Molly, I'll try to get back, but don't worry if I'm sidetracked. I mean to walk to Boston and get to Marek's in time to catch him as he's going to sleep. Does he have a significant other these days that you know of, Lakshmi?" Lakshmi shook her head. "He's pretty inscrutable in that respect."

"You leave anything in the shop you want me to pick up?" Again Lakshmi shook her head.

———

Fred walked to Charles Street from the Boston side of the river. By eleven the only light left in the sky was artificial. Clouds had blown in earlier to cover a tentative moon. Rain threatened. The trees along the riverbanks were already welcoming it, bending and thrashing their leaves.

Oona, the aunt from whom Marek had inherited the business and the property, had been a canny investor. She had bought the entire building whose first floor comprised the shop, once Oona's and now Marek's. The second floor was still illuminated: Oona's old living quarters, now Marek's. Fred pushed the buzzer next to the building's back door and waited. He tried again three minutes later, waiting still longer before he tried the door: locked. Inside the glass window, the light on the shop's alarm box glowed green, where it should be red. The shop itself was dark.

Fred let himself into the back hall. The door into the shop was ajar. He allowed his eyes to rest and reach toward darkness before he eased in. Light shining in through the front window, from the street, allowed him to see how things had been mishandled— overturned or pushed aside. The displacements were intelligent ones, not the exasperated trashing mess that the frustrated amateur leaves behind. The place had been searched in a hasty but thorough manner, by someone looking for a specific thing. Within the shop itself, the door to Marek's back room also stood open. The proprietor, Fred knew, always locked and unlocked this with a key he kept on his person.

"I'd better see how young Marek is doing," Fred muttered to himself, staring into the worse jumble that had been made of Marek's inner sanctum. In the gloom he made out the white gleam of today's mail, including the letter from Alphonse Bird Galleries, whose envelope, torn open, lay exposed on top. Fred could read it, or take it, or leave it, but it was Marek's problem—if Marek was still able to have problems. The kind of wreck made in the office tended to encompass people as well.

Fred raced up the back stairs and was held up briefly by the locked door into the second-floor apartment. The stairs and hallway were rose and old gold, and the interior of the apartment's entrance hall a blaze of French gilt furniture against an opulence of Turkish rug, into which Marek's blood was pulsing tiredly, chiefly from a deep cut bruised into the side of his head. He'd been hit hard, and often, after being caught naked on his way between bathroom and bedroom: a towel lay near him on the rug, old rose and gold. Marek was still breathing, but just barely. He was so badly damaged he might be beyond help.

When Oona lived here, the place had been so plain as to be austere. Her phone had been in the bedroom.

———

Fred was holding the towel to the worst cut on Marek's head when the medics clattered in with their folding stretcher.

He was drinking coffee in the kitchen when the first cops arrived.

Chapter 12

Majesty of majesties," affirmed the lobby of the Royal Court Hotel, doing its best to drown out the words of the prophet of Ecclesiastes. "All is majesty," the clerks at the reception desk almost crooned into the phones.

Room 611 did not respond to the house phone. Fred idled over to the desk of the concierge and asked his old friend Mr. Sanhedrin, "Has Alexander Small been called back suddenly to London? I don't get an answer from his room. It's ten-thirty, so I've already cut him a half hour's slack."

The concierge checked his monitor. "Try our Regency Room," he suggested. "Perhaps Mr. Small is taking breakfast there. He is still with us."

Fred took the stairs up to the sixth floor. He had not had a chance to change his clothes, but as far as he could judge he had been able to keep Marek's blood off his blue knit shirt and khaki pants. He'd had a harder time keeping himself from being escorted without ceremony out of the police station and into its annex in the lockup. There had been too many questions which his simple answers had not satisfied.

The sixth-floor corridor was filled with imported maids pushing trolleys filled with sheets and towels, soaps, shampoos, and virgin Kleenex boxes. Fred timed his move to coincide with the making-up of room 611. When he walked in, a chubby and sullen Irish girl with a name tag pleaded, "Beg pardon, mister." She'd just begun to strip Small's bed.

"I won't disturb you, Maureen," Fred Small assured her, glancing over the surfaces of furniture and taking in the pair of silver-backed hairbrushes monogrammed *AS*, the straw twit hat, the *Burlington Magazine* opened and lying on its face, the carton of Chinese takeout, the tossed newspapers exactly where they had been the day before, and the spare pair of shoes. "I just need something from my suitcase. Don't mind me, Maureen."

The suitcases were under the hanging raincoat in the open closet area: a pair of matched tan leather ones with, Fred noticed as he crossed the room, combination locks. He lifted and tried them furtively and found that both were empty; felt the empty pockets of the coat before snapping his fingers and saying, as he turned, "Stupid! I unpacked it!"

Maureen continued to struggle with the bed while Fred went through the bureau drawers: the socks, the shirts embroided with the initials *AS*, the underwear. Not even in the desk was there a scrap of paper to indicate Small's wider acquaintance or purposes. Fred scratched his head. "I can't have left it in the bathroom," he complained.

Indeed, the bathroom provided nothing more than male condiments and a floor littered with soap wrappers and coiled towels.

"Well, I am frankly puzzled," Fred told Maureen, glancing around the room a final time. "I'll check my car. I could have sworn..." He noticed the message light blinking on the phone next to the bed as Maureen beat the pillows into a shape resembling herself. "I'm late as it is," Fred said, picking up the receiver.

Marek's voice advised him, "We must offer more."

Fred hung up, telling Maureen, "Wouldn't you know it?"

"Shall I be doin' the bat'room then, mister?" Maureen asked.

"It's fine," Fred said.

"Will there be anythin' else you'll be needin', then?"

"I'm as right as rain," he answered.

———

Lakshmi was waiting for him in the park in front of the brown stones of Cambridge's main library. After the downpour of the night before, the weather had cooled. A light wind blew across the puddles in the streets, playgrounds, and parking lots. Lakshmi was in a blue denim dress that could accommodate up to six months of pregnancy. She was shaken and subdued. Fred sat next to her on the granite slab she had chosen, which was attended by a mangy group of pigeons.

"You'll have to make yourself available to the cops," Fred warned. "Mainly because they'll be looking for you. Marek is still unconscious and may not live. He's in Mass. General, in intensive care. Don't tell them I called you this morning; just say I found you at lunchtime, now, and told you Marek had been hurt. Call and offer to go in—wherever they want. They're not above pulling a stunt if they think it might help them, so be prepared to go talk to a pair of detectives at Marek's bedside while they watch for you to be overcome and confess.

"They'll know you worked at Marek's, and may even think you still do. It's up to you what you say, but my counsel is, stick with a limited version of the truth. Tell me this: do you have keys?"

"I threw them in his damned toilet," Lakshmi said. "The alarm and the front-door key were all I ever had. That holy of holies, the back room, only Marek had—*has*—the key to that."

"Someone took Marek's keys," Fred said.

"Then that person can get in and out whenever he wants."

"No, the police put locks on everything," Fred said. "Until Marek wakes up, I am regarded as either a suspect or a concerned friend, they're not sure which. They'll ask you to look around and see if anything's missing. If it turns out to be homicide, they'd love to lay their hands on someone trying to hock one of Marek's Ming vases. And listen, Lakshmi, I'd just as soon, and I know Clay would rather, you not mention the job you're doing for him."

Lakshmi folded her arms and recited, "Yes, Mr. Hricsó and I had words. He is an artist! It meant nothing. I took advantage of my temporary freedom to begin serious work on my doctoral thesis, which shall be entitled *Lady Eastlake: The Voice of Reason in the Censor's Shadow.*"

"It sounds like a thesis," Fred agreed.

"Don't think I'm not sorry about that bastard Marek," Lakshmi said. She shuddered. "They aren't going to arrest me, are they?"

"They'll probably act like they're going to; it's one of their stunts. But there's no reason for them to do that. Keep fear and guilt out of your responses and you'll do fine."

Lakshmi stood and picked up the briefcase she'd been guarding behind her calves. "I'll leave this with Molly, in case they become inquisitive. Should I mention Small, or not?"

Fred said, "I've been pondering that question. I didn't give them his name. So as far as you go, I'd say no. You can always pretend to remember him later. But don't deny it if anyone asks, 'You ever hear of a man called Small?'"

"Then I'll get busy. What I'll do—since I've supposedly just found out he's sick—is I'll go immediately to the hospital to visit Marek. They'll take it from there, I guess, once they know who I am. They'll have someone there, watching?"

"Undoubtedly," Fred said.

"Can I buy flowers at that market across the street?"

"Intensive care won't let you in with flowers," Fred objected.

"I'll look better—*it* will look better—with flowers."

———

Clayton was climbing the walls and hitting the roof. Fred's knock was answered almost with a snarl—a snarl that came to full voice when Clay saw the School of Constable issuing from its wrapping.

"You mock me," he said.

It was three in the afternoon, and things were quiet at the Silver Spur. Fred had exchanged greetings with Pig Lee, who was sitting at the desk in the lobby, dressed in a powder-blue playsuit and eating sunflower seeds from a paper packet while keeping his eyes on the desk monitor. Fred said, "Lee, listen, my guy in four-thirteen—he's strange, but he's a decent guy. He wants to pay the room charge, and he'll pay in cash. You never expected him to stay on."

It was wrestling that Pig Lee was watching on the monitor. The channel could be switched over to keep tabs on the halls and staircases, and maybe on certain rooms as well. Room 413 was clear of surveillance, though. Fred had checked it out of habit as soon as he found Clay established there, the morning before the auction.

Pig Lee craned his neck to look around Fred at an altercation occurring in the parking lot, between two people who had both tried to put their cars in the small shade of the same tree. "What is wrong with some people?" Pig Lee asked Fred. "You see that?

With a whole parking lot to park in? Listen, your guy is not a problem. He tips the girls. He paid in cash up front. We moved his car to where we can watch it better for him. He's a piece of cake. If he wants to live like the prisoner of Zenda, hell, it's a free country. I wouldn't. But that's me."

—◀▬▶—

Fred put the School of Constable in its old place on the desk and opened the window blinds. Sun scattered the dust between the slats.

"Did Marek Hricsó die?" Clay demanded.

"Not the last time I checked."

"There must be not a whisper of scandal!" Clay raged. "Do they not understand?"

Fred said, "I don't. The drawings are already scandalous. Why should a little more hurt? Whatever your secret agenda is, Clay, if I don't know what it is, I sure can't help you. What's the plan?"

Clay focused on his own earlier question. "He will live?"

"Maybe. The head wound was really bad; he lost lots of blood. Serious internal bleeding too. The plan was for him to die."

"Who did it?" Clay asked.

As long as Clayton had decided to pace up and down the open part of the orange room, Fred sat down. Aside from the man's suitcases and spare suit in the closet alcove, and the book on the windowsill, there was no sign whatsoever that the room was inhabited.

"I don't know who did it," Fred said. "Could be a friend of his."

"Small?" Clay asked, pausing to glare as he spoke the name. "Small has no reputation in the trade. I am uneasy, Fred. Uneasy. Uneasy about everything."

Fred reminded him, "I met Small. Even using tools, and having the advantage of surprise, he couldn't do that much damage. But something's going on. I went to his room afterward to ask questions. He wasn't in, and hadn't been, I'd say, since the night before."

"How do you know?"

"His toothbrush was dry. Towels, sink, bathtub, washcloth, all bone-dry. Marek's voice was on his message recording, saying he'd need more money."

"Interesting," Clay said. "Now, however futile the exercise might be, Fred, if you will indulge me—I overlook your outburst—

I should be grateful once again to concentrate upon my hidden agenda. As you know, my methods do occasionally lead to triumph."

As he lectured, Clay's pacing brought him to the second armchair, where he sat down on the orange vinyl, grimaced at the School of Constable, and pulled out the desk drawer, taking from it a sheet of Holiday Inn stationery on which were written notes in his neat hand. "The names of the trustees of, and some contributing well-wishers to, the Runnymede House Museum," he explained, passing the sheet across to Fred. "I have them from my relative, Parker Stillton. You will not need to speak with him. He continues to be distressed, feeling that I refused the honor of membership on the board only because I am a snob. Why would I deny such an allegation? How else is one to maintain one's integrity?"

"Eighteen people?" Fred asked, looking the list over. It was complete with names, addresses, phone numbers, and the nicknames by which the persons preferred to be addressed over cocktails.

"That is merely the first rank," Clay admitted. "They will undoubtedly lead to others. But we must begin with what we have. I am concerned about our deadline. What do you think of the work Miss Thomas is doing?"

"She's exactly ten hours into a job that could take years. And at the moment she's concentrating on Marek's problem. What else did you learn from your distant cousin, Parker Stillton?"

"'Learn'?"

"Who's mounting the legal challenge? How, and on what basis? What is its merit? Is there in fact an order to exhume the body? Is the long-lost son in town? All the information I have so far was filtered through John Columbo. So what else did he tell you?"

"Ah," Clayton said. "I should have asked him those questions? I had no wish to discuss our purchase with him. Therefore I pretended that my interest was purely a social one. I have the names, but from here on I rely on your discretion. It is dangerous to ask questions, given that those people are all so close to one another. Who speaks to one speaks to all."

"Before I do anything else, I am going to spend an hour with these drawings," Fred announced. "So if you'd like a change of scenery..."

"Excellent idea. I shall purchase some socks and shirts. Although the staff has agreed to take care of my laundry, one does need a change of scenery now and then. Fred, it was ungenerous of me not to afford you the intellectual stimulus of studying this curious trove. By all means, take an hour with them; take two! If it will suit you, I shall return at six."

Chapter 13

You'll find everything under the spare bed," Clay said, poised at the door. "Also, in the top drawer of my bureau is a sack of cotton gloves. I need not tell you that the human skin exudes deleterious fats, as well as sulfuric acid." He departed in a cloud of glory.

"Under the bed?" Fred asked the closing door. The room was still, and too warm. He adjusted the air conditioner to a more comfortable level before prostrating himself in the narrow space between the beds and reaching under the spare, his bare arm rasping across the grit that lies embedded between the piles of cheap orange carpet in a whorehouse bedroom in Fall River, Massachusetts. His fingertips met sleek cardboard with metal corners: a box—no, boxes. Eight of them were arrayed in two rows: flat gray boxes with hinged panels, twelve inches to a side and about four inches deep.

Fred mused aloud, pulling the boxes out and onto the carpet where he could see them, "How did Clay find archival-quality storage boxes in Fall River?" Each box bore a gummed label in its upper-right-hand corner, inscribed, in Clay's neat, cuneiform chop marks, with a Roman numeral between I and VIII. Fred hefted the boxes and chose number VII, which he carried to the desk after shoving the rest back in place under the bed.

The top drawer of Clayton's bureau contained not his socks and shirts and handkerchiefs, but a small office-supply store: several pairs of tweezers, glassine envelopes of many dimensions, a tape measure, folded sheets of rice paper, pencils, and, on the right-hand side, a flobby wad of thin white cotton gloves of the kind

Mickey and Minnie used to wear back in the good old days before safe sex. A paper bag on the floor between the bureau and the desk, marked SOILED in heavily blocked penciled letters, held the castoffs. "Neutral pH. Heaven forbid a work of human art should bear a human stain," Fred said.

Clay, though marooned in Fall River, was not wasting a second. Whatever the nature of his personal mission, it had driven him completely out of character. His normal practice after a coup, or what might turn out to be a coup, was to spend the next few weeks or months in a serious gloat of inaction before proving his success even to himself. But in this instance hardly any time at all had passed—what was it now, only three days?—since Fred delivered the drawings into his hands, and here he was, working like an accountant at tax time. While persons unknown had been scrambling Monday morning, the day after the sale, to throw a cast of lawyers into the spokes, Clay had located a supply house—yes, that was its label—in Worcester that would deliver by messenger.

The cotton gloves were one-size-fits-all. They resisted Fred's large, square hands, their pores straining as he pulled their hems down to the base of his thumbs. They fit like hospital nighties.

"Box *Septem*," Fred announced to himself, sitting down to it where the School of Constable could kibbitz.

The shock he felt when he opened the box was similar to what some longtime nineteenth-century traveler must have experienced on returning to Paris after Haussmann had meddled with it. It had been organized. Where crooked narrow streets and tumbling shanties had once crowded the *hôtels particuliers*, sprawling churches, and lazar houses, a regimental cleanliness now opened up dangerous tree-lined avenues to the cleansing action of the government's crack cavalry. These new avenues radiated outward from the political *nombril* where palace and seat of government and Nôtre Dame sat next to the *préfecture de police*.

The first thing Fred saw was a white sheet marked with Clay's penciled notes: BOX VII—*39 sheets. Group 1. 12 sheets. Venice. Brown paper. Watercolor. All roughly 9½ x 12 inches. All numbered verso, in ink, as follows:* —, *4, 5, 6, 7,*—*9,*—, *13, 14,*—, *22, 23,*—, *32, 33, 34. Group 2. 9 sheets. And so on.*

"We *have* been a busy boy," Fred muttered. If the contents of this box was any guide, in just three days Clay had managed to sort, and label, three hundred some drawings. He flipped over the cover page. Below it lay a neat stack of transparent glassine envelopes, each bearing a small gummed sticker with a number. The creases in the first sheet showed that it had once been folded in four, and it still bore four spirited sketches in watercolor, one occupying each rectangle defined by the folds. The upper left showed billowing green curtains at an open window giving onto a balcony, beyond which was a haze of buildings on the far side of water. *Bedroom at Venice. T.* was inscribed in pencil across its lower edge, above the crease. *Shaft of gold, dawn,* the pencil continued, crossing the divide; *DANAË.*

The other three panels attacked their subject with an almost brutal haste and skill, portraying the imprisoned woman sleeping in her tower, but even so discovered and impregnated by Jupiter in his disguise as a shower of golden light or money. The artist's speculation was direct and uninhibited, as if he had been a witness to the event. He had invented a female at once opulent and acrobatic, her head and arms and lower legs confused by sheets as she entertained the attentions of the C.E.O. of all the gods, her torso offered up in an attitude the Supreme Court could only have characterized as displaying "*all pious abandon.*"

"Holy mackerel," Fred said. In one image the bed's roiled curtains were green; in the next, crimson; in the third, a lighter green, with the penciled caveat, *color shifts to suck the gold of dawn.*

Fred fingered the glassine envelope open and slid the sheet out, keeping it flat. The paper was stiff but not of the heart-stopping brittleness that would have signified that its acid content had burned it to the edge of self-destruction. The envelope, though transparent, had had the effect of imposing a slightly clouded cornea across the vision; naked, and with real light on them, the quartet of sketches grabbed and held and entertained the eye with the energy of their impulse. But it was obvious that they were not drawn from life.

Fred turned the page over. At the top right was the number *4* in ink. Numbers, *1, 2,* and *3* were somewhere else. Below the numeral, in pencil, was written *Bread and Cheese. Bottle of Ale.*

Dinner. 2 small glasses of Red. Glass of Gin and Water; below that, in another notation, was *Tuesday 3 o'clock. Miss Santorelli.*

"Bread and cheese must be lunch," Fred concluded. "We don't know what Turner had for his dinner, aside from the wine. Let's see…"

The next leaves, marked on their backs 5, 6, and 7, demonstrated to Fred's satisfaction that Miss Santorelli, once sent for, had done her sturdy best to realize, with her own body, the postures Turner had imagined at first light as the Venetian sun rose out of the Adriatic Sea. Sheets 9, 13, and 14 strongly suggested that after a lapse of many hours, the lady had tried again, matching her exertions to the frank insinuations of the dawn of a new day.

The images were free of symbolism and of all those silly and mawkish sentimentalizings by which Europeans had for so many years justified, and thereby perverted, their yearning after vital human flesh; none of those *Soul's Awakening* prevarications for J. M. W. Turner, where the lovely maiden catches herself before surrendering herself to nudity and worse. The pall of civilization had not intruded here. Even the bed curtains defied good manners: they leered and juddered and applauded, soaked in sperm and light and the gulping cries of passion.

A second figure entered the frame in sheets 22 and 23, identified in the latter as Romeo even as the former Danaë underwent a change of name to Juliet. Romeo had taken over the role of Zeus, the incorporeal shower of light ceding pride of place to boyish flesh. Then came another gap, of eight, before in 32, 33, and 34 the couple became a crowd with the entry of a third person—Juliet's nurse—who flustered into the scene in a torrent of flailing shift that she was doing her best to get into in time. The drawing of these last was again patently imagined.

A knock at the door startled Fred out of his study. "Yes?" he called. He checked the time. Four-thirty. He'd spent half an hour looking at just a dozen pictures. There were some 280 more to go.

"Your tea," came a female voice.

Fred had opened the door before he realized that the gloves were still on his hands. "Mr. Daygah not in?" Daiquiri asked. She carried a tray on which were set Clayton Reed's Liberty tea cozy, two mugs, and a plate of cookies. Clay had brought his teapot with him, as he always did when he expected to be away from home for several days.

"Shall I bring it in?" Daiquiri asked. Fred had not seen her since he saved her life; nor had he noticed at the time how short her hair was cropped, or how she smelled of lavender and tobacco. She did not recognize him as she entered the room and placed the tray on the bureau.

"Put the pictures away if I'm gonna pour," she said. She was wearing a blouse only slightly less transparent than glassine. It allowed—even forced—her small breasts to be a part of the conversation. Below them a short, tight black skirt was accentuated by a frilly bib of apron, barely large enough to suggest what it covered. "Mr. Daygah is very particular about his fuck pictures," she said.

"I know it," Fred told her. He closed the dozen sheets of paper, all safely back in their envelopes, into their box.

"That's a good boy," Daiquiri said. "He in the bathroom?" Her voice could be Atlanta; at any rate it was urban, and well south of Fall River.

"He went out," Fred said. "But I could use some tea."

"It steeped five minutes like Mr. Daygah wants it, and I warmed the pot," Daiquiri said. She uncovered Clay's silver pot, poured into the thick white diner mug, and offered it to Fred, then stood by, hesitant.

"Mr. Daygah likes me to have some with him," she said. "Before I start work."

"Please," Fred said. "Take a cookie. Sit down. You feeling all right?"

"You're the one came in that night, when he had my wind cut off," Daiquiri said, nodding and sitting in Clayton's armchair, in the window. "I thought it was you. Thank you."

"You're welcome," Fred replied. He took his gloves off, and they drank tea. Both looked around the room in that curious intimacy which descends upon strangers in a motel room when they have only tea, and a violent episode, in common.

"It is very hot today," Daiquiri said. She chose a cookie and broke it in half. She returned the larger portion to the plate.

"It is," Fred agreed. "Yesterday was hotter, though. All that rain helped."

"He hates it if it looks like one of us girls might drop a drip of sweat," Daiquiri said. "Perspiration, you know. Glow."

"Well, heck, when it's this hot…," Fred began.

"Two hours is all I can give today," she said. She took another sip of tea and then put her mug on the tray and carried the tray into the bathroom. Water rushed into the basin. Daiquiri bent to wash her hands. "You want me to use the bed or the desk? If you're finished with your tea? What should I call you?"

"I go by Fred," Fred said.

"Fred, I can get started whenever. But like I say, my time is limited." She opened the bureau's top drawer and began to pull on a pair of gloves. "He wants me to do box Four today," she said.

"Use the bed so you can spread out," Fred offered.

The young woman carried a stack of empty glassine envelopes to the spare bed, tossed its pillows onto the floor, and brushed herself a flat work space. "Nobody touches box Eight," she warned. "That's all chalk, Mr. Daygah says. Even he won't open that one. He tiptoes around it like it might explode."

She knelt and rummaged under the bed until she found the box she wanted, which she then pulled out and placed on the bed's orange spread. She puzzled out the strokes marking the Roman numeral and affirmed, "Four. That's IV." Then, using her gloved fingers and a pair of tweezers, she began to lay out the box's contents on the bed one piece at a time, next to Clayton's covering sheet, whose neat heading read, BOX IV—*33 sheets. 3 x 4 inches. Watermark: J. Whatman. 1832.*

"Eighteen thirty-two," Fred crowed. "We've got a date." He was standing behind the woman, watching as she began to insert the first drawing into an envelope. She used exaggerated care, as if the ghost of Clayton Reed were crouched on her shoulder. Among the works on the bed, some were sketches in pencil, others were in color, and yet others in both. They showed a variety of single and double figures, all continuing to elaborate, in one way or another, the prevailing theme. When Fred reached out to pick up a drawing, Daiquiri held him back.

"I can't let you touch them, Fred, not till you wash your hands and put on gloves. I told you, Mr. Daygah is particular. And he is tough. Lord, I will never try to smoke another cigarette in room four-thirteen as long as I am alive."

Fred called from the bathroom, over the rushing water, "I'm going to copy the words down, once you have them in the bags."

"As long as you put new gloves on. Don't use the old ones. We run those through the laundry with the sheets and that."

Fred dragged the desk chair over to the bed and began taking down notes and phrases, forcing himself to disregard the images.

> 25 Drops of Cajeput oil in glass of Hot Water, if not
> relieved in 5 min. take 50 more.
> 2036 13 Jan
> L.N. 10. a year.
> Judd. St. Place
> Keep as evidence of the failure of mind? No. Rubbish.
> Discard.
> Bedroom. Petworth.
> Blue eyes.
> Miss Seagrave. Late. Drunk.
> Mrs. Bottome—3 o'cl
> Leaves of Rue bruised...treacle...Mad Dog
> Miss Ol...1.

"Look at these," Fred said, showing Daiquiri the reverse sides of some of the drawings from which he had copied notes. "You see this one, in black ink—where it says *Keep as evidence of the failure of mind* and all? Would you say that's a different hand-writing?"

"Looks like he's pissed," Daiquiri concurred. "Or *she's* pissed. Like maybe it's the john's old lady saying, 'This one goes to the lawyers. That way I keep the house and the car and the kids.' Some women are like that."

Clay, returning, found them at their task and inclined his head with approval. "We make progress?" he asked. "Will you join me for dinner, Fred?"

"I'm going to call Boston. Depending on how that goes, I may take your trustee list to Westport and, while I'm there, pay a call on a widow of opportunity."

Chapter 14

The rain of the day before had settled some of the dust along the dirt road leading down Cobb Point, but the road itself was the worse for wear, given the vehicles that had pressed in and back for Sunday's auction sale. What had then been a companionable cloud of dust in the air was now replaced by swarms of mosquitoes praising the sun for westering past the yardarm. They surged out joyfully to find the day's first really serious drink.

The stunted woods on either side of the road consisted of salt- and wind-limited oaks and buttonwoods, as well as a low pine that attracted spiders. Fred's car rattled. Mosquitoes rushed in the open windows, along with sticky air whose movement, at a jouncing fifteen miles per hour, provided no relief.

Abruptly the second-growth pubic fringe of woods gave up. The dirt track glistened between a pair of plump and gentle swells, green hills on which cows browsed. Above the hills hung a perfection of deep-blue evening sky with not a cloud admitted. Under that sky, another mile ahead, not visible from here, lay an equally blue and similarly exclusive sea.

"*C'est l'heure exquise*," Fred told the distant cows. "In these parts that means cocktails and cheese that has traveled a couple of thousand miles by air so it can be passed around at the optimum point of rot."

He rolled along to the fork in the drive where, last Sunday, a heavy chain had prevented traffic from wandering toward the left, or east. On that chain had hung one of a series of yellow AUCTION TODAY signs, with an arrow directing everyone toward the right.

The chain was gone now, like the signs. The left fork stood out, notable for being the road less traveled.

"'The tumult and the shouting die; the captains and the kings depart,'" Fred said. The drive led between white rail fences toward the crest of the green hill. The architect's plan had been for the visitor, upon reaching that crest, to pause and gasp in wonder at the effect. "Beam me up, Scotty," Fred said, letting his car stop at the edge of the cattle ditch that cut the road. Running out in either direction from this interruption, and continuing its purpose, a half mile's worth of ha-ha separated the pasture from the grand sweep of boxwood gardens that sloped down toward the hollow where, in silhouette before the elements, stood Runnymede House: unique in Westport for all that it was, stone for obedient stone, the slavish replica of Hintlesham Hall.

The Cobb Point Preserve Society had stuck one of its brochures on Fred's windshield during the auction. Fred found the brochure under his seat and read:

> Runnymede House is a faithful replica of Hintlesham Hall. Let us describe what has been termed "the epitome of grandeur," and we quote: a magnificent example of one of the Stately Homes of England—now one of the small luxury hotels of the world. Hintlesham Hall (registered in England—number 2477659) is a house of evolving styles; its splendid Georgian facade belies its sixteenth-century origins, to which the redbrick Tudor rear of the Hall is a testament built in the 1570s by the grandson of the third Duke of Norfolk. The Stuart period is represented by the splendid carved oak staircases...

"I reckon that's the redbrick Tudor rear," Fred told a cow who had stopped chewing long enough to stare in through his window. He tossed the brochure onto the backseat. "Two floors, eighteen bedrooms, six bathrooms, one kitchen, and all fake. Nice view, though."

The stately drive was compelled into a stately circle by a planting of stately rhododendron, ensuring that the visitor kept his distance from the redbrick Tudor rear while being drawn around the east wing toward the square, cream-colored Georgian facade. Runnymede House did the same thing the best Newport cottages did: it offered its rump to those who approached by land while opening its welcoming wings toward the sea, in honor of the quaint New England myth which holds that someday the Savior will return from across the sea, out of the dawn, to claim his faithful, having surfaced again in England.

In front of the house stretched an expanse of flat white gravel in which sat a few tubs of forced rose trees with battered red blooms. Two floors of white windows stared blankly down on this and on a clipped lawn, suitable for golf or croquet, that ended abruptly at the absorbent blue edge of the bluff. Either there was no place to park, or the whole thing was parking. Either there was no place to knock, or any of the dozen floor-length doors or windows set into the square bay formed by the wings would do equally well to raise a shuffling butler with an Uzi.

Fred chose the likeliest door—the biggest one, which happened to fall at the midpoint of the central wall—to park in front of and to knock on with his knuckles. Sea air washed around. Mosquitoes began gathering from the lawn and the rose trees. The door was of glass panels set in white wood. Behind it stretched a broad hallway hung with outsize English hunting paintings: white dogs, white horses, and white men in dull red coats.

Fred smashed a hunting mosquito into his neck and knocked again. Although Runnymede House was nowhere near the size of its pretensions, it reverberated well. A window opened above him and a maid looked out from behind a screen. Two bits said the original Hintlesham Hall did not have screens.

"Come out where I can see you," the maid called. Fred stepped back and looked upward, leaning against his car. The screen made a scrim behind which the maid was almost invisible. "There's nobody here," she said. "What do you want?"

"I came to see Lady Hanford," Fred shouted. "I was in the neighborhood."

"'Neighborhood'!" the maid exclaimed bitterly. She and Fred stared at each other.

"Lady Hanford?" Fred asked.

"What's that under your arm?"

"Something I want to show you," Fred said.

A corona of seagulls materialized overhead and paid homage to something Fred could not see, above the roof, beyond the woman he was talking with. She told him, "I am not buying pictures. I can't buy anything."

"It's the Constable," Fred said. "The one you were bidding on last Sunday." He unwrapped the towel, dropped it into his car's window, and held the panel on a slant so as to catch enough of the waning light for her to make out what it was. "You were the under-bidder," Fred said.

"Wait. I'll come down."

A flock of crows swept over the house from the direction of the woods. They settled out of sight, beyond the edge of the bluff, and fell to squabbling on the shingle. Something as dead as it was attractive to them lay down there. Above the house, the crown of seagulls lost its shape and followed after.

Lady Hanford wore jeans and a gray sweatshirt with the words DON'T ASK across its front in big black letters. She opened the door and ran her fingers through blond hair that had had a hard day. She was forty at least, and shockingly changed from what had appeared out of the Daimler at the auction. She looked like Paris wrenched back in time to before the days of Haussmann: grim and sad and mortal. "You might as well come in," she said. "But I can't write you a check. The whole thing's in—in what my grandmother in Toledo would have called a rannykazoo."

Fred followed her into the entrance hall, which showed no sign of having lost any of its furnishings to the hammer of the auctioneer.

"According to that thing they passed around at the sale," Fred mentioned, "the original Hintlesham Hall is in Constable country. Newmarket. Racing. All that."

Lady Hanford was walking down the center of the hall as if she'd lost her tour group. "I should offer you a drink," she said suddenly, turning left into a small dark room filled with stuffed animal parts, guns, hunting prints, mirrors, cabinets, silver trophy bowls, and antlers. The space remaining had large worn leather chairs in it. Fred's hostess opened a piece of wall and exposed rows of bottles, racks of glasses, and a sink with a fridge under it. She chose a bottle, opened it, and poured a tumblerful of bourbon that she handed to Fred. Fred propped the School of Constable on one of the chairs. He followed the lady's gesture and sat down in another, with some difficulty keeping the whiskey from splashing over the tumbler's rim.

"I stopped bidding at thirty-five thousand," the widow said. She looked at the painting before sitting on the arm of a chair near his.

"You won't join me, Lady Hanford?" Fred asked, raising his glass. She shook her head. "Please call me Jane. No. Grief does the same thing as whiskey, but better."

Fred took a sip and set the glass on a brochure describing guns for sale two months before in Newport. "I'm Fred," he said.

"He wanted to be burned," Jane said. "I could not bear to have him gone so absolutely. But he was right. I should have. Now…" She swept her right hand through her hair again and changed the subject. "They said it wouldn't go beyond three thousand. What did you pay, thirty-nine? Add ten percent on top of that, that's forty-two nine. Unless—I suppose you want your profit."

"The problem is," Fred said, "the painting isn't even worth three hundred. It's not by Constable."

"That's what everyone said," Jane agreed. She stared at Fred, then at the picture, puzzled. "On Sunday I didn't care. On Sunday I could afford not to care. I liked the scene, and the little hay cart, and all the weather. So many of my pictures were going to go into Bobby's museum, and the money I paid would go into the museum anyway, and I thought maybe I could deduct it…and then I got carried away."

"It isn't from Lord Hanford's collection, then?"

"No. I just like it."

"Truth is," Fred said, "I want to ask you about some other art that was in the sale. Being curious…"

"I know nothing. You'd have to talk to Isabel Cooney, the— well, she worked for my husband. But the whole thing is upside down now. Monday morning I got a call from my lawyer—I hadn't slept Sunday night; seeing all our things divided and turned to money, I felt as if one of my lungs had been ripped out—telling me, essentially, what boiled down to, Hold everything. Everything's on hold. Except that for the moment, Bobby's son has no objection if I want to live in the house. Bobby's son who, until he did whatever he did to turn things around, had been prevented by court order from even setting foot in Bristol County! I don't know what he told them.…

"But that's why I can't write you a check. You've heard stories, I guess."

Fred acknowledged, "It's the son who's suing to get everything back. What I wanted to do—now here it gets delicate—"

"Is it more or less delicate than having your father's body dug out of the ground to prove that his widow killed him?" Jane asked. "Is it more or less delicate than the stories he's spreading down at the Capstan Club; lovely stories that our lovely former friends, Bobby's and mine, are rolling in like dogs in a rotten..." She faltered.

"The son—he'd be the new Lord Hanford?" Fred asked.

Jane nodded, then shook her head. "My husband's title did not pass to his son. He was a life peer only. The son is Bobby Rotwell, the same name my husband started with. What happened I don't know, what suddenly came over Bobby. His people had made no objection to the sale. Of course he and I don't speak, but the lawyers did, and...but...what did you tell me your name was?"

"Fred. I want to leave the painting with you. I don't like to be sued, and you like the painting."

"I can't pay. And if I could pay, maybe it's not even yours to sell."

A telephone rang somewhere in the house. "There's no one here," Jane Rotwell said. She rose and went away. Fred did the same, leaving the drink and the painting where they were.

The disguise Fred chose was a pair of white canvas pants and some plastic topsider knockoffs. He'd pulled the car over and changed as soon as he reached the woods, beating mosquitoes off while he did so. The blue knit shirt was lacking a little embroidered nautical flag on its pocket, of the kind yachts run up at sundown, signaling "bottoms up." But it would have to do.

Within forty minutes he had blended into the crowd on the deck of the Capstan Club, the unexpected guest of a happily absent Parker Stillton.

Chapter 15

The graciously sporty inside rooms, white paint and teak and plaid and brass, were almost empty except for those moving to and from the bar. The main action was outside the wall of sliding glass windows, now thrown open to allow members of the Capstan Club and their guests to visit on the deck overlooking their own portion of the great salt sea. It was eight-thirty. Fred's hands were filled with refills for some of his newest friends: Spar and Kimsie Ballard ("Scotch on the rocks with lime, and a gin and tonic—be sure you tell Mario who they're for. He knows how we like them") and Pottston Clark (a stinger). For Fred himself there was a glass of the closest thing they had to plain old beer.

The crowd was all muscle and paunch and big blond breasts decked out in Bermuda tans with designer labels. The club had its own dock where members whose yachts were moored offshore could tie their tenders. The deck creaked with the temporary good cheer of wealth being distracted by gossip and the prospect of meat a good deal later, after the sauce.

Fred delivered the drinks and laughed uninhibitedly at the second half of a joke being recounted by a new person who had joined the group he served. "Missy Cartwright," Spar Ballard announced, "Fred Taylor. Friend of Parker Stillton's from the frozen north."

"Bud Taylor's an old pal of Biff's, from Hotchkiss. Any relation?" Missy Cartwright asked. Missy was a hard-tan woman in her fiftieth year who looked as if forty-nine of those had been spent on the tennis court she was still dressed for. Fred had recognized Spar immediately as the chairman of the museum's board, who had been introduced at the sale and had distinguished himself by buying a cornshucker. So Fred had started with Spar. Spar was in his mid-sixties, well heeled, and equally well stomached, though seagulls had taken his hair. Kimsie, his wife, was a mournful person who resembled an antique chair with its upholstery and stuffing removed. She'd done her best to patch in the old nail holes, but they still showed her to be a woman whose children (Buffy and Tucker) had given her a good run for her money, and her husband's.

"No relation to Bud," Fred confessed. They'd met already, he and Bud Taylor, after which introduction the latter had almost immediately taken the steps down to the dock to check out somebody's dinghy. Kimsie Ballard had forced the encounter, hopeful that Fred and Bud—who happened to be chairman of the membership committee this year—might be long-lost cousins. It had taken Bud Taylor a total of seventeen seconds to torpedo that canard. "My family is broadly traveled in this country," he concluded his brief speech of dismissal, "but Iowa...ah, someone I must chat with. Priority. Pleasure to meet you, Frank."

"Friend of Parker Stillton's," Spar Ballard reminded Missy, putting his free arm around Fred's back, as close as he could reach to the shoulder. "Haven't seen Parker, have you? In this crowd..."

Missy shook sixty-nine dollars' worth of someone else's work on her hair. "God, any new face," she sighed, and grabbed the wrist of the arm Fred was not using to carry his beer. "Where is your craft?" she asked, gazing hungrily seaward.

"Stay right where you are," Fred told her. "If I don't phone home, my woman is gonna think I am somewhere in the boondocks having a high old time."

"She lets a lovely man wander away on his own?" Missy asked.

Fred winked, tore his arm away, and partied through the gathering until he reached the bank of outdoor Lexan shells that offered telephones under the eaves, where the deck cornered to find a side entrance.

"Who's John Ruskin? What did he do?" Terry demanded once she understood it was Fred who was calling.

"He was a guy in England who wrote books about art," Fred summarized. "'Truth to nature' was his winning idea. Why on earth...?"

"What did he do to Lakshmi?"

"What?"

"She sounds like she's going to kill him."

"Lakshmi's there? Can you put your mom on?"

"Not till you tell me what John Ruskin did. They won't let me listen."

"Terry, go get your mom."

"But you haven't—"

"Honey, I haven't got a clue what your mom and Lakshmi are talking about. John Ruskin's been dead for a hundred years."

"If he's dead, then what is Lakshmi's problem?" Terry protested, and the receiver dropped with a crack.

"The only thing missing from this setup is your sister Ophelia," Fred said after Molly and he established the basics. "I wish you were here with your eyes and your ears and your nose and your memory for detail. I'm posing as Parker Stillton's guest—that's a cousin of Clay's—and I'm meeting people in droves like there's no tomorrow. The names go by so fast I may have some wrong, but I have exchanged words with, I think, Pottston and Sundown Clark; Whitey Gosling and his wife, May; Dizzy McCall and her man, whom I think she called Crash; one Muffin Fingerhold, who's parading around with guests, visitors from France: an art nouveau female called Toots Sweet and a man who makes over-the-sofa-size jewelry, Henri Par Venue. Also the chairman of the board and his wife, and—"

"Is this call *about* something?" Molly asked.

"Just starting with local color. The big story of the evening, which is relayed in loud whispers and with rolling eyes, but always just out of my hearing, explains why Jane Selden is not part of tonight's madding crowd."

"Who's Jane Selden? Kathy's sister?"

"What? You're as bad as Terry. Who's Kathy Selden?"

"Kathy Selden," Molly said slowly. "The reason you don't get half my jokes, Fred, is that you don't have a head for names. I'm about to go into a whole routine about a pretty girl jumping out of a cake, and you don't even remember Kathy Selden. I'll give you two hints. Debbie Reynolds? *Singin' in the Rain?*"

"Oh," Fred said. "No, Jane Selden's real, not Hollywood. She married Lord Hanford in a December-May romance, became his Lady, and followed him to this ridiculous house he bought in Westport. They came into forty-seven best friends who needed a captive lord and lady to give them reassurance of their own natural-born class down at the Capstan Club. They even rode to hounds together sometimes, chasing imported foxes around Cobb Point. See, at the Capstan Club you can get yourself elected chairman of the membership committee, but they can't make you baron of anything.

"All I've been able to get so far is what Dizzy McCall whispered to me in a voice dripping with prurient sympathy: Lady Jane simply can't show her face among her suddenly *former* friends. It would be in such poor taste, Dizzy said. Unheard-of!"

The blobs and knots of Fred's new friends eddied, unraveled, and re-formed. One bubble burst and Missy Cartwright shot out of it, heading in his direction. "There's my date for the evening," Fred said. "Listen, Molly, got a pencil? Can you take something down to pass along to Lakshmi?"

"I bet you're all dressed up in a sailor suit," Molly gloated. She did not need to be seen licking her lips and leering with her green eyes. "I'll put Lakshmi on. She's right here, on the porch."

"Just pass this on," Fred said. "Tell her there must have been an inventory of Turner's drawings when they came into the National Gallery. The library at Harvard must have a copy. There's—just for fun…" Missy spied him and started over, waving. Fred waved back, holding up a hand with five fingers spread. "Anyway," Fred went on, "if she can find that, tell her to look for a group of watercolors done in Venice. I don't know when, but they'd be on brown paper, nine by twelve inches, and numbered on their backs."

"Talk about needles in a haystack! Didn't you tell me there were nineteen thousand drawings?"

"We've got to start somewhere. These were already numbered on their backs, long ago, I'm guessing by the artist himself."

Missy Cartwright pointed at her own empty glass and, from her distance, gestured at Fred the question of whether he was not ready for a refill. Fred waved a yes and nodded for good measure.

Missy trotted toward the line attending the bar, her tan limbs set off by her tennis whites.

"The numbers we're missing," Fred told Molly, "are One, Two, Three, Eight, Ten, Eleven, Twelve, Fifteen through Twenty-one, and Twenty-four through Thirty-one. You got those?"

"Gottem," Molly confirmed. "Terry, if you and that dog are going out, Sam goes with you…No, Prince Charles is not enough. You have to take a human. If Sam doesn't want to, I wouldn't mind roamin' in the gloamin' myself in a while. Maybe Lakshmi too. Don't answer back. I'm talking to Fred. No, you can't talk to Fred again. OK, I'll tell him. Get lost now."

"How's Marek?" Fred asked.

"He's hanging on. The same. Lakshmi was with him most of the afternoon. Terry wants you to visit her at camp. You coming back tonight?"

"I may be swept into the social whirl. But if a large man crawls into your bed, don't shoot before you see—"

"I'll shoot when I'm good and ready."

"Oh, also," Fred remembered, "tell Lakshmi in her travels to keep her eyes open for the name *Petworth*. My date approacheth with a foaming flagon. I'll call in the morning if I'm not beside you."

———

"You haven't seen Biff, have you?" Missy asked, putting the mug of beer into Fred's hand as he hung up the phone. "You'd know Biff. He's the one with his nose between the tits of anyone here with tits who's under nineteen."

"I haven't noticed anyone of that description," Fred helped.

"He was here when I came," Missy said. "Fred, leave us sit down. I am beat. Three sets this afternoon." She led him down some wooden stairs into a space under a grove of locust trees, where an English-style teakwood park bench was bolted to a subterranean plinth. She carried two glasses of whatever she was drinking. They sat on the bench and she inquired, "Who you with again?"

"Parker Stillton."

She looked vaguely around.

"Someone said you were on the board of that new museum," Fred remarked.

"Runnymede House Museum," she affirmed carefully, keeping the syllables from tangling in teeth that were trying to go crossways. "What else is there around?" she added. "I mean that's got any kind of class or interest or appeal or—you know—*je ne sais qwa?*"

"Thought I'd see Isabel Cooney here," Fred prodded. Their grove of locusts was on the same side of the Capstan Club as the parking area. Under the trees the flabby dust was studded with bottle caps. The grass was mowed, but the ground crew had not gotten this far.

"I have not had a good fuck in three years," Missy Cartwright announced before taking a long drink from her glass. Ice cubes shivered against her teeth. "Who or what is Isabel Cooney?"

"Curator. She'll be the director of your new museum."

"Oh. That little red-haired chippie that worked for Lord Bobby? Why in the world would she be here at the Capstan Club?" Her tone of voice was ancient and obvious, signifying, Why wouldst thou seek amongst us for the help?

"You know where she lives?"

"Who?"

"Isabel Cooney."

"Search me, as the bishop said to the actress." Missy Cartwright placed a hand on Fred's knee, shifting her seat toward him on the bench until there was no white space left between them.

"For some reason I thought I might find her in the house there, with the widow," Fred said.

"Jane the plain fortune hunter," Missy answered. She snickered salaciously. "You know, she's not nobility, no more than that red-headed Cooney-catcher. No. Jane's just an American girl with a twitch, and her nose where it didn't belong. I guess, coming from out of town, you have not heard about the little local brouhaha?" The frank hand on Fred's knee moved up. Missy Cartwright drank, her glass steady in the other hand, then spat a lime seed into the dust. She leaned closer as her hand rode up even farther. "I know I can trust you not to tell tales out of school," she assured him. "You see, I myself am on the board, and my husband—did you happen to meet him? Biff Cartwright?—he's the museum's attorney, so between the two of us I get the inside dope.

"Jane Selden found herself a nice rich lord three times her age, and she waved her firm round high white fanny in his face and nailed him to it. You know what I mean when I say *nailed*?" Her hand flicked, testing absently, before it settled down again at the top of Fred's thigh.

"We all did our best to welcome Lady Bobby—you have to, with family—but everyone knew he was making the same mistake all old men do whenever they find young tight female flesh on either side of their ugly nose. That bastard!" She dropped her empty glass on the ground and reached for the other, full one, which she had placed beside her on the bench.

"Now, we had heard there was a son, some mysterious thing, but we'd never seen him," she said. "Lord Bobby never mentioned him, and she—Jane—would only drop hints, as if he were some awful kind of monster." She looked down in surprise at where her hand had crept to, and left it there. "But it turns out Lord Bobby Junior is an absolute charmer!"

"You've met him," Fred said, standing to drain the remainder of his beer. "I'm empty. What can I get you, Missy? Oh, then you must have been part of that famous auction last weekend?"

Missy held on to Fred's arm and fixed him with eyes bubbling with mischief and gin. "Bought a few lamps for the guest house. Didn't have anything to sell. No, our gift is in kind. It's going to be what we call a working board. Lots of meetings. No, but listen, this guy, the son—he's not a lord yet, but we're all so used to it, we call him Lord Bobby Junior anyway. It's only a matter of time. He's full of ideas! If—well, I should tell you, he hated to do it, but he *had* to challenge the will. His plan—and he talked to the board last night, because we were all upset and didn't know what to think, with things happening as fast as they did. Lord Bobby Junior told the board, why don't we simply plan to use Runnymede House itself for the museum? Why build anything new? Runnymede House is already there, and it would be perfect!"

"Except the widow's in the way," Fred pointed out.

"He's working on that," Missy whispered, standing by pulling herself up Fred's arm. "That's him now. See the green Mercedes pulling into the drive? You recognize it, of course, since you're a friend of Parker Stillton's. That's Lord Bobby Junior with him."

Chapter 16

It was like the moment in a lavish production of *Aïda* when the audience first understands that they're bringing an elephant in. Everyone smells it first. A wind of alarm and joy sweeps through the place, almost a panic, as the audience looks to the exits through any one of which, according to the director's whim, or the beast's, the animal will make its appearance. Forgotten by the extras on the stage are all the little worries about panty lines or gaps in their body paint, or the uncontrollable wobbling droop of their spears. The diva rocks back and forth on the horn of a high C-flat. There's no turning back now, folks, because here comes the tenor, at climax, joined to his elephant; and everything's ready to blow.

Bobby Rotwell slammed the Mercedes door and laughed at the world's good fortune. He was an Elgar *Nocturne* of comfortable tweed, dispensing from his person perfect English weather: a cool evening breeze after the shower has passed. He threw his head back when he laughed, tossing blond curls still fragrant from a mother's lingering caresses.

"God, look at all that," Missy Cartwright slavered.

The other man called, climbing out of the driver's side, "We don't lock anything here. We're all family at the Capstan Club." He closed his own door. Fred recognized him as one of the overtall, overthin men of indeterminate age but overdeveloped teeth who had been scattered through last Sunday's auctiongoers. Parker Stillton was dressed in Fred's own disguise, except that his loafers, instead of having been turned out cheap by political prisoners in Sri Lanka, were tooled from Italian leathers chewed to supple perfection by maidens at Gucci. The pants were linen. The blue knit shirt bore on its breast a nautical pennon that translated as *Fill'erup*. Parker Stillton was the real thing.

The two men, jostling against each other with the familiarity of boys accustomed to contact sports, finished a confidential exchange of views, confirmed it with a final bark of laughter, and walked toward the Capstan Club. The deck on the far side of the building had fallen silent as soon as the car slowed, and already small groups of courtiers, glasses in hand, were drifting out of the club's front doors, converging toward the new arrivals.

"Excuse me," Missy Cartwright panted, dropping Fred's arm like last year's model. Rotwell was a middle-sized man of obvious physical power and ruddy, outdoor good looks. Missy's move toward him was almost headlong, her tennis dress twinkling. But she was only one of the awed crowd being drawn ineluctably in his direction.

Fred stood under the locust trees and watched. The man was magic. He knew what he had, and he wielded it with absurd ease, rubbing it in by appearing to be unconscious of what he possessed. "Animal magnetism," Fred remarked aloud to the empty air.

"Yes, ain't it," said a rocky voice behind him. Fred turned to the companion he hadn't heard approaching: his new friend Kimsie Ballard, mournful wife of Spar, the chairman of the board. "Lord Bobby Junior appeared in town on Monday morning," she went on, "and immediately everyone's compass started to spin, on account of his chorus-girl hair and that laugh you could use to cut meat."

They watched while the group that had formed around Rotwell figured out how to get itself through the door without any of its members losing precedence. Rotwell's grand gestures signaled reassuringly, There's plenty for all.

"You don't like him," Fred guessed.

"I have no opinion of Lord Bobby Junior," Kimsie replied. "Did Parker not notice you here? Your being his friend and all?"

"Everyone's attention seems to be stuck on the young laird," Fred reminded her. "I'll go in and do what I can to say hi. May I get you anything, Kimsie?" She shook her head and leaned against one of the locusts.

The new boy's charm had not rubbed off on Parker Stillton. Fred found him holding a glass and standing alone in the empty game room, bemused by his sudden catastrophic isolation. The entire party had moved back to the deck, trailing Bobby Rotwell.

"Parker," Fred greeted him heartily, thrusting a hand out. The tall man gazed a question before reciprocating. Fred continued, "Fred Taylor. I work with Clayton Reed."

The man's handshake was firm and pleasant, businesslike. "Didn't I see you at the sale?" he asked.

"I can't say you did," Fred said.

"It was a huge success," Parker Stillton said. "Clayton did not participate. I made out like a bandit. Landed a tax deduction of thirty-nine thousand dollars, minus the auctioneer's commission, for a painting I picked up as a lark for a couple of thousand bucks at an auction in Newton, Mass."

So the "Constable" had belonged to Parker Stillton. "I heard the sale was all bollixed up afterward," Fred said.

"I'd love to know who bought it," Parker pressed on, oblivious. "Someone in the back of the crowd. Just for fun I asked the people at the auction house, but of course they stood mute. Their 'fiduciary responsibility to the purchaser,' and all. Just like they won't tell the buyer that the picture was donated by me." He rested his drink on the rim of a pool table and gazed through the room with the bar, out to where comfort and joy reigned on the darkening deck overlooking the bay.

"With the court order, of course, we'll learn who the buyers of record are, and Lord Bobby Junior's determined to proceed with it. Redress the imbalance. Dissipate rumors of foul play. But some people, for instance the rug dealers, paid cash, loaded their ponies, and headed for the high ground. They will be difficult. My advice...but Fred, what brings you here?"

Fred asked, "What does he hope to gain?"

"Who?"

"Rotwell. The son. The man you call Lord Bobby Junior."

The question seemed to strike Parker Stillton as odd. "We want to see justice done. It is not a matter of money, not for Lord Bobby Junior. However, the Runnymede House Museum, coincidentally, may stand to gain considerably. No, no, Lord Bobby Junior has a considerable fortune of his own, left to him by his mother."

Fred asked, "But then what's the beef? I've heard rumors, naturally. It sounds complicated."

"We are contesting the will," Parker said. "It is quite simple."

"Would have been simpler *before* the sale," Fred noted.

"True. Interesting gray area, the whole business, which may be where I come in. I specialize in matters pertaining to charitable organizations, governance, that sort of thing. But just the same, I'd love to see Clayton's face when you tell him what my Constable brought me as a tax deduction. Where is he? He called me the other night, and when I called back there was nothing but empty phone. I'd been holding off telling him till I could do it in person, but when you said you worked with him I thought, Hell, don't waste it. Where is he?"

"Said something about a wedding," Fred confessed.

"Just make sure you tell him. Clay took one look at my Constable, said 'humph,' and pronounced, 'It's a fake.'"

Fred asked, "How are the son and the widow getting along?"

Parker Stillton snorted. "A man with a sense of humor!"

"He's really saying the old man was murdered?"

Parker Stillton closed his mouth and looked wise. He shook his head, then took a drink, and put his glass back where it had been. He said cordially, "I have the honor to serve on Lord Bobby Junior's team. Perhaps I should not have spoken about it, but you're almost part of the family. However, ask me no more, please. Lord Bobby Junior and his people in London assure me that they see no conflict of interest between his concerns and those of the Runnymede House Museum. Please understand: beyond that, I rest mute."

Fred telephoned Clayton from a booth next to a Store 24 perched on the edge of a marsh outside Westport Center. "I get two opinions describing the state of affairs down here," he reported. "Opinion one is it's a rannykazoo. Not so—only a brouhaha, runs opinion two."

"You say you are in Westport?"

"Just barely. I was trying to feel things out by talking with folks associated with the museum venture. I've met a half dozen of them. The problem is, like you, I can't put a question to anyone without giving your game away. They're all in each other's pockets and beds and law offices, and nobody knows which is which. I'd hoped to try the smoking-room horselaugh and shout, 'Say, did you hear about all the pornography at the auction? Who dumped that?' But that would tip the wink to somebody, let them know we care.

"I've seen the son," he went on. "About forty, same as the widow. If I were casting *Macbeth* I'd hire him like a shot for the part of the First Murderer. All huntin' and shootin' and easy money: cool customer, rough stuff. His smile is as the smile of ten."

Clay said, "So you talked with him?"

"Thought I'd ponder it first. Parker Stillton represents himself as one of the lord apparent's legal team. Did you know that?"

"No." Clay tapped his pencil at the Fall River end of the conversation. "Fred, we must talk. Will you come back to Fall River?"

The Silver Spur's parking lot held six cars, including Clay's Lexus. Fred made it seven and pushed into the lobby, where a fat old man he had not seen before sat at the desk, wearing an undershirt and poking at a mole on his neck. The man looked malevolently at Fred as if the mole had been Fred's idea.

"I'm with Mr. Daygah in four-thirteen," Fred told him, letting the fat man nod him along upstairs.

Clay, in his crimson dressing gown, let Fred in. The pressed green legs of his pajamas showed underneath, extending toward slippers modeled on those of Peter Rabbit. "The Constable's off our hands," Fred said.

Clay closed them in and stood worrying while Fred crossed the room and took one of the armchairs. He said, "There is no legal merit to the demand from the auction house. Not yet, at least. That's all bluff on their part, to make things easier if and when Rotwell's court order comes through. The auction house has to run interference. And Myron says however that plays out, if what we bought proves to be not out of the estate, there's nothing in our way as far as title goes. It is not interesting, but from other sources I happen to know that the Constable was not in the estate.

As to the Turners, if he can find me, the only thing left is for the plaintiff—Bobby Rotwell—to sue us directly. We could return to Boston now, and put all our attention on this matter, but for one thing: the unresolved issue of the dealer Small," Clay continued.

"Small's not a problem," Fred objected.

"Not Small himself, but the implications of his appearing on the scene. Fred, you are not thinking. Try this: Marek Hricsó, under duress, told Rotwell who I am and how to find me on Mountjoy Street," Clay said. "My supposition is consistent with the man you described to me. 'First Murderer'? You factored in that possibility?"

"Holy shit!" Fred said. "Of course you're right, Clay."

Clay continued evenly, "Why not assume that Small and Rotwell, both of them English, are working together? There has been no improvement in Hricsó's condition, Miss Thomas tells me. Granted, we do not have certain knowledge of the identity of Hricsó's assailant, but you said yourself...I see no reason why we should not draw this inference.

"I am glad to be rid of the so-called Constable. It was an embarrassment. I will not ask what you did with it. I prefer to imagine it floating facedown in the Atlantic, a piece of old furniture panel with incoherent and palpably new paint on it!

"There is too much at stake. I have hope that something will come of Lakshmi's efforts. Despite the overalls, she strikes me as a competent young woman. You, Fred, must espouse the active mode. I shall remain here with my prize, an anchorite cut off from the busy world, until all danger to the success of my project has passed. I shall continue to direct my full attention to these drawings. We have two, perhaps three days more in which to make of them a presentable package, which must transcend all scandal and red tape. I still hold out hope that I may present a *virgo intacta.*"

Fred broke in, "You're right about Rotwell. Let's assume he's dangerous. What did Lakshmi find concerning the will? She called this evening?"

Clay made up his mind and crossed to the window, where he sat down in the second chair. He crossed his legs and fidgeted with long fingers at the lapels of his robe, then fluttered his hands like the messenger in a Greek tragedy who arrives with bad news only after the chorus has announced that the whole world is covered with corpses.

"My blackest fear is this," Clay revealed. "While you are moving and shaking, Fred, I am forced into a life of contemplation. For me contemplation and suspicion are almost synonymous. Suppose that the dealer Small did not just tardily *guess* that the package I purchased might be of value; suppose, rather, that he *knows* it is. Fred, I must know. Find Small. He will be the weak link. Feel him out. Learn what he might pay for the package. Indulge any subterfuge you think will lead to our goal—that is your strength. Should he mention a figure of twenty to thirty-five million, we'll know he is warm."

"Dollars or pounds?" Fred asked. "Oh, never mind. At that level, it doesn't matter. You want me to go to London after him?"

"Call me if you do. I may ask you to look in at the Tate or the National Gallery."

The covers on Clayton's bed were already turned down in a crisp welcoming triangle. His book lay ready on the night table. Fred stood and stretched.

"If you should go to London…," Clay added, "well, there is time. We will talk. The first thing is to find Mr. Small. It is almost midnight now. There will be an early-morning flight out of Logan. You will leave me a message at the desk?"

"Mr. Daygah. Four-thirteen," Fred said. "I get it. After the painter."

"A nom de plume," Clay confessed. "No, better, a *nom de pinceau*. You recognize the allusion. A predicament similar to mine was endured by Degas in a *maison close* in Paris in, what, eighteen eighty? He escaped tedium by executing monoprints of the subjects offered. I suspect Turner of similar flights, at similar houses, among London's dockyards. A change, I myself even find, offers a—"

"I'll be off," Fred said.

Chapter 17

Fall River is a sprawling and grubby city, its size limited on one side by the polluted shores of Mount Hope Bay, and on the others only by poverty and exhaustion. It had boomed with fabric mills in the 1800s, later burned, and been bankrupt by the 1930s. Since then the city's energies had gone into becoming accustomed to this state of affairs and learning to package itself as "living history."

The midnight traffic heading north out of Fall River on route 79 was sparse and fast, joined by a few large trucks and more smaller ones only when it fed into 24. Fred drove warily. The road was broad and flat. It had been designed to dull the senses of travelers in order to promote the area's only thriving industry: wrecking. Every half mile a blackened, overturned car had been pushed into the scrubby fringe of woods that edged the road. Discarded wheels lay in the median rift between the northbound and southbound lanes.

Fred let the faster traffic do its thing and dawdled along at the speed limit. He turned the radio on and got white noise interrupted by clicks that were too irregular to be Morse code. Fifteen miles out, he found himself alone on the road and slowing, as he approached the top of a hill, to acknowledge the visual commotion ahead. Red and blue lights played against the underside of the low cloud cover. When he crested the hill, he saw a half dozen police cars parked at odd angles in the trough of the valley, their headlights pointing into the dense brush that filled the median separating the northbound from the southbound lanes. A few cars and small trucks were backed up ahead of him, halted by the interruption. Rifle fire cracked, and Fred braked more rapidly. More cop cars were now converging on the scene from the opposite, southbound lanes. It was all lights, no sirens. Men crammed the roadway ahead of where Fred stopped his car: uniformed officers shuttling through the lights. Another echoing shot was followed by a yelp of pain. A black form slunk speedily into the bushes on the far side of the white panel truck that was Fred's closest neighbor. The truck boasted BEST SEAFOOD, NEW BEDFORD.

There was no pushing through this, and given the heavy brush in the median, and the shooting, no U-turns or heading back, either. He'd be picked off in whatever this was—it looked like a battle in a drug war. The commotion was now magnified by the overhead thwapping of a tilting helicopter. Fred climbed out of his car into a melee that resembled setup time at the tent circus, but with somebody shooting. An officer fired steadily into the median's brush, his bullets bringing howls and snarls and a thrashing of branches. Another man shot. The moon came out, then thought better of it.

Radios in the squad cars sputtered with indecipherable emergency. Fred ambled over to the seafood truck, whose driver ate French fries out of a Big Boy container while he watched the show that was blocking his deliveries.

"There's no return fire," Fred observed. "Who've they got trapped in there, escaped convicts from Bridgewater?"

"Dogfight," the driver said. He bit off half a fry before shoving the rest into his mouth and talking around it. "Wild dogs living around here. As bad as the Serbs and Croats. Somebody called in a fight between the Berkley pack and East Taunton. My money's on East Taunton every time. Ten to one. You on?"

Two rifles fired in quick succession. "Got her," shouted two men. Then, "That's the lead bitch. They're running," somebody called.

"I'm out of my depth," Fred said. "No offense."

Thirty or forty dogs burst out of the bushes and ran across the northbound lanes. A volley of free fire killed and maimed some and stampeded the rest into the imperfect cover of a marshy stretch to the east of the road, which led toward an abandoned Dairy Queen done up in plywood.

"Jesus, that's gonna change the political ecology," the driver said. Two fire engines traveling abreast, their lights swinging and sirens blaring, heaved into sight, racing the wrong way toward them in the northbound lanes. "What's that, the U.N. arriving now? What are they, fuckin' lonesome?" the driver complained. "What were they gonna do, spray them with hoses?"

A few officers wandered cautiously among the downed dogs in the roadway, firing into their heads with pistols.

"They're all excited now," the driver said. "We're not gonna move for an hour at least. I get depressed, watching my tax dollars at work. I'm gonna take a nap."

The sparse traffic was backing up behind Fred's car. The size of the crowd of lawmen was only growing, streaming down both sides of the highway from the north now, pooling and milling in a dangerous mix of officers, cars, and guns. Fred wandered toward the median, where the main action had been. A hectic strobe of lights showed scattered leaves and a few twitching dogs. The officer who had been busiest with her service pistol called out, "I'm goin' in. Any of you jokers want to keep me company?" Pistol at the ready, she started down the embankment and shot a yelping dog point-blank. "They play dead," she shouted. "Don't trust 'em. Half of them have rabies."

Two others joined her, men carrying rifles. Their encouragement and instructions sounded from the undergrowth after they were out of sight, punctuated by occasional shots and howls. The moon came out again, blackening the dogs' blood in the roadway. The yelps of the survivors roiled from in back of the Dairy Queen. The crisis over, they had remembered who was who and started fighting again.

Fred found a uniformed man who did not seem to be showing off or playing with his equipment. He pointed toward an anomaly in the space that had been churned up by the fighting animals. "Human body there," Fred explained. "Unless it's a deer, but I'd guess human."

Fred started down the embankment. The uniform dithered awhile until, about six yards behind him, its large feet followed through the burdock and buttercups slippery with dew. Yes, it was human, or had been: slight and male, wearing the maimed rags of a brown suit too heavy for this climate at this time of year.

One shoe was off. The belly had been laid open so that the club-striped necktie conflicted with the entrails, while at the same time subtly complementing them. One hand was already eaten off, or at least elsewhere. The balding head, its face upturned, resembled one of the starchier vegetables after wild dogs have fought over it.

"Yep," Fred told the young officer puking beside him, "it's human." He backed away. If he showed any further interest, he'd be here all night and well into the next morning. "I'll get out of you-all's way," Fred said, and walked slowly back to his car to sit and stare into the sky until he fell asleep.

———

"Mr. Small is no longer with us," caroled the female concierge behind the desk at the Royal Court Hotel. Mr. Sanhedrin had been replaced.

"He left? I was supposed to meet him for breakfast. I've been waiting for him in the Regency Room. Check again?"

The concierge gave a sigh to rival the one delivered daily by Queen Elizabeth II over her morning *Tatler*. This woman needed no further troubles. She was already exhausted by years and disappointments and failed hairstyles. She went through the motions of punching number codes into her keyboard and reading from the screen. The name on her tag was Mrs. Wen.

"Mr. Small left us yesterday afternoon at approximately four o'clock," she confirmed.

"You saw him yourself?" Fred asked. "He leave a forwarding address? Anyone with him?"

Mrs. Wen stared at an uncouth opening in the empire miles behind Fred—the one place, normally covered by the Union Jack, where the sun don't shine. Fred shook his head ruefully and walked back to the Regency Room, arriving at his table just in time to be served the English breakfast he had ordered, complete with Daddies Sauce.

———

Marek's face looked like a Turner sunset. He lay on his back, his skull bandaged, being fed from a tube and drained by a tube. He was visible behind the glass partition that separated his room from the corridor. The uniformed cop in the hall looked up, registering where Fred's interest lay.

"Friend of yours?" the cop asked.

"Friend, colleague. I'm the guy who found him."

"So you're a hero," the cop concluded, angling for a fight.

Fred shrugged. "He looks bad."

The cop chewed on something he was imagining, which had large seeds. "Sit with him if you want," he invited. "He's as much fun right now as Jerry Seinfeld. You see that show?"

Marek Hricsó's room smelled as if they had already started to embalm him. It was without flowers or inedible fruit. Fred pulled a small, straight-backed chair around the bed and sat with his back to the window. Marek's shallow breathing seemed coached and involuntary. "'Blood, toil, tears, and sweat,'" Fred said, the words forming a hazy image in front of his eyes, something like Turner's *Fighting Temeraire*, a warship going through flames to its final berth.

The twitches in Marek's face were not the result of comprehension but merely the tracks of impulses struggling to find their way through damaged nerve paths.

"Bobby Rotwell," Fred said. "Robert Rotwell. An Englishman. Traveling with Alexander Small, the London dealer." Marek breathed in. A long time passed. He breathed out. Above him on a shelf a box held a shifting pattern of busy green lights that showed what was going on in every part of Marek except whatever part it was that housed his will to live. The man's hands lay obediently on top of the light blanket, just where the nurse had placed them. His arms were badly bruised.

"Mr. Robert Rotwell," Fred tried one last time, bouncing the name off what was left of Marek. He sat in the room for a half hour until a nurse came in to change the bags.

"I reckon I can't ask what his prospects are?" Fred asked. "For living, that is, or for gaining consciousness?"

"They like you to talk to the head nurse about that kind of thing," he answered, checking Marek's pulse. "She won't tell you anything."

Fred said, "I won't disturb you." He left the nurse and Marek to their work.

———

Billy Pasquale, in back of the reference desk, told Fred, "Your friend Molly's across the street at Starbucks drinking *caffè latte con carne*, she said. You're bound to catch her there. She left five minutes ago."

"Am I all right parked in your lot, or will they tow me?"

"We know your car," Billy said. "We wouldn't dare. Molly would kill us."

It was not until he was halfway through the park that Fred realized it was the weather itself that was chill and gloomy. Molly looked up from the table where she had spread that morning's *New York Times*. She'd dressed in a pink sleeveless shirt with wide black buttons and—Fred learned when he leaned around the table in order to kiss her—a broad green skirt with daisies on it.

"Square dancing later?" Fred asked.

"Love to."

"I'm sorry. It sounded like an invitation, but it was just a stupid remark. I'm so sorry. I feel like an oaf and an idiot. Someday. But now I have to go back to Fall River."

"Get coffee if you want some. I want one of those yuppie dry things dipped half in chocolate, too. I have ten minutes to burn."

"What's the news?" Fred asked.

"Burundi has stopped being the place where everyone wants to be."

Fred brought back his purchases and sat across from her: Molly's yuppie thing and orange juice for himself. "I'd meant to spend some time with Sam," he said. "And Terry wants me to see her camp, which I haven't done. I feel like a heel."

"The summer's not over."

"No, but I can't see where it's going, right at the moment. I'd been thinking, planning…" Fred let the thought run out. "I don't like just dropping in and out of the house randomly," he explained. "How can anybody depend on that? I mean, kids."

"It's just since Sunday that you've been tearing around," Molly reminded him. "It's not long. They're in camp all day. Who's excited?" She dunked the naked end of her yuppie thing into whatever it was she was drinking, swished it, and lifted it to her mouth.

"Terry's so good at establishing herself stage center," Fred went on. "Sam gets crowded into the wings. And in Cambridge he has no friends."

"Fred, what's the matter?" Molly asked.

"Marek's very bad."

"I know. Lakshmi keeps me posted. Which reminds me, last night she left me a copy of whatever she FedExed to Clayton Reed, in case I saw you first."

"It's at your mom's house?"

"No, I brought it to work with me," Molly said. "I never know when you're going to swoop out of the clouds, say hello, take a bite of the chocolate end of my yuppie thing, and unswoop."

Fred put the last bite back on her napkin. "I'll get another."

"I had all I wanted."

"Terry was funny last night," Fred said. "On the phone. She demanded to know what the scoop was on John Ruskin, claiming you and Lakshmi were whispering secrets about him and wouldn't let her listen."

"It's a good story, but I don't have time to tell you now," Molly said. "It's not crucial to what you're doing. But by the way, Ruskin was one of Turner's executors."

"No kidding?"

"Lakshmi got a copy of Turner's will at Widener. It's amazing what you can find in a decent library."

"So Ruskin was at the bedside to catch the last gasp of his beloved master?" Fred asked.

"No, when Turner died Ruskin was in Venice," Molly said. She giggled. "He loved Venice—the site of his greatest triumphs! He'd honeymooned there, years before. Gotta go." As they stood up, she added, "Follow me to my desk, and I'll give you your papers. Lady Eastlake was there too. During the Ruskin honeymoon in Venice. According to Lakshmi."

Chapter 18

Jouncing into Boston on the Red Line, Fred took a quick peek at his copy of Lakshmi's initial report to Clayton—ten pages of Xerox copies in addition to her own printed cover letter.

Cambridge, Wednesday

Dear Mr. Degas:

Mr. Rudenstine is a dear. I have the use of a computer, so you will not have to decipher my miserable handwriting.

Turner's will: I attach a copy, but I'll tell you what happened. It was a nightmare of codicils and loopholes and places where he changed his mind. The man left money, quite a lot. It's kind of sweet: Turner wanted to found a home for "decayed" artists. But the lawyers got most of the money.

It looks more and more as if the material we are concerned with was a part of Turner's estate—so I need to figure out how it got *out* of the estate and *to* where it is. So, who are the people involved?

I was right. The will was contested by family. After five years of fighting in Chancery (you recall Dickens's *Jarndyce* v. *Jarndyce*?) between the family and the National Gallery—that's Lord Eastlake, remember? I said he'd be in the middle of this!!—here's what happened. The money was gone. The real estate went to the family. The painter's father had had two brothers, Jonathan and Price; and Price's son Thomas

Price Turner—our Turner's cousin—was the ringleader who contested the will. When the dust settled, the family got Turner's houses, all his engravings, his copyrights, and whatever money was left after the Royal Academy got its share (that's Sir Charles Eastlake also).

The deal the family made with the National Gallery was that the museum could have all the original paintings and drawings. *But:* Charles Eastlake, the museum director, was rabid against—forgive me if I use shorthand—dirty pictures. (I can prove it to you, but not here.) He was a big censor, and he refused to endanger public morality, as he saw it. So if the museum could not accept the dirty pictures Turner left behind him, my theory is that maybe the cousin kept them.

So possibly the moral of all this is, look for descendants of Thomas Price Turner of Exeter, England, the cousin.

But we also want to note who Turner's executors were, because any or all of *them* might have been left alone with the collection during those five long years when the lawyers were tearing at the estate. And any of them might have run off with the package. Here they are: William Frederick Wells of Mitcham, Surrey; the Rev. Henry Trimmer of Heston; Samuel Rogers of St. James Place; George Jones, R.A.; Charles Turner, A.R.A. (I got hopeful about that name, but he turns out to be no relation); Thomas Griffiths of Norwood; John Ruskin the younger of Denmark Hill, Camberwell; Philip Hardwicke of Russell Square; Henry Harpur; and then finally Hugh Andrew Johnston Munro. It's a big mess, and I may have it wrong. You can go through it yourself. The main thing is, it still looks like the bulk of the original work went to the National Gallery.

HOWEVER—as you read through all these whereases and inasmuchases, in the will itself, you will notice some other names standing out! Then, as now, historians always disregarded the women. Turner's wills and codicils do contain the names of females, who would all be cut out entirely in the long run, but whom Turner himself tried to provide for over and over: "Hannah Danby, residing with me," and "Sophia Caroline Booth, late of Margate." There's also, in the earlier documents, before the codicils start

coming thick and fast, mention of an Evelina Danby or
Dupree, and a Georgiana T. Danby, who are described as
daughters of Hannah.

What do you think?

According to Molly, the old wives' tale everyone's heard
is that after Turner died, his wife destroyed his dirty pictures.
If there's any truth to the story (and granted that Turner
was unmarried), WHO ARE THESE WOMEN? Aren't they
worth a look?

Frankly, I think we'd save time by going straight to a
scholar who knows the whole Turner story. But I have your
strict orders to keep my inquiry under tight security. So I
do and I will. I'll summarize all this tonight when I call
you, and you'll tell me how to proceed.

Faithfully, L. Thomas.

Suddenly, and unaccountably, it had become blazing hot by the
time Fred emerged from the subway at Charles Street's elevated
station. The river's blue challenged the sky and matched its
scurrying clouds with sailboats. Fred glanced downriver toward
Mass. General, where Marek lay, before clattering down the iron
catwalk of stairs to Charles Street. The late-morning crowd was
either window-shopping or hurrying back to the office with iced
coffee. A few serious decorators bustled importantly, and empty-
handed, into and out of stores specializing in new or antique
perfect accents for those hard-to-furnish corners.

Two lampposts down from Marek's, a police detective lounged.
He was disguised as a flagrant punk, with leathers and spiked
purple hair and silver chains hung from his lips and ears with
safety pins. He was reading a comic book about breasts from outer
space and listening to any conversation that developed in front of
Marek's padlocked shop.

Fred confided to him, "In my student days in these parts—
there were about fifteen of them, altogether—the way you could
spot a cop doing surveillance was that he'd be pushing a broom
up and down the same block all day."

"Man, I'm readin'," the cop said. "Man, you know where I can
score?"

Fred sat at the counter at Chico's, the next block down, and ordered an orange soda from Marilyn. "Marek looks bad," Fred began.

Marilyn shook her head. She was a broad, strong woman in vertical pink and white stripes that extended into her hair. Her right arm was tattooed with a menagerie of insects, her left with birds on their much larger scale. The rest of her, she had several times hinted, she would gladly show off as well—but not here.

"I sat with him for half an hour," Fred said. "He's not conscious."

Marilyn handed him his drink. Six other people sat at the counter, and she had to cover takeouts too, shouting the orders in to Chico, who worked behind the square window in the partition that closed off the kitchen area.

"Everyone's stunned," Marilyn said. "I mean, who's safe?"

"Does anyone have a theory as to who it was?" Fred asked.

Marilyn turned away to snatch an egg-salad sandwich from the service window and whack it down in front of an old lady at the end of the counter. "Enjoy, honey," she said. Then she had to dispose of a takeout before she had a moment for Fred.

"Everyone likes sex," she announced in a hoarse whisper. "Rough sex is what everyone says, rough sex that went too far. It's what everyone says, but that's the culture we live in: we start blaming the guy who gets clobbered. Then you ask them, Do you know for a fact that Marek Hricsó went that way? Turns out nobody knows a thing. There's no lover anyone knows about who might have turned mean. And who knows—whose business is it anyhow whether the guy's even gay or straight?"

"Ketchup?" the old lady with the egg salad called.

When Marilyn came back to Fred, she continued, "That sweet little girl who works there—whipped cream and strawberries and legs like a climbing vine—what's happened to her?"

"I can see your point," Fred said. "So no mysterious wandering curly-haired Englishman or anything? No Burmese prince with an exotic ax to grind?"

Marilyn shook her head. "The people want dirty stories. Ask the *Globe*. You got a buck-fifty?"

Fred took the next street over up Beacon Hill and stood at the top of Mountjoy looking down. He'd been surprised here once before by John Columbo, when his guard was down; now he took his time staring into the shadows along the street. With the sun this hot and high, the contrast tended to dazzle. Fred waited under a tree until he was sure, then sauntered slowly down the street, looking into the parked cars on both sides.

The interior of Clay's house was dim and cool. The telephone was ringing. Fred picked up the stack of mail where it had fallen inside Clay's front door and carried it to his desk, along with the stack of Lakshmi's research. The telephone stopped ringing. Fred filled a mug with water from the bathroom sink and poured it on his begonia, wilting in the half-window that gave a view of the lower legs of passersby on Mountjoy Street.

The office was Fred's but it was in Clay's house and—except for the begonia, a gift to Fred from Molly—filled entirely with Clay's business. While the back room stored paintings, the front was devoted to bookshelves, file cabinets, and pictures they were studying. So many captive paintings in such close proximity lent the space an almost animated air of striving.

The Turner painting Clay had bought—that shocking expanse of articulated canvas—had been swept away so briskly by Roberto Smith that its existence now seemed unreal: a phantasm or night-mare. In due course that painting would come back to Boston from New Bedford in a van and find a simple temporary frame. Clay wouldn't order the real thing until he had lived with the picture for a good while.

Dirty old man: Turner had left his paintings and his drawings to his nation, provided for them to be respected, kept together, and properly hung. He had tried to leave his fortune to help comfort the last days of old artists down on their luck, but with the aid of greedy lawyers, his cousin had finessed him. Turner'd been thwarted at every turn. He'd wanted to leave protection for a pair of women too, but there, once again, according to Lakshmi, both the dead artist and the living women had been buggered by the law.

Fred called Clay. "I'm coming down," he said. "I'd meant to be there much sooner. I don't normally share your reticence on the phone, but in this case…let me just say, the man can't be talked to."

"The one from the sceptered isle? Not having heard from you, I'd presumed you were on the plane."

"Too late," Fred told him. "I'll check the mail and come. Be there by two-thirty or three."

"There's been a setback," Clay guessed.

—⊷⊶—

Fred fanned the mail and set circulars and normal business to one side. The envelope with the eagles on it was from the Alphonse Bird Galleries. Bird's designer, starting from the auctioneer's heavy emphasis on Americana, had taken note of the happy coincidence that an *eagle* was also a *bird*. The letter was not even registered or certified, but had simply been stuck in at the door slot by the courier. Bird's effort had been perfunctory at best. Fred tossed the letter aside.

Fred asked himself, If Small led Rotwell to Marek; and if, for the sake of argument, Rotwell did for Small—*who*, in the first place, told Small that Marek had what he wanted?

A square parchment envelope addressed to Clayton in a nice curving script became more interesting when Fred flipped it over and saw the embossed golden heraldry of the logo and address of the Royal Court Hotel. He flipped the envelope over again and checked its face. The stamp was not canceled. It had been delivered by hand.

"I suppose this is evidence," Fred said aloud. "I shall herewith, and inasmuch as, tamper with it." He slit the envelope's side open with his pocket knife, remarking, "Saliva caught in the adhesive gum, no doubt. They've got a thousand tricks to try now—and they've gotta do something all day. We'll leave the saliva intact."

The signature on the heavy ivory card read *Alex Small.*

Tuesday

Dear Mr. Reed:

I am in Boston briefly, on a confidential matter that concerns you intimately. I am at your service, room 611, Royal Court Hotel.

Small's business card fell out after the larger note, complete with the little red graphic of the Burlington Arcade.

"Clay was right. Marek gave us away. I suppose there's a Mrs. Small," Fred said, "who despite her worst fears, may even now be trying to explain to the little ones why Daddy hasn't called to say happy birthday to Neddy."

The telephone rang. Fred picked up his things and made tracks.

Route 24 offered a Burger King not far from Taunton, a half dozen miles from where Fred had spent much of that early morning. He let the counter jockeys give him a couple of burgers with accessories and sat down to them, pulling out Lakshmi's research. He'd noticed, under the many tight pages of Turner's legal problems, a memorandum headed:

FRED: MEMO CONCERNING SIR CHARLES EASTLAKE

Listen, Fred? This guy Eastlake is a criminal. Look what a prude! There's only one painting in the world I ever loved enough to get stopped in my tracks by. I don't know about pictures and—sorry—I couldn't care less. But I saw this one in London last year and it gave me the cold shivers. I love it. It's Venus. The painter's Bronzino. Italian, fifteen-something. Do you know the picture? Well, in case you don't—everyone's naked. The main figure is Venus, who's sort of sitting, crouching, kneeling so you see her whole front, and she's kissing about a twelve-thirteen-year-old boy. Well, maybe sixteen, because he's gotten so tall he has to crouch down so his precious round fanny sticks out to the edge of the frame. He's Cupid. With wings and a fanny. It's all sex. You can see he's gotten too big all of a sudden, the way he's wrapped around his mother, and his hand's on her breast. Very sweet—it's his mom, after all. All around them are kids and old people making allegorical faces, and doves and the rest of it. I love that picture. I love everything about it. It's almost electric.

Now. When Eastlake hung it in the National Gallery, listen to this. Venus had to wear a silly transparent diaper somebody painted on. It's not like Bronzino had given her pubic hair they had to cover up; there's not even a hint of cleft! The mere fact that her two legs came together—her limbs, I suppose they would have been called then—that fact alone was too much for the English lords. There's a memo Eastlake sent to the keeper, a man named Ralph Wornum, the guy in charge of the nitty-gritty, telling him not to print the word *sensual* in the catalog. Those hypocrites. Here they are, just legislating their prurient disregard—not just of women, but of sex itself, as if sex has to do only with women.

As for the boy, somebody painted a mask of leaves across that sweet ass I wanted to bite. You are *supposed* to want to bite it—that's the whole point! What was Eastlake thinking of? He made a weird and lovely thing into a dirty joke.

The Venus was vandalized by prudery, and Eastlake showed it in state that way, pretending all that censorship was the painter's own work! Fred, take a memo from Lakshmi Thomas to Sir Charles Eastlake and all his gang: If you can't stand sex, leave it alone for others to enjoy!

L.

Chapter 19

Clay's room at the Silver Spur was a scene of cottage industry when Fred opened the door in response to Clayton's "Come." Three people were at work, all in white gloves. Clayton, in the white linen suit, stood at the windowsill, where he had spread out an array of drawings in their glassine envelopes. He was writing notes, using a clipboard. Seated at the desk was a statuesque woman of middle age, dressed like a cocktail waitress at a place that sees far too many wandering businessmales on expense accounts. Daiquiri, dressed briefly and transparently, was kneeling beside the spare bed, placing drawings in glassine. She waved at Fred without breaking her concentration; he wandered over and filched two of her empty envelopes. "Ah, Fred," said Clay.

"We need to talk," Fred told him.

"Ladies, when you reach a good place to pause and take refreshment...?" Clay suggested graciously.

The woman at the desk said, "Mr. Daygah, I wouldn't guarantee it, but—no, what the hell, I guarantee it. It's three, maybe four chicks at most in box Six."

"A 'chick' is a woman," Clay informed Fred. "Go on, Mrs. Smith. On what do you base your conclusions?"

"Body type. See, the girls are gonna change their hair every five minutes, so you can't go by that. That's where you were making your big mistake. And God knows your guy isn't being cute about getting their faces right. Come here. I'll show you."

Clay stood behind Mrs. Smith and leaned over her work to study it with her. Daiquiri, rising to a crouch, began putting her own work away while the other woman instructed their host. "Concentrate on body types, like I say. Length of legs and arms. Athleticism. The prominence of bust, hips, bellies. Some of these gals have been around awhile. I sorted them into three piles that I'm sure of. See? Woman One I call Jazz, don't ask me why. I just think of her like that. Number Two is Little Potbelly; and here's Three, who I bet was tall. See the length of this shin? Sad, all these people working so hard, dead so long ago. You work and you die and you're gone. It's just sad. Who knows who they were? Girls working. These in the fourth pile, either they're too indistinct to judge from or there's someone in the way."

"Beg pardon, I am forgetting my manners," Clay said. "Fred, I would like you to meet Mrs. Juno Smith." Mrs. Smith was rising from the desk with her hand out.

"Fred de Toulouse-Lautrec," Fred said, shaking the hand of Mrs. Smith while being careful to leave intact her long golden plastic fingernails.

"Finished with box One," Daiquiri said. "That's all of them except box Eight, which no one's supposed to open."

"Thank you so much," Clay said. "I shall arrange with you later? Will you both join me for tea at five-thirty? If you are free of other obligations?"

"Small is dead," Fred announced as soon as they were alone. Clay's color went greenish gray against the white suit. He slumped into one of the orange chairs; Fred took the other.

"He was found by the road south of East Taunton, and driving home, I happened onto it. I was close enough to make some observations and I managed to overhear some talk. First, he had no papers on him, so he won't be identified right away. Second, the cause of death is going to take some time to establish because of the condition of the body—which I need not go into. I heard talk about gunshot wounds, but those were probably inflicted after death. A hit-and-run was the first thought of the medics on the scene. But Marek also looks like a hit-and-run victim right about now.

"Small was trying to get in touch with you," Fred continued, handing over the two glassine holders into which he had slid Small's letter and its envelope. "There may be other prints on them aside from mine, so let's keep everything in the glassine."

Clay stared at Small's message. "'Confidential matter,'" he read. "It sounds like a blackmail note. Can you deny, Fred, that occasionally my suspicions are well founded?"

Fred nodded in agreement. "It's phrased so that whatever is of foremost importance in the recipient's mind will be betrayed to the sender. It's supposed to make you break for cover and run with what you care most about. Then the hunter picks you off."

"So I was right. Marek told Small for whom he had purchased the Turners," Clay concluded. "...Ah, I understand. Very droll. Not Fred but *Henri* de Toulouse-Lautrec. Because of Toulouse-Lautrec's sojourn in the rue des Moulins and so forth, living and painting among the *filles de joie*. Very good, Fred. Levity. But back to the matter at hand—"

"Small dated his note Tuesday," Fred said. "It was late Tuesday night that Marek was beaten. I'd visited Small that morning, you'll remember. By Monday, Small already had Marek's name."

"Very well," Clay allowed. "But incidentally, Fred, it is no longer any mystery how Marek was identified so quickly as the purchaser. Your good Lady Molly telephoned and informed me: the *Globe* did one of its social-interest numbers on Monday, quoting 'a private dealer, well known in certain Boston circles,' who reveled in the chance to report that all the so-called Curiosa had been purchased by one of the city's colorful own. There followed a snide sentence of innuendo that I shall not bother to repeat. A public auction, after all, is not called a public auction without reason; we were correct to remain *hors de combat* and incognito.

"So long as I continue not to be found, it may not matter that Marek revealed me to be the purchaser for whom he acted. True, you may say that there is a homicidal maniac at large. Are we not to assume that Rotwell is responsible for Mr. Small's misadventure? As he is for Marek Hricsó's?"

"Yes. I think Rotwell dumped Small, or Small's body, on his way to or from Westport. Rotwell was in Westport Monday, and if I remember correctly what Missy Cartwright said—"

"Missy Cartwright?"

"A woman—a board member—I met at the Capstan Club. Rotwell talked to the new trustees in Westport on Tuesday evening; then he was there again on Wednesday night. John Columbo, or one of his ilk, is almost certainly the 'private dealer well known in certain Boston circles' who retailed the dirty story to the *Globe*."

"That's settled, then," Clay said. "We may both now concentrate on the question of how my Turners came to be in Lord Hanford's collection. You have studied your copies of Miss Thomas's discoveries? She suspects Charles Locke Eastlake. But there are others. Apart from the overalls, what do you think of the maiden efforts of Miss Thomas? Do you not find her cast of mind to be somewhat on the literary side? More suited, perhaps, to fiction?"

"Before we start in on comparative research," Fred dodged, "let's notice that we're in a room with a set of drawings that may have led to one death already, and two if Marek dies."

"Correct," Clay conceded, folding his hands and gazing at the closed blinds of his window. "One of us must therefore visit with Mr. Rotwell."

Fred agreed. "Your cousin Parker knows where he is."

Clay pursed his lips. "That would be too direct," he objected. "I prefer that we not surface unless we must—and *until* I must. As the poet Horace would advise us, let Rotwell fall under his own weight. If our inferences are correct, he will try to reach me. But how shall he find me? I am here."

"I'll wait for him at Mountjoy Street," Fred said.

"In that case, let us bait the trap correctly. Fred, take my car and park it in my space. Let it be clear to any who care to know that I, unafraid, am in residence at my home."

———

Approaching Boston, Fred hit a heavy slog of bad-tempered traffic on route 3 that forced Clay's Lexus to an air-conditioned dawdle. This late in the afternoon, the trouble should be heading out of the city, but road crews were busy interfering with the surface. It was not until shortly after five that the car was at last docked in Clayton's space next to the house. As Fred unlocked the door and fiddled with the alarms, the telephone stopped ringing.

Clay kept the building at an even seventy-two degrees in summer, wanting the paintings not to be subjected to extremes of temperature, though in general a painting can stand whatever a human can.

Unless she had other business out in the world, Molly should be home by now, at her mother's house. Fred would give her time to get her shoes off and think about supper for the kids before he called. He showered in his bathroom and changed into a clean version of the same summer uniform he had been wearing: khakis and blue knit shirt.

Sam answered the phone on the second ring. "Sam," Fred began. "How's tricks?"

"I'll get Mom."

"Two minutes of your time first," Fred demanded, sitting at his desk. "Since I never see you, because nobody is where they usually are, including me. How's the swimming going?"

"All right," Sam said.

"What else are you doing at that place? Which I'm going to visit when I can. Archery? Baseball?"

"I made a pot. Next week we glaze it and fire it—that's what it's called when you cook it."

"You made it on a wheel?"

"Yes."

"Terrific. How big is it?"

"I can put my two hands around it. Well, I'll get Mom." That end of the phone fell silent. Fred swung back and put his feet up onto the desk. From where he sat he could survey his begonia and the small window's worth of Mountjoy's foot traffic.

"Ho, Fred," came Molly's voice. "Had a hot day?"

"Tolerable. I'm at Clay's, I don't know for how long."

"Then we'll maybe see you?"

"Can't tell. I am truly not good company. I've been forced from the contemplative into the active mode, which would be fine if I had something to do."

"What are you up to?"

"I'm waiting for someone. This thing Clay's doing is a honey of a research problem, worth a year of quiet work, but he wants it tied up in three days. Because of the circumstances, I can't even stand anyone in a corner and ask questions. Can you believe Clay doesn't have a single book about Turner? Give me a quiet hour anywhere, and—"

"Isn't Lakshmi helping?"

"She's great. But she doesn't know where to concentrate. How can she? This isn't her field. She's English lit, remember? She's going to keep churning up names of irrelevant people and chasing mysterious dark women named Hannah Danby and Sophia Caroline Booth...."

"Who's Admiral Booth?" Molly asked.

"Not *Admiral* Booth. Sophia."

"Fred, wait a minute. Sunday night. Remember when you called from that place you were staying in Fall River with Clay and the dirty pictures—the Silver Sperm Motel? You asked me, 'Does the name *Admiral Booth* mean anything to you?'"

"I did?"

"Admiral Booth. I swear it on Mom's place mat of Windsor Castle before the big fire."

"Oh, yes," Fred remembered. "There was a scrap of doggerel on one of the drawings, about Admiral Booth standing to."

"Then who's Sophia? There's the admiral and now Sophia," Molly insisted.

"I don't know," Fred said. "According to Lakshmi's summation, Turner tried to leave some money to her in his will. Six minutes with the right books and I'd know. Maybe Lakshmi got somewhere today."

The pause on Molly's end of the conversation was eloquent of female collusion. "She spends a good deal of time with Marek," Molly admitted.

Fred watched the lower legs of people cross his window. Most of a dog passed as well, going uphill in front of a man's sandals, flat feet, and hairy calves.

"And did you ask me to watch out for Petworth? The word hasn't cropped up," Molly said.

"Petworth? Oh, yes. One of the drawings was labeled *bedroom* or *my bedroom. Petworth.*"

"Surely it wouldn't be a person's name," Molly mused. "Like the butler's? As in, 'Make up my bedroom, Petworth'? It's much too hobbity. Lord and Lady Petworth? They'd be embarrassed, wouldn't they? Except, come to think of it, Mom did mention a castle called Cockermouth. Never mind, Sam. I am talking with Fred. It's not your business. Fred, Petworth could be a castle, like Cockermouth."

"Or Lady Cockermouth's maiden name," Fred helped.

"Honey, if you're still stuck in the active and/or uselessly irrelevant mode tomorrow, I'll see what I can scare up for you," Molly promised. "When Lakshmi comes tonight, shall I tell her to call you at Clayton's?"

Chapter 20

Fred put the phone on the floor next to his couch and slept for an hour until Clay's call woke him. Was he there? And if so, was he all right?

"Sleeping," Fred told him.

"No developments?"

"It's been a quiet evening. I'd feel more optimistic if we'd baited the trap with more than your car."

"You will keep me informed?"

Rotwell's call did not come until eight-forty. "Mr. Reed?" he asked in the cheerful manner of the master insurance salesman. "Glad to catch you. Sorry it's late. You're a hard man to reach."

"Yes?" Fred threatened, using the penultimate-sounding cadence familiar to those who collect for dubious charity over the phone.

Rotwell had good news. "Bobby Rotwell," he cheered. "You don't know me."

"Rotwell?" Fred speculated. "How did you get this number?"

"Mutual friend. I'll be brief. I am the son of the late Lord Hanford," Rotwell gushed. "Frightful bother and all, Mr. Reed, it must seem, but would you mind terribly if I popped 'round?"

Fred let his hesitation dawdle. "What do you want?" he asked finally.

"Issue of art. Opportunity. Better if I pop 'round. I am twenty minutes away, no more. It would be most frightfully kind. Much in common. I am in Boston rarely, and my time in this country is brief. You will not regret what I have to put to you."

"I'll have time for you in half an hour," Fred announced. "I can give you fifteen minutes."

—————

The disguise Fred chose was one of Clay's satin dressing gowns, this one of royal blue. It was small on him, but fortunately Clay liked them large, so with the cuff turned down, the fit was not ridiculous. Fred took a quick look around Clay's first-floor parlor, checking the terrain. The furniture was crowded and fussy, either too heavy to throw or so light it would shatter rather than do any real damage. The china would smash but not stun.

If Rotwell was someone who knew what he was looking at, the paintings hanging along the walls would be enough to do the stunning. Clay changed them according to his mood, never all at once, and certainly never worrying about a decorator's sensibilities. The drapes at the bow windows were gold, and the Oriental rugs tended toward a nondescript faded pink. Whatever the furniture was, if it had cloth on it, nobody noticed—not with the paintings in the room.

A moderate-sized Bierstadt Wind River landscape hung above the piano, as pink as the rugs; next to that was a Dod Proctor nude, a female dancer, looking like a Tamara de Lempicka; then a pair of Dutch flower pieces from the seventeenth century, in which birds battled with insects; and beside them a huge Rothko universe of yellows and lavenders that Clay had acquired by some means Fred had not induced him to divulge. The Rothko was a fabulous thing, more modern than Clayton would usually consider buying, and of a monetary value far beyond what he would spend on anything. Clay had hung it as a mortification because he could not understand it.

The room was eccentric, and in its own way uncomfortable. It needed Clayton's brisk, nervous presence to give it focus, his worked elegance to settle the threat of the suspicion, Is this a joke? Molly called the amalgam postbachelor modern, or postmodern bachelor. Fred was too large for the spaces between the furniture, and his edges too square, even in the borrowed dressing gown.

"Don't overdo," he said to himself, as he noted the placement of the silver sherry tray on a piece of furniture for which Clay undoubtedly had a name. The two decanters on it were filled, with six glasses at the ready should the need for them arise.

Fred ran his eye once more around the room. Nothing was exposed here that Clay would not want seen by a stranger. The prize of his collection, the Vermeer, was in the library, on the far side of the kitchen. It was now the only Vermeer in Boston, and no more than six people knew of its existence, two of whom, the husband-and-wife team who cleaned, had no idea what it was.

The buzzer at the front door rang twenty-five minutes after Rotwell's call. Fred said, "One moment," through the kitchen intercom, then let the man wait five minutes.

On approaching Clay's town house from the street, the visitor was presented with a shallow yard filled with ivy, through which a short walkway gave onto a masonry staircase leading either down to Fred's basement aerie or up to Clay's stoop. Since the house stood on the corner of Kew Garden Street, it had windows on one side as well as on the front and back, and what was in effect a side yard with parking spaces for two cars. While they waited, Fred inside and Rotwell on the porch, Fred took a look out the windows. Clay's car was alone in his space, under the guardian sign reading 56 MOUNTJOY: TRESPASSERS TOWED. If Rotwell had come in a car, Fred could not identify it.

"Sorry," Fred said when he threw the door open to Act 1, Scene 3 of the Noël Coward play, wherein the male romantic lead sweeps in to steal everyone's heart. "Conference call," Fred confided. "Rotburg, you said your name was? What are you selling?"

Rotwell was holding out his big, red, square right hand, on which gleamed a gold ring that might fit the dents in Marek Hricsó's face and body. All else was tweed and self-indulgent barbering, and risky good times. Fred let the hand hang in the air just a moment too long before he accepted it.

"Lord Hanford's son," Rotwell reminded him. His eyes did not show whether, two nights before, they had registered Fred standing under the locusts next to the Capstan Club or, from afar, talking with Parker Stillton in the game room. Unless he was talented (like Molly) or trained in recognition, Clay's blue robe should be enough to throw him off in this new place.

"Well, come in," Fred said impatiently. The man's arm was smoothly muscled, though not unreasonably so, with power developed by a variety of vigorous and graceful actions—swimming, perhaps, or polo, or wrestling. "I promised you fifteen minutes," Fred said. "Who is Lord Hanford?"

Fred led his guest down the hall, past Japanese hanging scrolls of melons, moons, and reeds, and into Clay's parlor. "Let me take your coat," Fred offered before seating the visitor on a loveseat. "Boston is hot."

The man surrendered his jacket with easy grace. The cuffs of his blue shirt were held by fat gold satyrs' heads with ruby-colored eyes. They, like the golden curls, were a brutal assertion, like an English breakfast: fried toast, Daddies Sauce, and all. The man was as vulgar and dangerous as he was attractive.

Rotwell had not expected the question "Who is Lord Hanford?" It took him aback, and he requisitioned several moments to recoup while looking around the room to get his bearings.

"Very nice," Rotwell approved. "My father, Lord Hanford, was also a collector."

"Your father has passed on," Fred prompted testily. He leaned forward in the armchair he had taken. "You are selling his collection. What was his area of interest? Sherry?"

"Never touch it!" Rotwell shouted. "Ha! Ha! Excellent idea. Just the thing for a hot evening. Sweet, if you have it."

Fred poured them each a glass from the darker decanter while Rotwell planned his approach. The Englishman accepted his glass, told Fred, "Here's how," and raised it to his lips, watching Fred closely. "I'll be frank with you," he began. "I am here to *buy*, not sell."

Fred leaned back in his chair and glanced complacently around the room—the opening move that signals, Nothing I have is for sale; I am already far more comfortable than I need to be.

"See here, we are both in business," Rotwell confided—*his* opening move to claim the existence of an even playing field, in spite of his opponent's having declared that there is no game.

"*I* am not in business," Fred remarked. "What is *your* business, Rotwell? Is it *Lord* Rotworth? I never could follow that hooha."

"Rot*well*," Rotwell said through his teeth. "Dad's was a life peerage only. His title died with him. Ha! Ha! One piece of his baggage I won't have to carry. Let someone else warm his seat in the House of Lords. But now you mention it, this brings me to why I am here. I see we can both be frank, so I won't bore you with pussyfooting." His big grin invited Fred to find and enjoy a double entendre in the word: *Pussyfoot* would have been an even happier maiden name for the celebrated Lady Cockermouth.

Fred said, "Well?"

"A lot of Dad's things were sold last weekend in Westport, south of here. Maybe you heard something about it? At a benefit auction for the Runnymede House Museum. Hobby of his. Ha! Ha!"

"Yes?" Fred prodded, taking a sip of his sherry for effect. Surely no one drank sherry after dinner, except under duress.

"Now, the sad fact is, Dad and I had not seen eye to eye for some time—I won't bore you with the details, ha! ha!—and the gal he married when he hit his dotage, she and I never hit it off, d'you see? Therefore, out of respect for the little widow and all, ha! ha! and not to make waves, I kept my distance, didn't go to the sale—not, in the circumstances, *done*. D'you see? Ha! Ha!"

He waited until Fred said, "Gotcha," before continuing, "But I am a sentimental man." Rotwell chuckled, looked sad, and gave a grin. "Excellent sherry," he said. "May I?" He crossed to the decanter and poured for himself, offering more to Fred, who shook it off. Standing at the table, the decanter still poised in his hand, Rotwell went on. "I am a collector also, ha! ha! in my small way, and Dad had something I wanted. Something, actually, of mother's, which should have come to me when she died; but I shan't bore you with little family troubles. There now, I can't say it plainer than that." He leered in the lopsided clubman's expression that sends the after-dinner signal to the ladies: if you don't withdraw, somebody's gonna get gang-raped among the port and cigars.

Fred said, "Where do *I* come in?"

The telephone rang on the table next to Fred's chair. It gave him Lakshmi's voice. "One moment," he told her before putting his hand over the mouthpiece and whispering apologetically to Rotwell, "Tokyo."

"Yes?" Fred encouraged Lakshmi.

"John Ruskin cataloged all the drawings for the National Gallery," she blurted, almost breathless with excitement. "He managed to get his name on every single thing Turner ever made. What's with this guy? Didn't he have a life? I got out Finberg's inventory and took it with me to Mass. General—"

"I'll call you back a little later," Fred said. "Something to get rid of first. You'll stay at the same number?"

"At Molly's mom's house."

"I'll be only a few more minutes," Fred assured her, and hung up. "Yes?" he prompted Rotwell. "Your mother?"

"The plain fact is, ha! ha! I made a tactical error," Rotwell admitted. "Someday I will learn not to let sentiment sway me! Wanting to save the widow embarrassment, I employed a man to represent me at the sale."

"Ah?" Fred said.

"Whether by accident or by design—I shall never know which—my man failed to arrive until it was too late. Or so he told me. Ah well, ha! ha! Water under the bridge now."

Fred stood and moved toward the doorway, ready to escort his visitor into the hall. Rotwell stayed put, proving his right to do so by holding up the glass he had not finished emptying. He talked on smoothly.

"I soon learned—a man in my position learns what he wants to—that what I had hoped to buy—a parcel of watercolor paintings and drawings—had been purchased by a Boston antiques dealer. I'll not mince words, ha! ha! The drawings were, many of them, erotic in nature."

"And your mother did them?" Fred asked.

"Good God no, a relation. Distant relation."

"I repeat, where do *I* come in?" Fred asked brusquely.

"Don't toy with me. I know the man sold you the pictures afterward."

"He did?"

"For a fraction of what I had authorized *my* man to pay."

"You must have been disappointed," Fred allowed. "What was the name of the relative?"

"They said you were slippery," Rotwell blustered, standing and holding the sherry glass as if he might toss it. "I came for those drawings, Reed. What will you take for them? Name your price. I know what you paid."

"All I can do is convey an offer to my principal," Fred said.

"What do you mean, your 'principal'?" Rotwell shook with anxious wrath, his engine idling on too rich a mixture.

"Mr. Reed is out of town," Fred explained. "I am Fred. I do odd jobs."

"Where is Reed?" Rotwell all but shouted.

Fred said, "He calls, and I pass the odd message along, if it seems important. I'll tell him what you said, but from past experience I know he'll take you more seriously if you make an actual offer. If he's interested, he'll get back to you, or ask me to. That is, *if* he even has what you want. You have an address, a card, a phone number?"

Rotwell went crimson with rage that he turned off again so quickly it flickered. "I'll be back," he said shortly, now that Fred had been placed correctly, if tardily, among the servants.

"He'll tell me not to let you in again," Fred warned. "I did it this time only because you made your business sound important. Important to Mr. Reed, that is. Now I see that it is important only to you."

"You tell Mr. Reed to call me," Rotwell demanded furiously as he blundered along the hallway to the street door. "I shall be at the Royal Court. It is an hotel."

Chapter 21

Clayton had to be called first. "He's come and gone," Fred reported.

"Yes? Yes?" Clay asked. "Is he the man we take him for? You revealed nothing?"

"I revealed nothing but suggested everything. Yes, he's the man we take him for. I'll sew it up fast: failed son of a great man, full of charm; anger so close to the surface it's ready to bust through. That's my judgment. Also, still my judgment, he knows what you have, and what its importance is, and its value. He's a desperate man, therefore a fool. He's prone to take big risks. He tried a truly dumb finesse at the auction, and we were just lucky. The man he sent to act for him—reading between the lines, I'd say it was Small—literally missed the bus."

"He told you a lot," Clay said, amazed. "But please remember: we are on the telephone. Use code, if you can."

"Bobby's a candid, open-faced boy," Fred confirmed. "A boy in his forties, but stuck with the boy's position because first the old man wouldn't die, and then, even before he died, he cut the kid off."

"He made an offer? Or what was his play?"

"The best he could manage, with me keeping him off balance. He expressed serious interest. I told him I'd pass news of that interest on to you. He's at the Royal Court. It's where Small stayed, too."

"Our own intermediary was mentioned? The wounded one?"

"Not by name. Both of us sailed innocently across the subject. He didn't say how he got to you, and I didn't ask. A man that frank can only be a liar. But on the theory that even a liar tells the truth half the time, since words and ideas are limited in this world, we've got to at least look into something else he said: he claims he has a genetic right to the drawings. They were done by a distant relative, he says, though he won't name that relative. They should have come to him from his mother, according to him."

"But this is wonderful!" Clay chortled. "From this we go straight to Debrett. *Debrett's Peerage.*"

"I know what *Debrett's* is," Fred said.

"And you conclude that he knows what the drawings are?" Clay asked. "And knowing that, he trusted a *middleman* to act for him? At a benefit auction in a foreign land? How much was he able to spend?"

"Those are all questions he may be delighted to answer," Fred said. "He demands that you call him. But don't do it. Not until we both sleep on it and talk it through between ourselves, and decide whether there's anything to be gained by it."

"So you come south tonight?"

"When our man left he was what Molly's daughter Terry calls 'jumping mad'; if he finds a bomb, he's liable to come back and toss it through a window. I'll stay here. Tomorrow Molly can take five minutes and get the boy's mother's line out of *Debrett's*, in case that's of any use. As far as your talking to him…

"If he knows what the pictures are, and I say he does, the hope of getting hold of them is reason enough for him to stall settlement of the estate. He didn't block the sale because he thought he could steal them—or, as you prefer to put it, get a bargain. Who knows what the rest of his plan is? He could be just striking out blindly, reacting in fury because he lost the fortune he was counting on.

"My question, Clay, is, given that what you want is a publishable clear title, is it worth it to you to consider buying him off?"

Clay mused, "An amusing tête-à-tête that would be, in which neither of us would reveal what both of us knew—that is, the real nature and value of the collection—while both strove to set a price on it, even as neither could be certain his title would stand up to rigorous scrutiny. As an intellectual exercise alone—"

"Don't call him," Fred ordered. "The man is brutal, but he's not without intelligence."

"We shall sleep on it," Clay agreed. "This was excellent work, Fred. And while you sleep, you will be vigilant for bombs?"

Fred had been talking from Clay's kitchen, tugging the receiver of the wall phone around on his shoulder while he tried to make a meal out of the supplies in Clayton's cabinets and refrigerator. He'd settled on noodles and butter and two cans of smoked oysters and had the water boiling by the time he was finished with Clay. Cold Perrier from Clay's fridge would take the place of the sweat Fred had given up over the course of the long day.

Terry answered the phone on the first ring. "Terry, you are a monster," Fred said. "It's after ten. You should be asleep."

"Mom's worried about you," Terry said.

"I'm great. I'm already great and I'll be perfect after my noodles are cooked." He gave the pot a stir.

"Mom, it's Fred," Terry called, and then she whispered to Fred, "They're on the porch downstairs, under my window, telling secrets about John Ruskin. It's like he's Captain Hook, or that hunchback with the name that sounds like diarrhea medicine."

"Fred?" Molly asked. "You can get off now, Terry."

"I'm talking to Fred."

"You're finished. Hang up." At Terry's extension the receiver made a smack of obedience.

"Whatever you and Lakshmi are talking about," Fred began, "you've got Terry hooked."

"We try to keep our voices down, but she and Prince Charles sit in her window, listening at the screen. Your mysterious stranger came? You OK?"

"Hungry, which I am fixing. If you hear a crash and a scream, it's just me draining my noodles."

"Lakshmi's waiting to show you something. You coming back to Cambridge?"

"I need to stay here tonight. The guy's a loose cannon. What word on Marek?"

"No change. Hold it a minute." Fred put his noodles into a bowl, added butter and salt and pepper, and dumped in the two cans of oysters, all the while listening to the distant sounds of a whispered conference. He stirred and tried a bite. "Lakshmi says can she come to Mountjoy Street?"

"Why don't you both come?" Fred said. "I haven't seen you, really, honey. Much as I hate your mother's house, I miss—"

"I'm going to bed," Molly announced firmly. "OK, Lakshmi, see you tomorrow. Tell Fred I said hi."

"Listen, before you go," Fred called, but he had to dial the number again to get her attention.

———

Lakshmi chained her bike to the railing of the steps, unloaded her briefcase, and carried it up. She was dressed in minuscule blue shorts and a hooded yellow sweatshirt that she peeled off before entering the house. The thin white undershirt below it tried to follow suit. Fred feared for her life.

"Come in," he urged. Lakshmi was panting like a dog at the foot of the cypress where it's treed a wounded convict; each new drop of falling blood adds to its frenzy.

"This is fun, what you do," she informed Fred as she dropped her bag on the hall floor and stared as if a trance had fallen over her. Gazing from left to right, she drifted along the hall and was drawn into the parlor, where she stood gawking.

"Holy Mother of God," she whispered, shaking her head. Her round breasts shook under the stretch of flimsy cloth. "He's alone with all this? Mr. Reed's not afraid they're going to eat him?"

"He doesn't even know they want to," Fred told her. "It's hot. Beer or soda water? Ice? Anything?"

"Hot tea," Lakshmi ordered. "Where did I lose my stuff?"

She retrieved her briefcase while Fred put water on, and by the time he had the Lapsang Souchong steeping, she had spread her notes out on the small table in front of the loveseat where she had installed herself.

"I want it weak," she demanded. "Pour me some and come here. This is exciting. Remember last night? Molly said you'd called with a list?"

Fred put her cup on a coaster next to her work and sat in the space she made available for him on the loveseat. She was proud of herself, and dying to show off. She took a sip of her tea and said, "Perfect. Now. Molly gave me this list of twenty-two drawings you were looking for amongst the nineteen thousand and told me, Good luck. Well, especially since I spend most of the day with Marek. But it's peaceful in Intensive Care, and I can work. I just bring my books. It's sad, like the place Mr. Reed is working, but I can concentrate there."

Lakshmi took another sip of her tea, then a larger gulp, and continued, "So you were perfectly right. Finally, in nineteen-oh-nine, the National Gallery in London published two volumes entitled *A Complete Inventory of the Drawings of the Turner Bequest, arranged chronologically by A. J. Finberg.* So I grabbed those from Harvard's library and took them with me to the hospital and—did Molly tell you it was John Ruskin who arranged all the drawings? The son of a bitch, I have to admit he helped me—anyway: I started looking. And I found them!"

"You're kidding!" Fred said. "You mean we can tie them together—what Clay has and Finberg's inventory?"

"The group you asked about, the drawings Mr. Reed has, are on brown paper, yes? Nine by twelve inches?" Lakshmi reassured herself.

"Right," Fred said. The lust of anticipation that leads the scholar all too seldom to the satisfaction of anything real now inched itself into the room and stood, winking in a glistening nudity of coyness.

"Just to put you on the page," Lakshmi said, "the whole collection starts, volume one, page one, in seventeen eighty-seven, when Turner is twelve years old! Twelve. It's a copy of an engraving by someone else. Can I use your bathroom?"

"You do love to hold center stage," Fred muttered while he waited for her to come out of Clayton's bathroom. "Enjoy riding upon a little suspense, do we?" He gazed at the heap of Lakshmi's notes but left it alone. The life of the researcher had few moments of such romance; why spoil it for her?

"OK," Lakshmi said, bustling into the parlor again. "Sorry, I thought I was getting my period. Find yourself in a place like this, it's the first thing you think of: 'Truth to nature.' No? Yes? Take that, John Ruskin. But I'm all clear. Where was I? Yes. Look here. I finally hit pay dirt at seven tonight, in volume two, page one thousand twenty-six." She rooted through a stack of Xerox copies and pulled out two pages with their corners folded together. "I had to follow the man from the age of twelve until he was sixty-four, in eighteen thirty-nine. You should have heard me scream! The nurses came rushing...."

She and Fred leaned over the first page of her copy. "There are twenty-nine drawings in the Finberg group, which he's calling group three-eighteen, but don't be confused by Ruskin's numbers, or Finberg's, or whatever—see, they're described here...."

"Bingo," Fred said. "Lakshmi, you're terrific! The ones from the Turner Bequest are published as *Brown paper: large, All about nine and a half by twelve in size. Body color used in all.*"

"And see how all but three have numbers on the back, like Mr. Reed's?" Lakshmi crowed. "In italics, there at the end? Anything in italics they figured was Turner's own handwriting. So don't pay attention to the first three in the group. Look at their number Four, called *Interior of Theatre.* See? On the back Turner wrote, in ink, the number *One.* Then there's *Two* and *Three*—scenes of Venice—then they're missing his *Four* through *Seven*, which Clay has in Fall River—excuse me, I mean Mr. Reed. I get excited."

"I'm excited too," Fred agreed. "I'll get what I have." The page on which he had scribbled his notes on the Venice watercolors was downstairs, in the pocket of the shirt he'd changed out of. Carrying her Xeroxed pages, Lakshmi followed him down the spiral staircase that led from the entrance hall into his office.

"This is where you do what you do?" she asked.

"When I'm not tearing around the world. Let's match your list against mine." They leaned over his desk side by side so they could move their eyes from Lakshmi's printed pages to Fred's scrawl.

"Number One is the interior of a theater," Fred said. "Two is the Campanile by moonlight, Three is the Piazza, Saint Mark's—the one with the horses, you know it?" Lakshmi shook her head. "Then in Fall River we've got number Four, which is studies of Turner's bedroom in Venice with some ideas about Danaë being raped by Zeus; and Clay's Five, Six, and Seven go into the same subject, but with the help of a model, Miss Santorelli; then we're doing Saint Mark's in Eight, Nine is Miss Santorelli again, in Fall River, Ten and Eleven we're in church again, Finberg's Twelve is fireworks—given the context, I'd love to see those—Thirteen and Fourteen, in Fall River, are Miss Santorelli wrestling with the dawn and either winning or losing, according to one's point of view...."

They ran down the two lists, taking special note of Finberg's number Twenty-six, *The Lovers.* Number Thirty-one, bleakly described for the National's trustees as *Interior with Figures*, was followed by the catalog's notation *These were contained in a parcel endorsed by Mr. Ruskin, 'A.B.34 P.O. Color on Brown. Bad.'*

Fred said, "Very interesting. 'Endorsed by Mr. Ruskin.'"

"Mr. Ruskin was endorsing all over the place," Lakshmi said. "Mr. Ruskin was a goddamned nightmare, wrapping things up and writing his evaluations on them. On these what he decided was *Bad*. And so they were branded. When you read the book's introduction, you'll see, Fred. 'Truth to nature,' indeed. Mr. Ruskin had his precious opinion about everything. On some he'd note things like *Rubbish*."

"Or *Dangerous Rubbish*," Fred recalled. "That's got to be his label on the whole Fall River package—on some canvas you didn't see, Lakshmi, that was wrapped around the drawings. You don't by any chance have the Finberg here with you?" he asked.

"It's too much to carry. I leave everything in Marek's bedroom."

"I'd love just three minutes alone with an index," Fred said. "Tomorrow, will you do this for me? Look for those two names, Sophia Booth and Hannah Danby."

"You don't think my list fits with yours?" Lakshmi asked.

"I should be firing off rockets," Fred said. "I'm sorry, I got side-tracked. Of course it fits, Lakshmi—it's perfect, and thank you. In fact, it's a clinching argument as to *what* the things are. You've proved the drawings Clay has are by Turner. Nobody could want more, for a start, at least. Clay's going to turn somersaults of happiness, which will look to you more like a man saying 'Tut.' It's just that even though we've hit this double, we still have to make it safely home. And there are problems, especially now we've proved that Clay's group comes from the Turner Bequest. Because now we also know it is supposed to belong to the National Gallery in London. So what was it doing in Westport?

"But listen, hell, Lakshmi, let's be happy with what you did! The correspondence between this piece of Clay's collection and Finberg's list is fine; it's what we used to call back in Iowa a honeymoon fit." Fred shook her hand gravely. "I should bust a bottle of champagne on your head, but it's late, and I'm driving you home," he said. "Don't argue. It's a bad world, but your bike will be safe here till tomorrow."

Chapter 22

By the time the Lexus reclaimed Clay's parking space, the brick of Beacon Hill was giving up the last of the day's heat and letting a cool midnight settle on Mountjoy Street. Many of Beacon Hill's guests and residents were trying to get value from the change by strolling the steep, tree-lined walkways. Many were in couples, some even in threes.

Fred locked the car door and glanced at Clay's house, at the one light he'd left burning in the first-floor parlor, which gave a glow to the pulled drapes. The glow alone, however, did not give the house the feeling of being inhabited. Lakshmi's chained bike would have served that purpose, but she'd refused to be separated from it, insisting that she wanted to ride it home until finally agreeing to let Fred balance it in the trunk of Clayton's Lexus.

"How can the man want all this?" Fred asked aloud, staring angrily at the establishment that was keeping him from Molly and her children. "The more Clay has, the more there is to watch. Then he goes into the house and he's trapped with it all. Trapped. Like Molly's mother. Marek. Daiquiri."

Fred began walking slowly down Kew Garden Street, heading around the block. If he had to stand sentry duty, he reasoned, why not do it from the outside, where he could move and see into the shadows? Wait in the cage along with the crown jewels, and it's not long before you start to *think* like one of the crown jewels— or, worse, think you *are* one of them.

Fred took his time, checking each car, prospecting into the deep shadows between buildings. All were residences, though some also contained offices. No moon showed tonight. The dark sky sat in its space, stained by Boston's smudge of urban light.

Fred mused as he walked, Clayton's insistence on keeping the pair of us under cover is cramping me to the point where I almost can't do anything useful. We've been blown way off course by interruptions. Nonetheless, I've managed to get hold of a key to link the Turners to the published record.

We bought the damned things last Sunday. Monday afternoon I should have called the auctioneer, identified myself as Marek's principal, and asked—for God's sake, Alphonse Bird knows me well enough to trust what I say, within reason—and asked who consigned lot whatever-it-was. Could he confirm that it came from Lord Hanford's estate?

Not that it's Clay's fault that Rotwell turned up and started the fur flying. And damn his eyes, I should give Clay credit for spotting the pictures. No one else did, though somehow Rotwell knew what they were.

Yes, now we can prove they're by Turner—but that's trouble too, since our proof threatens to make them the rightful property of the British government.

And where, I wonder, is Isabel Cooney in all of this? As Lord Hanford's curator and now the director designate of that museum, she'd've had all the time she wanted with what we bought. Hell, the watermarks are even English! Here were three pounds' weight of English drawings she should have spotted as Turners, wrapped up in a painting that screams out what it is once you know what you're looking at. For the audience at the sale there's some excuse: the deceit of packaging.

But even if she was ignorant of what the collection was, Cooney ought to have a file on it. Unless it came through Rotwell's mother's line, where did Rotwell senior buy it? From whom, and for how much? Did *he* not know what it was? Unless there was something shady about his having it, and he knew that, it should all be an easy, open book that Cooney would let me read from in the right circumstances. Why not?

Clay writes Cooney off as a fool. At the sale she just looked like one of those fresh female faces at the desks in every New York gallery, who're only doing this until they find steady work in a soap opera playing Helena Bonham Carter by day and office slut by night.

———

Fred had wandered two blocks on Kew Garden Street, and now turned right on Spittal Mews to cut uphill two blocks behind Clayton's house, in his present disguise as a Beacon Hill resident who wanted to put off for as long as possible the moment of locking himself in with the partner and the air conditioner. The mews itself was all endangered elms, and ivy, and the surviving members of vanishing breeds of elite cars that nosed their hitching posts or looked to lick salt from the carriage mounting stones left over from the Tory era.

"So instead of chewing the fat with Isabel Cooney," Fred complained aloud, "my head's tied up in a tangle of irrelevant genteel folk stretching from the Capstan Club trustees back to Sir Charles and Lady Eastlake and John Ruskin and Turner's trustees and executors and sweethearts. God!"

He looked into Cranmore Road, both ways. The members of Beacon Hill's neighborhood preservation society, nostalgic for their spiritual London home, had kept the street narrow enough to be an alley. Its pavement was brick. It was lighted, like the rest of the neighborhood, by gas lamps under any one of which Mr. Hyde might lounge, basking in a sulfurous London fog.

I'm up to my eyes in red herrings, Fred thought to himself. False starts and loose ends, any or all of which might lead to another irrelevant tangle. Item: When I was there last Wednesday night, where was the Hanford woman's Daimler? Item: What about the mysterious, sinister chauffeur who gets the sallow cheeks of John Columbo's behind pulsing with lurid expectation? Item: We've got Hannah Danby and Sophia Booth toddling along, holding hands with Bobby Rotwell's mother's great-aunt....Meanwhile, Clay has his secret deadline, and I wait for the reappearance of a chortling male Goldilocks whose neck should have been broken at least a week ago. His presence drags in another dozen stories that are all in the way of our simple goals: Keep what we bought, and prove what it is—that's done, at least—and where it comes from.

Fred reached the corner of Cranmore Road and Mountjoy and looked uphill, then down. When you're this pig-ignorant, his brain grumbled to itself, everything you don't know seems like the tip of the iceberg that what you're looking for is hiding under. You ask yourself, Who was the woman Alexander Small had in his bed in the Royal Court Hotel last Tuesday? Hannah Danby? Sophia Caroline Booth? You ask yourself—jiminy! What's John Columbo doing in those bushes?

The pair of yellow leather legs glowed under the magnolia across the street from Clayton's front door.

It took seventeen minutes for Fred to come up behind Columbo quietly enough not to break his amateur concentration. It had been necessary to go another block on Cranmore, turn downhill, cut into a narrow alley, and climb spiked brick walls dividing tiny gardens filled with the plants that cater to dry shade and money— and to do it without sounding alarms or disturbing either conscientious dogs or the dangerous old ladies who maintained Beacon Hill's neighborhood watch. Fred crossed the last three feet of ivy and stood on the far side of Columbo's tree, three feet behind him, listening to him breathe.

"Asshole," John Columbo said. He reached into a pants pocket and pulled out a crumpled pack of cigarettes. Tonight's T-shirt was black, so his moving arms seemed almost disembodied. The cigarette was lit by a lighter that glowed red plastic briefly while its flame was working. Columbo blew smoke and groused, "…the fuck is he doing?" He smoked for a few minutes in silence before smacking something against his chest with his free hand and muttering, "I'd have seen a light come on if he came in the back, which he wouldn't do. That's the basement." He tossed the end of his cigarette into the street. Fred's hand on his shoulder made the man gasp and fart; beyond that he did not move, waiting instead for a quick death.

Fred drove his fingertips into the muscles. "You lost?" he asked.

"Oh, shit!" Columbo said, turning. "Fred, don't do that! You scared me!"

Fred demanded, "What do you want, John?"

"To talk with Clayton Reed. Where the fuck you come from, I don't know. Reed drove in a half hour ago and then disappeared, somewhere between his car and the stairs."

"That still doesn't explain your being here at one in the morning," Fred said. He gave the shoulder a renewed squeeze. "Save us both time and trouble. What do you want?"

Columbo hesitated and started a pout. Fred bunched the back of his T-shirt into one hand and with the other grabbed the seat of his yellow pants, hoisted him into the air, and began swinging, letting his goggling head brush the tree trunk.

"I can toss you or drop you or smash you," Fred said. "Any or all of those. I'm busy. What are you here for?"

"Let's go inside," Columbo tried, swinging. Soon he would puke. Although his arms were now flailing, he remained oddly passive. "I have a buyer," he said.

The craziness of the moment almost made Fred drop the man, but instead he hauled him vertical, righting him and letting his scrambling feet find the ground. "You made me nervous, hiding here," Fred told him. "We got rid of the Constable. It turned out not to be right after all, John, between you and me, so you're better off."

"The Constable, hell," Columbo said, sputtering with indignation. "The Constable like shit! Get out of my way, Taylor. I'll do my business with Clayton Reed."

A light came on on the second floor of the building that the magnolia guarded. Fred said, "Let's take this to a quieter place. You got your bag with you?" As Columbo was shaking his head to deny it, Fred reached into the dark pool of vegetation under the tree and grabbed the canvas bag by its shoulder strap. He slung it across his back and started across the street, then, changing direction, headed downhill. "By the river," he said.

John Columbo followed his bag. It rustled with papers and clumped with about eight pounds' worth of solid objects. "What does Mr. Reed want to sell?" Fred asked.

Charles Street, when they reached it, was not busy, but it was peopled. A few of the bars were still open. Fred jogged them down Pinckney Street, cut over to the Fiedler Bridge, led the way across the parkway, and found a place in the grass far enough away from the next loving couple to allow them to whisper their own sweet nothings.

Fred prompted, "What you want to say begins, 'I have a buyer…'?"

"I'll take my bag now," Columbo said sullenly. His face was as gray as the dusk next to the river, and it held a mean hint of triumph. Fred shrugged and waited, the bag's shoulder strap well twisted around his left arm.

"Think you fucking had everyone fooled," Columbo snarled. He smiled. "Thought we had a little secret, didn't we? Little Freddy-Boy and little Clittie Reedy with his weedy dickie all tied in a knot. He doesn't want all the nice people to know?"

Fred prodded, "You have a buyer for what, John? I have things to do."

"Dirty pictures, asshole! Think you're so cute."

"Fill me in," Fred said.

Columbo threatened, "Think I don't know who Marek bought those drawings for? Think I don't fucking know why you hung around the sale? To throw everyone off the scent. You think I was born fucking yesterday?"

"Marek's in a bad way," Fred mentioned, standing up with the bag.

"I know everything," Columbo said, bursting with spite. He sprawled on the dry grass, backed by the black river, watching his bag swing on the end of its strap. "It's too bad about Marek. Marek plays with rough people." Columbo grinned and shuddered, watching his bag swing. "Ask Clayton Reed if he wants to make a better offer than the *Globe*—no, than fucking *People* magazine—for the story of who really bought all that pornography."

Fred said, "You can collect your bag tomorrow at the main desk of the BPL." Columbo, stunned, sat with his mouth open in disbelief.

Fred walked three paces before he turned back and added, "Empty your pockets. And don't talk. Blackmailers I don't talk to. I put them in the river." When Columbo hesitated, he did the job himself, rolling the man over on the riverbank. Finding nothing of interest, he tossed the wallet, cigarettes, and change back on the grass and warned, "Don't look for your bag before noon."

Chapter 23

Fred peered into Columbo's bag before emptying it onto Clayton's parlor rug, under a lamp near the grand piano. A mess of things, and sheets and scraps of paper, fluttered down. The stuff that was not his business Fred put back quickly, paying it no attention. What Fred wanted would be on paper.

Unless he's just fishing, Fred thought, using that good old line *All is discovered*. He didn't say anything that couldn't be a lucky guess; after all, already by Monday afternoon, he was speculating that the drawings might be the big score of the sale.

Columbo kept thoughts, and information, the way a rat in a library insulates its nest. The bag was his traveling reference desk and diary, filled with call slips from the BPL, cash-register receipts, scraps of paper fringe tugged off Xeroxed posters, pages copied from books about artists, and many copied leaves from price guides, as well as corners of used napkins with penciled notes. *Carl*, said one, with a phone number; another, *M's Bdy. Mvie? Dnr? Pier IV??* The notes to himself tended to be written in shorthand and then smudged. The bag had disgorged a pile of papers it would have taken Fred months to understand, but most or all of it was irrelevant to anything he cared to know.

Fred started to separate the printed copies from the scraps, then the obviously private, or impossibly obscure, from the receipts and business cards. Clay's carriage clock chimed the single note that signaled 2:30 A.M. as Fred turned to the Xeroxed pages and started those.

Start with *what's* on his mind, then look for *who*, Fred advised himself. Which is coincidentally what's easiest to read. It would save time if the guy believed in staples or paper clips.

Most of the pages came from one or another of the annual auction price indexes. These provided a survey of where Columbo's interests had lain over the past weeks or months. Two pages recorded Hoesslin sales, and Fred's sorting turned up five pages of Constable prices as well. So Columbo had looked hard and hopefully at the possibility that the Constable in the Hanford sale would turn out not to be a dud—even though he should have seen and discounted it when it sold to Parker Stillton in Newton less than a year before.

Columbo's hopes and fears sifted from Fred's hands onto the growing pile until Fred banged head-on into what he had most dreaded. Page 1912 from a Meyer's price guide snickered with Columbo's marginal notes in ballpoint pen. Across from a *TWOMBLY, CY (A) Untitled* (oil and sand on canvas, £220), and above *TURVILLE, Serge de (F)*, two oil paintings by *TURNER, Joseph Mallord William 1775–1851 (GB)* were listed. The dates and locations of the sales were reported only by number codes, which Columbo had translated in the margins. *Landscape: Woman with Tambourine* had sold in Christies' London salesrooms in April 1989 for £1,000,000 (FF 10,000,000; $1,818,180), and *Seascape with Squall Coming Up* at Sotheby's London in November of the same year, for slightly over a million dollars. But that second one was small, Fred noted. Just seventeen by twenty-four inches. And Columbo had to go back that far just to *find* a decent oil by Turner offered at auction. A major one—there was no possible doubt that Clay had at least ten million dollars, represented in the oil painting alone.

It was plain that John Columbo had come to a late, and bitterly angry, epiphany. His traces were easily followed; his thinking, depressingly clear. He'd made pages of frantic copies from Turner's reproduced sketchbooks, the sheets smeared in his haste to snatch the books out of the copy machine and put in more. Six further sheets copied from Leonard's *Annual* proved the focus of Columbo's study, and its transparent motive.

"A lot of people named Turner in the art racket," Fred remarked aloud, taking the pages of Turner prices to a chair where he could sprawl in comfort. "You got your Alan Turner, born in nineteen forty-three; Frank James and Francis Calcraft and George; H.W. and Helen Maria Turner; Jonathan, Charles Yardley, Julius, Rogers, Kenneth, Robert, Shirley; William Turner of Oxford, and good old Ross Sterling with the field of flowers that thinks it's a Hassam. But Holy mackerel! Look what you can scrape in at public auction for a single, solitary watercolor by our boy J.M.W. Here's an eighteen thirty-five landscape sold at Sotheby's New York for four hundred ten grand. Dollars. Money."

Fred let his mouth hang open so as to equalize the pressure between the still air in Clay's parlor and the riot of wind inside his head. "Jeekers," he said. "I told Molly a dozen of the good ones would pay for her mother's house? Just *one* would do it. And Clay's got three hundred! Enough to buy all of Fall River and get change."

The front door's buzzer sounded, and Fred, glancing hastily around for something to use as a club, went for the door. Visible through Clay's spy hole, Columbo's yellow legs shone under the porch light when Fred snapped it on: he'd stepped back a pace, ready to rush forward when the door was opened. Fred turned the light off again, and Columbo started hammering on the wood with his fists and feet.

Fred trotted to the kitchen and called into the intercom, "Sit on the top step, John. I'll come out." He waited while Columbo hissed and whispered counterarguments, then repeated, "Choose. The top step or the sidewalk. Or keep making a racket and wait for the boys in blue."

Through the front door, Fred watched Columbo come to his decision. He tried sitting on the top step, decided that was a posture of defeat, then walked down to the sidewalk, where he stood defiantly. Fred opened the door and called, "Be with you in a jiffy."

The Xeroxed pages, and everything else he knew he didn't want, he shoved back into Columbo's bag. He kept only the handwritten notes and ephemera to look through when he had a chance.

"You've saved me a trip to the library," he told John Columbo, stepping outside and closing Clay's door behind him. He descended the stairs and gave Columbo his bag, then turned to go in again.

"You bastard, that's *it?*" Columbo shrieked. "You think I did all this work for nothing? That's it?"

"I guess I could kick your teeth in, John," Fred suggested. "The blackmail approach kind of bothers me."

"Listen, that was just a feeler," Columbo said. "That wasn't serious. OK? OK? Don't get your panties in a twist. I want real money, and Reed's going to pay. You wanna know why?"

Fred took a seat on the top step. "Let's not disturb the neighbors. What's on your mind?"

Columbo was scrabbling around in his bag. He jerked out the sheaf of Xerox copies and leafed through them before glaring at Fred—if Fred was reading his expression correctly in the street-light's dusk—and declaring, "So. Now you know what I'm thinking. You sons of bitches. You won't ride this gravy train alone. I'm not the asshole you take me for, Fred. I know this business, and I know this town. I can fuck this up for you but good."

"Let's keep our voices down," Fred reminded him. "Unless— shall we walk down to the river again?"

"I want one million dollars cash," Columbo demanded in a hoarse whisper.

"A lot of people share that feeling," Fred told him. "The folks who run the lottery depend on it. What makes your own particular wish unique?"

Columbo paced to the foot of the stairs and pushed his face toward Fred's. "I know what Marek Hricsó sold you," he said. "Forget the garbage, you cute son of a bitch. I mean the bundle of drawings. I know what they're worth since I know what they are. You thought that with Hricsó out of it, you were clear. You were almost right. That and a million dollars means you're clear. Five minutes after I tell the guy where they are, and what they are, he slaps a court order on you, and you and sweet Clayton Reed have fuck-all."

"'The guy'?" Fred asked.

"The guy you and Reed have been hiding from all week. The son, the new Sir Lord of Hanford, who's the rightful owner of all of it. I tell him where the drawings are and what they are, unless…now, shall we go in and ask Reed if it's worth a million to him to keep things as they are?"

Mockingbirds started singing in the green gloom somewhere not far away. It's going to be another scorcher, they called.

Fred said, "You talked to Marek on Tuesday, after you and I enjoyed a drink together?"

Columbo patted the front of his pants. "I'm not below a little prostitution," he said. "Hell, for a million bucks? Do I wait inside or here? You got any coffee?"

"No coffee. Two pieces of advice," Fred said. "We're not friends, but I'll give them to you anyway. The first is, when you threaten, you show your hand. You're a fool to tell your opponent what you plan to do. The second is—and I warn you to take this seriously, John—Bobby Rotwell is a dangerous man."

"Yeah, right!" John Columbo guffawed. "Tell Reed he has eight hours to respond to my offer. Hell, he knows he can break up the collection, walk a dozen of the watercolors to London, sell them there, and make a profit even *after* he pays me. Twelve o'clock noon. I'll call or I'll come."

"Tell me how to reach you?"

"Fuck you," John Columbo said.

———

Fred slept on his couch until the door's buzzer woke him at six. He dragged himself up the spiral staircase to the hall, where he spotted Lakshmi waving through the spy hole. She'd changed into a loose pink sundress and was clutching a paper bag in one hand and her briefcase in the other. The bike was already chained to the railing.

"I couldn't sleep, I'm so up," she called. "I couldn't wait. I had to tell you. Fred, did I wake you? I'm sorry. I brought doughnuts and coffee. You like coffee?"

Fred led her in and sat them both down at the table in Clayton's spartan kitchen. They opened paper wrappers and cartons and started to spill coffee and powdered sugar.

"OK," Lakshmi said. "Here's the deal I made with myself: days I do Mr. Reed's research; evenings are mine. There are three hours yet before the library opens, so that's mine too. It's a beautiful morning out there, Fred; you should see it. This is my time too, I figure—but my own research right now, it turns out, is really straddling Mr. Reed's, everywhere I look. I can't help noticing—"

"Your *own* research?" Fred interrupted.

"Lady Eastlake. I told you. She'll make a fabulous thesis. She knew everyone, wrote just enough, and hasn't been worked on. You have sugar?"

Fred found her some in a cabinet. She stirred it into her coffee with one of Clayton's Revere spoons, which she then chewed absently.

"So I try to be fair to both him and me," Lakshmi continued, "but they overlap, so—so at night I'm reading Lady Eastlake's journals, and last night what do I come on but January second, eighteen fifty-two, and she's talking about Turner's funeral. Listen to this—"

She reached into her briefcase and pulled out a sheet of yellow paper on which she had written notes in pencil. "She writes about what people were saying about the will, and Turner's bequests, and then she says, *To his own only daughter he has not left a penny, though his housekeeper gets a hundred fifty pounds a year.* Fred, have you ever heard about a daughter?"

Fred shook his head.

Lakshmi went on, "And I quote, *His life is proved to have been sordid in the extreme, and far from respectable.* So it was a big surprise, to people who knew him, that he turned out to be really a dirty old man. But listen, there's more: *It is odd that, two days before he died, he suddenly looked steadily and said he saw Lady Eastlake.* This is still Lady Eastlake writing in her journal, remember. She adds, *This the woman who lived with him, and whose name he passed under, in a quarter where nobody knew him, told his executors.* Then she goes on about the executors, who are all men. What do you think?"

Lakshmi took a bite of doughnut and breathed clouds of powdered sugar.

"It sounds like you've found us three women to follow," Fred said, counting them on his fingers. "A daughter neither you nor I ever heard of before; and a housekeeper; and a woman he was living with under the *woman's* name, in a place where nobody knew him."

"It's five women," Lakshmi corrected him. "People only look at the men. It's men, men, men. Men can't even *count* women when they see them. Somewhere in the universe, maybe on Mars, there's a library as big as Widener filled with the books women didn't write, since who knew they were alive? *Five* women, Fred.

If Turner had a daughter, guess what? There's a mother too: woman *four*. And then here's Lady Eastlake, appearing to the sick old painter in a vision, while he's dying, like a patroness for his soul. Woman *five*. Listen, here's my idea. The question you're forgetting, what everyone's forgetting, and part of what Mr. Reed has to figure out, is how these drawings got to America from England in the first place...."

"Now don't get confused. I'm still thinking your bad guy is Lord Eastlake. All these puritans—you know what they are in secret. I'm betting he took them. Then, later—Sir Charles Locke Eastlake and Lady Eastlake didn't have any children to leave things to when they died, but they did have a favorite nephew you've probably heard of, also called Charles Locke Eastlake, who's one of the big names in American furniture design in the eighteen eighties. My theory—"

"Lakshmi," Fred stopped her. "My head is already filled with red ants that are not friendly to each other. I should give Molly a call before she decides I've gone to China. Would you hold that thought?"

———

"Petworth," Molly said. "I've got Mom working on Petworth."

"Oh, crikey," said Fred. "Honey, I just called to say hi, and good morning, and to remind Terry and Sam that I was supposed to go fishing with them tomorrow and tell them I'm sorry but it may have to wait. I'm sorry. I want them to know now in case they get a better offer. We'll talk later, OK? I'm sorry."

"The summer's not over. I've got my research assignments. Did Lakshmi get there OK?"

"She got here, I took her home, and she's back again," Fred said. "She's hooked on her research. She's worse than the Ancient Mariner."

"Admiral Booth," Molly said.

"Who?"

"Forget it. Lakshmi's got a truth-to-nature honeymoon story. Get her to tell you the tale of Effie Ruskin."

Chapter 24

Who in hell is F. E. Ruskin?" Fred demanded, hanging up the receiver.

Lakshmi snorted sugar and glanced at her wristwatch. "The story of the Virgin Wife," she intoned. "Poor Effie—Euphemia Gray. Effie had the bad luck to fall under the cold spell of that pervert John Ruskin, boy wonder, who ran around holding lighted candles at Turner's shrine. Turner was forty-five years older than Ruskin, and he was a heap big noise in the politics of English painting by the time Ruskin was a student at Oxford. So Ruskin, as you know, hitched his wagon to Turner's star when he started writing books and lecturing on art, and he made a name for himself very young."

Fred put his remaining coffee into a saucepan and started it reheating. Clay would not have a microwave; he feared that the rays, somehow prospecting around corners in the house, would infiltrate and subvert the cells in all of his paintings.

"So Ruskin, very young, was known as the coming art critic, and his bloodless theories, which I won't go into since I hate him, were perfect for the age of the Crystal Palace prude. All of civilization was somehow expected to rise above sex. But try as he might, he couldn't help it: he was human. Even Ruskin had urges, only his urges were toward little girls. He spotted Effie Gray when she was thirteen and he was twenty-one. She happened to be sick at the time. He haunted her and courted her until, when she was twenty, in eighteen forty-eight, he married her. Since she was from a *nice* Victorian family, she'd been kept in the dark about the realities of barnyard life as they applied to humans, and her father handed her off to a groom almost ten years her senior, who was expected to clue her in."

"Well, when she took her pants off for her new husband, John Ruskin threw up his hands and shrieked, 'Yuck, woman! That ain't Greek! What's all that hair and confusion?' Wait, I'll read you…"

She dug through her papers while Fred poured his coffee back into the paper cup and then got a carton of eggs out of Clayton's refrigerator. "Scrambled eggs?" he offered.

"Sure. Now, this is the guy whose taste and judgment in aesthetic matters were already famous. 'Truth to nature,' don't you know? He'd published two volumes of his *Modern Painters* and— yes, here it is. Six years after the wedding night, Effie was still a virgin-in-waiting. First Ruskin had said they'd wait until she was twenty-one; then that they'd just hold off until she was twenty-five; then finally that she was mentally unfit to be the mother of his children, which by then I can well believe! Lady Eastlake persuaded her to sue for divorce. Effie's only recourse was to go on her own—and so she had to write her dad an explanation that would conform to everyone's nice upbringing."

Fred broke eggs into a bowl while Lakshmi read. "*My dearest father…yadda yadda yadda…even now I was unwilling to tell you all, fearing your anger against John Ruskin who has so ill treated and abused me, and his Parents who have so seconded him, although so far they are innocent, not knowing the gravity of the offense with which I charge him and from which proceeds all the rest. But they have been most guilty in the education they have given him…yadda yadda…Feeling very ill last week and in the greatest perplexity about my duty to you…I went and consulted Lady Eastlake.*

"Now, Effie Ruskin and Lady Eastlake had been friends ever since they met in Venice, not long after the Ruskins' wedding, and I think even then Effie must have found some miserable way to ask, 'Am I really so different down there from every other human woman?' and Lady Eastlake told her, 'Honey, *where* have you been? You're fine! Just one of the club.'"

The butter spat in the pan. Fred dropped in the eggs.

"Back to the letter," Lakshmi pushed on. "*I have therefore simply to tell you that I do not think I am John Ruskin's wife at all—and I entreat you to assist me to get released from the unnatural position in which I stand to Him. To go back to the day of my marriage the tenth of April eighteen forty-eight...I had never been told of the duties of married persons to each other and knew little or nothing about their relations in the closest union on earth. For days John talked about this relation to me but avowed no intention of making me his Wife.*— Meaning, of course, giving her the friendly screw she had every right to.—*He alleged various reasons, Hatred to children, religious motives, a desire to preserve my beauty, and finally this last year told me his true reason (and this to me is as villainous as all the rest), that he had imagined women were quite different to what he saw I was, and that the reason he did not make me his Wife was because he was disgusted with my person the first evening, tenth April."*

Fred said, stirring eggs, "I'd say poor kid, except she was twenty-five. The situation did its best to keep her a kid, granted. You'll find plates in the cabinet; get some that don't have gilt edges. So this is the same fastidious golden-boy art critic Ruskin, who within two years of his divorce—"

But Lakshmi, on a roll, rolled on and over. "Ruskin threatened to beat her, sure. He could do *that*, but he wouldn't sleep with her. The formal complaint was impotence, as Effie's family and lawyers worked it out." She clattered plates and selected a couple to bring to the stove, holding them out while Fred spooned on the eggs. "Ruskin hotly denied that he was impotent and offered to prove his virility to everyone's lawyers. That's nice to imagine, isn't it? See, what John Ruskin loved..." She smacked the plates onto the table and flung drawers open until she found some forks. "Well, suffice it to say that years later he was haunting another little girl, with the wonderful name of Rose la Touche. He was still hoping to find one with a marble crotch like the statues in the Victoria and Albert Museum. And he wrote to a friend—the actual letter exists—and said, *Have I not often told you that I was another Rousseau?* Which means, if you are unhappy enough to know your Victorian lit like I do, that the way Ruskin got off was to think cruel thoughts against women as he masturbated."

Lakshmi opened Clay's refrigerator and leaned into it, concluding, "This is the expert the National Gallery selected to sort through the Turner Bequest with his sticky fingers. Do we have any sauce for these eggs? Ketchup? A-1?"

At seven-fifteen Fred put the dishes into the sink and told Lakshmi, "Excuse me while I make a phone call."

"That's OK. I'm going to tear over to the hospital, say hi to Marek, and be at the library when it opens."

By now Clay must be up and dressed and tucking into whatever the Silver Spur provided in the way of a breakfast that was free of stimulants. "Here's where we are," Fred told him when he answered the phone.

"Not on the telephone," Clay begged. "Things are too close and tense."

"Closer and tenser than you think," Fred said. "Don't waste time arguing your fear of wiretaps. OK? First—good news! We have a definitive positive fit between one group of drawings and the published record. You'll get the paperwork by FedEx later this morning. It's spectacular, and it's plenty to rely on for a start. You will want to refer to your box Seven."

Clay, on his end, was breathless.

Fred went on, "However, the same evidence ties the collection to the Turner Bequest, which makes the issue of rightful ownership—"

"Never mind," Clay broke in. "This is excellent. And you are convinced yourself?"

"Absolutely."

"I was so close to despair," Clayton said. "Now, relying on your assurance, I shall make plans. Federal Express will deliver by ten-thirty? Excellent. Excellent. Anything else?"

"There are outstanding issues. In the bad news department, after the son demanded that you telephone him, then—you recall who bought the Hoesslin?"

"Yes."

"Two visits with him late last night. At his instigation. He demands a large present."

"Indeed. His reason?"

"He has a million reasons. He put things together and says he will find his reward either here, by noon, or from the presumptive heir apparent."

"He's dreaming or demented. Incidentally, have you seen this morning's Boston newspapers?"

Clay did not subscribe to the *Globe* or *Herald*, and his *New York Times* had been canceled for the duration of his exile. "Anything I should know immediately?" Fred asked.

"In due course," Clay said. "I am trying to think of how to respond to this new wrinkle."

"I like the Duke of Wellington's solution," Fred replied.

"'Publish and be damned,'" Clay quoted. "Our guess is, anyway, that the son already knows what Mr. Hoesslin wants to sell him?"

"Yes."

"We will disregard his deadline. It is impertinent, unnecessary, and irrelevant. It is also outlandish and more than imprudent from the point of view of Mr. Hoesslin himself. A million reasons? The man must be touched. Fred, spend some quiet time with the morning paper and then drive down or, better, telephone again. After I see the evidence for myself I shall decide whether, and how, to proceed."

"A message should go to the son," Fred said. "And better earlier than later, before he begins moving around the world. He'll be quieter if he thinks he has some hope."

"Very well. I shall rely on you to unravel the Boston end. Think of something," Clay directed, and broke the connection.

Fred called the Royal Court and told Bobby Rotwell, "I'll try to meet you in the hotel dining room at nine. What do they call it, Coronation Street? The Throne Room?"

"I want to see Clayton Reed."

"You may get me," Fred said. "I'll do my best. If not, wait for my call."

Boston was ticking like an old house opening its pores to the threat of heat. Fred walked uphill toward the State House. There was still barely enough freshness in the air to inject a mistaken optimism in the morning's foot traffic as it converged on the central point of Boston's former glory. Fred cut through Boston Common, bought himself a *Globe* and a *Herald* at the Park Street subway station, and found a shady bench to sit on while he checked through them.

Subtracting filler and fluff and style, and making allowances for leaps of logic, the two stories that pertained stood out with depressing starkness. Clay was a step closer to losing the Turners. In response to an inquiry by Lord Hanford's estranged son, Mr. Robert Rotwell, Spar Ballard, the District Attorney of Bristol County, had ordered the body of the late Lord Hanford to be exhumed. Mr. Rotwell had refused to talk with the press, instead referring all inquiries to his spokesman and attorney, Parker Stillton, who had not returned calls. Lady Hanford, also, was not returning calls.

Independent of this matter, unremarked by the *Globe* but delighted in by the *Herald*, was a follow-up piece on the bizarre and brutal death of an unidentified man in the Taunton area, evidently caused by wild dogs. The victim had been a man in his mid-forties, dressed in a brown suit of English make. His shoes had come from Rutter's of London. Speculation was that the man was either English or an American Anglophile traveler recently returned from the U.K. Local men were forming vigilante posses to fill in where the forces of law and order had so clearly failed. The wild dogs were warned that their days were numbered. Residents of the affected area were counseled to stay in their homes for the next few days.

Fred folded the papers and left them on the bench. The news had told him nothing he didn't already either know or suspect, aside from the amusing sidelight that the D.A. of Bristol County was, as well, the chairman of the board of the Runnymede House Museum. He was also a respected member of the Capstan Club family that had opened its arms to the new Lord Bobby, dropping the American-born Lady Hanford in the same gesture.

Fred looked across the green Common, and the Public Garden, toward the squat majesty of the Royal Court Hotel. He had nothing to say to Bobby Rotwell. Let him wait and stew and hope and talk to his lawyers and eat bangers and a fried slice.

"I'll go see Molly," Fred announced to no one, and he popped into the subway station, ready to roll until he recalled that he should call Clay in an hour, at which point he might have to establish speed in some direction. "Hell, I'll just drive down there,"

Fred said. "Except if I've got an hour, why not use it myself to find out how we got those drawings?" He dithered back and forth angrily on the stairs leading into the noisy underground, while crowds of people eddied around him, heading for work or shopping. If he went to the Boston Public Library he couldn't use the stacks, and Columbo would probably turn up, look over his shoulder, and confirm his guess. There wasn't time to get into Cambridge and back.

Fred started walking swiftly toward Mountjoy Street. "It's all paper," he told himself. "The money, the drawings, the research— nothing but paper. To quote another Victorian who got stuck on little girls, *It's nothing but a pack of cards.* Paper, paper, paper— have I lost all sense of proportion? There's a dead man, Small; and another man, a colleague of mine, halfway killed."

Marek lay on his back, his head tilted toward the glass partition. His eyes were open. He was alone except for his tubes and his blinking monitor; the corridor's guard had gone away. Fred stepped quietly into the room and looked down at the patient. Marek's face was thinner. There was no way he wouldn't lose weight, being fed from a tube. His eyes did not register Fred's presence.

"Hey, Marek," Fred said. "Good to see you." Next to the visitor's armchair, away from the bed's tubes and contraptions, was a small table, on which rested a pair of green volumes with call numbers inked onto their spines. "Lakshmi left the Finberg inventory here," Fred remembered. "Marek, I came to see you, but it turns out I am a son of a bitch after all. What were those names I wanted?" He crossed the room, sat himself in the chair, and was picking up the top volume of Finberg's catalog when the nurse came in.

"Didn't see you there," she said. "You Mr. Harxo's brother? A friend?"

Fred nodded his head.

"We're a little better," she said, "aren't we, Mr. Harxo? Didn't we talk today? Do we want to say something else?" She leaned over Marek's bandaged head.

"That's terrific," Fred said.

The nurse pulled a green spiral notebook from the pocket of her uniform. "Do me a favor," she said, handing it to Fred along with the pen clipped to it. "Anything else he says, write it down, with the time. Do you mind?"

She opened the book and showed Fred the single entry: 8:35. *Fred. Fred. Fred Taylor.*

"An officer was stationed in the hallway last time I stopped by," Fred said.

"He was here earlier," she told him. "I guess he went looking for this guy Fred Taylor."

Chapter 25

Where they'd look for him was at his address in Charlestown; that was all they had from the driver's license he'd shown them when they started asking serious questions at Marek's, last Tuesday midnight or Wednesday morning. Though he had not actually lived there for some time now, he was an owner of the place—and he liked to keep his options open. In the meantime the building's occupants, a pick-up group of veterans of this and that, would cover for him without needing instructions.

Slope Burgy took the call. Fred hadn't checked in for a month, and as far as the guys knew, he was in Peru or Kamchatka. But Slope knew his voice right away, just as Fred recognized his own husky and belligerent "Yes?"

Fred said, "I wondered, anyone looking for me this morning?"

"Yes," Slope growled.

"There now?"

"Up the street a block, in a dry cleaner's van. *Princess Lahdidah Studio of Dry Cleaning*, if you can believe it."

"They introduced themselves?"

"Real friendly."

"I got nothing that needs cleaning," Fred said.

"You'd have to give it to them yourself if you did. Anything else? Anything in the lockbox you want?"

"I'm fine," Fred said.

There'd been no need to ask whether Slope had passed on Clay's or Molly's number or address—but the police might have picked up on Fred's connection with Clayton Reed by churning through Marek's papers, wanting to get a head start if and when Marek turned into a homicide rather than a mere attempted. If they wanted him that badly, he'd have to stay away from Clay's place. And from his car too, unless he was willing to spend the next day and night swept up in someone else's agenda.

Fred had placed his call to Charlestown from a pay phone outside the drugstore on Charles Circle. Now he called the Cambridge Public Library to ask Molly to meet him in the park out front. Even while dialing, he had begun to skim through Finberg's *Inventory*, the haste of his frustration making him clumsy with the books he had spirited out of Marek's hospital room.

He clattered up the iron stairway to the Red Line stop and stood in the hot wind above the river, listening for the roar of the train as he studied the index. What were those women's names? Booth, Sophia Caroline: no such name was listed. Nor was there any Hannah Danby. But *Petworth*—here, finally, was something to pursue.

The train arrived before he could find the first Petworth entry: a sketchbook of 1805–6, it turned out after he took his seat, done when the artist was thirty. The sketchbook was described as being *bound in calf, with four brass clamps. The paper is white, and prepared with a wash of grey, except the two leaves at beginning and end of book. Water mark of drawing paper, 'J. Whatman, 1794.' Water mark of fly leaves, '1799.' Size of page, 10 x 5¾. Turner's label on back:— '37 studies for pictures Isleworth.' Mr. Ruskin's endorsement:—'Five studies for pictures. May be shown as it is. One leaf cut out, where a real leaf of herb is laid. The study cut out was of vegetation at Warwick.'*

That sanctimonious son of a bitch had cut a page out of the notebook! And branded it, as well, with his editorial opinion. Pages 4, 6, 9, 29, and 31, Finberg reported, were all sketches that related to the painting *Thames at Weybridge*, which belonged to a Lord Leconfield at Petworth. So. There was Petworth, a place, not a person.

Then next, from 1809, among a set of loose drawings, came a *view of Petworth House, from the lake—See oil painting 'Petworth,*

Sussex, the seat of the earl of Egremont—Dewy Morning.' Exhibited Royal Academy, 1810, and now at Petworth House (Lord Leconfield). So Petworth was a *house*, in Sussex, and already it had two names of people attached to it, Lord Leconfield and the Earl of Egremont— if you could call those names. Really, they were titles. Anyone could be hiding under those.

Having crossed the river, the train was already underground, jostling noisily into Kendall, when Fred hit the big payload, under Ruskin's officious "endorsement," preserved for all time, warning that what followed was *of hardly any value:* a so-called Petworth sketchbook done in 1830, when the artist was fifty-five, containing a number of studies of the place. It was followed by 116 watercolors, all done that same year, inside the house and outside, on its extensive grounds. Like many of the group Clay had with him in Fall River, these were watercolor on blue paper, about 5½ x 7½ inches. The catalog's descriptive titles suggested a riot of subjects: *White and gold room at Petworth House; The Red room; Twilight; The Lake at Petworth; The red lady on a couch; Bed, with crimson silk curtains; An interior with figures.* According to Finberg's notes, these paintings had been found in bundles dismissed by Mr. Ruskin as *rubbish, inferior,* and *worse.*

"Mr. Ruskin was feeling his oats," Fred told his neighbor on the rocking bench as she gathered her bundles to debark at Central Square.

"Long as he keeps his hands off *mine*," she threatened.

As Fred flicked through the pair of volumes, the vulnerable, fragmented intimacies of Turner's occasional notes and musings, even his recipes for medications, began to hold his interest less than the persistent editorial comments of Ruskin, who had organized the collection: *Coarse but noble; Not of much value; Chalk scrawls on grey. Rubbish; Tail and head of Fish cut off to get centre into sliding frame.* So the aesthete had even gone so far as to *cut* a drawing when it was the wrong size for a frame?!! Then, above a group of sketches done from a life model at the Royal Academy in 1832—*'stooping figure,' 'standing figure,'* and so on—came the revelation that Ruskin had written on the parcel, of its contents, *Kept as evidence of the failure of mind only.*

Fred looked up at the train's dark windows and concluded to himself, Hold it! Daiquiri and I—we found a similar note on one of the Fall River drawings. That phrase, *failure of mind*, sticks with me. Ruskin had his mitts on Clay's collection: this proves it. If a man boasted of having *kept* something—for whatever reason—it means he believed he had the power *not* to keep it. For Ruskin's diagnosis of failure of mind, the necessary symptom was that the painter looked at naked people and drew pictures of them. It was not an uncommon act, certainly, even in those dark days, but naked women were not, according to Lakshmi, John Ruskin's cup of tea.

The subway cars screeched and stopped in Harvard Square. Fred piled out with his colleagues into the glare.

—⁂—

When Molly came out of the library, the nondescript park achieved a sudden focus of friendly elegance. Fred rose from his bench to cast his arms around her. "It's all set," Molly told him. "I start my classes Monday evening."

"Classes?"

"Real estate. I told you. A better and brighter me will soon be selling shopping malls to unsuspecting con men from Nigeria." Molly's hair was different, maybe, as if she'd had it cut—maybe, or unless it was the heat. The curls were coiled in tighter. She was wearing a white dress covered with small pink roses, its fabric seeming to have been stolen from a child's tea set. She noticed the Widener Library call numbers on Fred's books. "You've been giving your business to our rival. I have tons of stuff for you. How come you wouldn't meet me inside?"

"Marek woke up long enough to say my name, and everyone thought, Let's get him!"

"Everything you want is inside."

"Right now what I need most is a car. Clay's is at his house, which I figure is being watched, and mine's in Fall River. I can't rent one without having my name float out into the electronic air. But if you wouldn't mind—"

"Take it," Molly said. "But give me ten minutes to unload what I've done for you for free, even though we're supposed to charge ten dollars an hour. My keys are inside anyway." She ran into the building, a woman on the verge of a new beginning in the heady world of real estate. She returned with a stack of Xeroxed papers that made Fred gag with dismay.

"Clay will have to reimburse the city for the copies," she said, "but my time he can have for nothing, as long as I get to see these famous dirty pictures. You'll go through all this stack, and here's what you'll find, if I'm right. True, Turner never married. But for years he lived with a woman named Sarah Danby. Hannah Danby, whom you asked about—Turner's housekeeper—was her niece. More interesting is the fact that Sarah had two daughters, named Georgiana and Evelina, who everyone either knew or knows were Turner's daughters as well, probably—or at least Evelina was."

"I'd heard a rumor there was one daughter," Fred said.

"Furthermore," Molly continued, "word got out, and became a general part of the Turner myth, that he used to have a bit more of that restless urge to you-know-what than there was an easy opportunity for in some circles; and why do you think they never knighted him, when he was the absolute king of the hill in painting? Because the cronies knew, right? That in spite of his sublime reputation as an artist, in fact, he was an old lech.

"Anyhow, the other woman, Sophia Booth—Turner died in her house in Chelsea. We're talking dockyard red-light district. And Turner was well known to her neighbors there, but not as a painter. In Chelsea he was known under the alias *Admiral* Booth."

"Oh," said Fred. "Admiral Booth. I remember."

"He was living two lives in two different houses," Molly explained. "He kept his paintings and Hannah Danby in a house on Queen Anne Street, and then, as Admiral Booth, he lived with his mistress in the other house on Cheyne Walk, Chelsea. To me he seems a sweet, sad old rapscallion. Even though he was a big success, his instincts were with the ladies, and with the decayed artists he wanted to leave his money to. I like him. He even wrote poetry. A lot of it is soupy and turgid stuff; the longest and saddest one he called 'The Fallacies of Hope.' He's worth understanding— his life, not just his pictures—when you have time and the cops aren't after you. And he's got some advice, Fred, even for you. Read it sometime."

She selected one page from the pile, folded it four times, and handed it to Fred, who tucked it into the pocket of his shirt. Squirrels raced in and out of the shade behind her.

"Petworth," Molly bustled on. Fred held his peace. Why wreck her moment by telling her he'd found it? "There's a half inch on that. I'll boil it down. Petworth is a country house in Sussex where Turner used to visit the third Earl of Egremont and his family until Egremont died, in eighteen thirty-seven. He'd been a big patron and friend, and Mom—where's that thing she faxed me? I mean, Egremont's being a major collector and a bit of a famous man between the sheets himself, some people said, why shouldn't all those drawings have been his? Anyway, Petworth House is only about forty miles south of London, so Mom went down there in a taxi. She's in heaven, being able to help with your work, right on the spot, in one of the stately homes! So she taxied down, and she's faxed me—yes, here it is!—a list of all the heirs of the third earl, which I needed so I could compare it with Rotwell's mother's people. We're getting there, Fred. Don't try to run. We can get all this personal info just from the National Trust, and now you can do whatever you want with it."

She'd been rooting around in her stack until she hit upon the greasy fax paper. "Mom says it's a beautiful home, full of Turner's paintings. The family's name is Wyndham, and they were Earls of Egremont until George, the son of the third earl, was made Lord Leconfield, in eighteen fifty-nine. He married Mary Blunt. Henry, his son, married Constance Primrose, and on down—you get all the kids, but you want to follow the line of the ones who owned the property, is my guess, until we get to Max Wyndham, who has the house now. He's the second Lord Egremont (that's not the same thing as the earl of, don't ask me why), and also at the same time the seventh Lord Leconfield, who married Caroline Nelson, and Mom says, why don't you telephone him? Or Mom will do it if you tell her what you want to know."

Molly tucked the fax back into the mix and pulled out the next sheets, her face clouding. "I put off telling you about Rotwell because I believe he killed his mother," she said. "I think he beat her to death, and my reason is the big silence that comes down over all the newspaper accounts of the family ten years ago, after she died. Her body was found in St. James's Park, battered to death, when the boy was thirty. You can read all the speculation and non-conclusion and denial, but it looks to me like a big buy-off. Having lost his wife, Lord Hanford saved his son and then disowned him, and essentially left the country. It's all in there.

See what you think. I can't read any more. All these stories of dead people start to make me very sad."

"But you found the mother's name?"

"Sure. In *Dod's Peerage*. Since England's an island and they all love nobility just as much as Mom does, you can look up anyone—so long as they have a title, that is—going back to Canute. You'll find my notes. Hanford's first wife was Marjorie Something Pack, daughter of Sir Thingummy Whoosit. Knowing that much, you can probably trace her all the way back to Sir Hampden Paulet of Nether Wallop, Buckland, in the sixteenth century, through whom she may claim relation to both William Shakespeare and Lady Diana Spencer Windsor, once Her Royal Highness the Princess of Wales. A high point of Mom's tour was visiting that poor girl's grave even though she wasn't a royal any longer when she died.

"Be careful with my car, OK?" Molly concluded, tossing Fred her keys. "And I'll need it tomorrow. Mom's coming home Sunday, remember?"

"OK," Fred promised. "I'd forgotten."

"Maybe that's not all you're forgetting." Molly leaned up to kiss a face Fred had not shaved. "Look, if you need to wreck my car by running over Bobby Rotwell, it seems to me that, reading between the lines, it might be the best solution for everyone."

Chapter 26

Molly's old red Colt was parked on Rush Street, not far from Wombswell Croft. Fred carried Molly's research to it, along with the two volumes of Finberg's inventory of drawings from the Turner Bequest. Lakshmi would have a fit when she found them missing—if she even noticed, that is, in the shade of the happier fit when she learned that Marek had spoken a coherent phrase.

Fred thought about how easily he could have killed Marek that morning if he'd objected to the news that Marek was coming around. With that guard on his wild Fred chase, was there any security at all left in Intensive Care?

He stuck his stuff and Molly's in the car and locked it, then gritted his teeth, shrank down a size, and went into Molly's mother's house. Prince Charles yipped with joy and came thwippeting down the stairs to address his ankles. Molly had done her best, but the house was beginning to look seriously lived in. Sam's swimming suit hung by its jock from the inside knob of the front door, where the boy would be bound to see and grab it on his way to camp—unless, of course, the door was already open.

Only one chair in Molly's mother's living room would hold most of a man, and that one was shrouded in a white slipcover. Fred sat in it and picked up the telephone's receiver. Molly's mother was the only person he had ever encountered in the world who sheathed her telephone receiver in white terry cloth, as if she feared she might one day get a call from Nicholson Baker.

When the desk in the Intensive Care Unit answered, Fred made a point of enunciating clearly, "The man who attacked Mr. Hricsó, in bed thirteen, may want to finish the job." He kept the message anonymous and brief, cut the connection, and then reached Clayton at the Silver Spur. "I'll be there in an hour and a half," he informed him.

"I shall have left," Clay said.

"Mountjoy Street is off limits," Fred told him. "I'm being watched for, and Rotwell will look for *you* there, not to mention John Columbo—"

"For God's sake, this is the telephone," Clay shrieked in panic, like a child seeing all his chewing gum disappear down the bathtub drain.

"This is a secure line," Fred assured him. "I'm not at your house. No one knows where either of us is. To continue: the police may be watching your place for me, on account of Marek. We should confer."

"I am leaving the Silver Spur," Clay insisted. "I find Miss Thomas's research concerning the Venice group, coupled with your own, utterly persuasive. As will others. I am determined to proceed with my plan, relying on you, my team, to press forward aggressively. My object is almost in reach. The question remains: how did these drawings get from the Turner Bequest into my hands?"

"I'll talk to Isabel Cooney," Fred said. "But since that's risk, I wanted to discuss it with you first. In any case, all our efforts may be useless if the courts—"

"Oh, tut," Clay objected. He waited, thinking, the tapping of his pencil in the ashtray providing the only evidence that he had not been spirited off to Mars. "The law is an ass, which may be of value to us. And Isabel Cooney is a fool. Even so, I will inquire as to where she may be," Clay said finally. "In order to do so, however, I must make an occasion to telephone Parker Stillton.

"Fred, our foremost obstacle is this morning's confirmation that there is to be an objection to our rightful title. Parker Stillton is our opponent, together with Rotwell, and his tame district attorney, Mr. Ballard. Goodness. If Rotwell's challenge to Lord Hanford's will prevails—"

Fred cut in, "The only way to derail Rotwell is to have him arrested for assault and murder. We assume he is behind what happened to Marek and Small. We could *threaten* to have him questioned if he doesn't lay off, but blackmail isn't dependable.

What's more, you say you want to keep the collection free of scandal. But you say you are leaving the motel? Clay, where are you going? Are you putting the drawings into a safe?"

"They travel with me," Clay said. "To New Haven. I shall put up at the Royal Court Hotel, New Haven. My time in Fall River has made me nostalgic for comfort of the old school."

"New Haven'll be a long pull in my car," Fred warned. "Let me explain some of old Betsy's tricks."

Clayton's answering expression was one that could only be heard as "Tchah."

"I don't want you traveling alone with all that value," Fred continued. "Granted that you prefer not to degrade the art by referring to it in financial terms, but a hundred million dollars' worth—"

"I shall be well looked after by two gentlemen I have engaged to drive me in their vehicle. They will be busy this evening so I leave in half an hour to accommodate them. You have met Mr. Lee and Mr. Sammy Rondo?"

Fred grunted assent.

"The issue of what to do to offset Mr. Rotwell's challenge, I simply leave in your hands, Fred. Please wait where you are while I endeavor to learn Ms. Cooney's whereabouts, if you feel you truly must…?"

"*Must* is exactly what I feel," Fred said.

Ten minutes later, Clay's call betrayed a bemused and suspicious man. "The most extraordinary coincidence," he marveled.

"Yes?"

"Ms. Cooney has taken a suite in Boston, at the Royal Court Hotel. For her convenience, Parker says, while she is being deposed."

"Well, blow me down," Fred exclaimed. "*Things come together*, as the poet Yeats used to say."

"Drat the poet Yeats! Stop Rotwell. I shall be in New Haven from, let us say, to be on the safe side, four o'clock this afternoon. Will you ask Miss Thomas to telephone me there at her usual time? Nine this evening. At the Royal Court, yes? I shall have dined by then. Stop Rotwell. That shall be now your first priority!"

It was as if a time machine had swept through the hot fields of MIT and reduced everyone's age by a dozen years. Sam's swimming suit dangling from his left hand, Fred wandered under the merciless sun, over baked lawns that stretched between the institute's buildings. Packs of children, something like five hundred of them, herded by counselors, raced or did archery or played volleyball, or engaged in treasure hunts or calisthenics.

Fred found a man who looked as if he could at least imagine being twenty, despite the pink playsuit he was wearing. He was standing under a tree, eating a sandwich. "Can you take me to your leader?" Fred asked him.

The man chewed and giggled. "You part of Living Fantasy?" he demanded. "What are you supposed to be?"

"Looking for Sam Riley," Fred said, holding up the swimming trunks.

The man in the pink playsuit choked. "The kid running around naked; that's Sam," he said. He glanced hurriedly around him, as if fearful, too late, of being caught in a joke that might nail him as a pederast.

"He needs the suit, or he gets demerits," Fred explained.

"Oh, you thought I was part of the camp!" the man concluded. "No, see, we just happen to be here, a bunch of us, using the campus. We met on the Internet, playing Dungeons and Dragons Galore. Everyone takes an identity. We have two days to find each other on the campus, just the weekend. I'm an elf. I came in from Worcester. You seen anyone looks like a wizard, dragon, oaf, wench—any of those things?"

"The weekend doesn't start until tomorrow," Fred helped.

"Oh, shit! No wonder," the man said, as the rest of him matched the color of his suit.

Fred interrupted an archery teacher and found out where to go: an office in an abandoned classroom building where a harassed genius talked into a telephone while scrolling data across a computer screen and opening mail and doing numbers on a calculator. She told Fred, "Sam Riley's an Aardvark."

"It's what I've been saying all along," Fred agreed.

"The Aardvarks should be swimming in five minutes," she said, without relinquishing any of her occupations.

"Where do the Aardvarks swim?" Fred asked. He held up the swimming suit.

The genius shook her head. "You'll never find it. I'll get you my trusty." Without breaking stride she whistled through her teeth, and Terry appeared out of nowhere, saying, "Hello, Fred."

"Will you take our guest to the swimming pool?" the genius requested.

"Sure thing," said Terry, and she trotted out into the heat, plunging directly across fields where her fellows were engaged in docile herd activities.

"They don't make you arch or pot or swim or run or anything?" Fred asked her. "You're not a Wombat or a Whale?"

"We're gonna be late," Terry panted. "That's all stupid. Miss Harriet lets me help her run the camp, but don't tell Mom. When I'm sixteen, Miss Harriet says, she'll even pay *me*, instead of *Mom* paying *her*. Sam's in there." She pointed out a low gray cement building into which a straggle of boys and girls was converging. Then she turned on a dime and ran off.

Fred found Sam alone, scratching his head in front of his open locker. "You're saved," he said, tossing the suit across.

"I was gonna try swimming in my shorts," Sam said, pointing out the blue pants he was wearing. "But they always catch you. Thanks, Fred. I better hurry." He stood waiting to change until Fred left.

Stepping from the blare of heat on the street and sidewalk into the cooling gloom of the lobby of the Royal Court Hotel was the moral equivalent of being hit on the head. Fred stood blinking and gasping gift-shop gentility before glancing around. He might have no memory for the odd passing name, but Isabel Cooney's face and figure he could remember, as well as her brief speech to the crowd at the auction for the Runnymede House Museum. She'd been tall and thin, with a southern Americanism not completely discouraged by Wellesley or Bryn Mawr. Despite the heat of that day, she had dressed in a dark-blue suit, with tailoring that emphasized her long legs, narrow waist, and emphatic chest and set off the French twist (or whatever it was) of thick red hair. So Fred was looking for these hallmarks as he scanned the lobby for the new director and then moved along to check the hotel's Cromwell Lounge and Guy Fawkes Powder Room. Of her speech he recalled only the opening words, which had been delivered with the same robotic charm of anyone trained to speak at a political convention: "We are all so thrilled and excited…"

If she had come to Boston to work, there was not much chance that she would be in the hotel at two o'clock, but it was a place to start. Fred went to his old friend the concierge. Mrs. Wen looked him over quickly and dismissed him as one she had dismissed before. He still had no heraldic emblem on his shirt.

"Isabel Cooney's suite," Fred said.

"Eight-twelve. Shall I ring?"

"Ring on," Fred agreed, and watched Mrs. Wen's face break into a surprised smirk before she handed the receiver over.

"My name is Fred Taylor," Fred said. "I am in town, and—"

"One moment," cut in a hearty British voice, emphatically male, equally charged with bonhomie. "Ms. Cooney has stepped out. Come up. We'll wait together."

Fred handed the receiver back to Mrs. Wen, who polished the handle with a Kleenex before returning it to its cradle.

The color scheme of the eighth floor was white with green and pink trim: spindly floral swags that were better suited to a birthday card than to decorate floors and walls. In its cruelty, the management of the Royal Court Hotel had hung mirrors opposite the elevators so that guests and their visitors could notice if they had shaved, and whether or not they had changed their pants in days. Since 812 was a suite, the DO NOT DISTURB sign on its door was larger than what you got for less on the sixth floor, had golden scrolls around its edges, and demanded quiet in more languages.

"Glad to see you," Bobby Rotwell boomed, beaming as he opened the door to welcome Fred into a white sitting room trimmed like a birthday card. Rotwell had noticed the heat to the extent of placing his light tan jacket on the back of a chair and rolling his shirtsleeves up to the elbow. Even his tie was off. His powerful ruddy forearms glowed with gold hairs. The room was large enough for a meeting between seven people who were not happy with each other. And there'd be more to the suite that Fred could not see through the closed doors: bathroom and bedroom.

"Sit," Rotwell ordered, letting his broad arm sweep across the room and the drapes and the view of the Public Garden. He waited while Fred chose a place on a small couch upholstered to resemble a birthday card, from which vantage point he was not obliged to look at a painting of someone whose work resembled that of Ross Sterling Turner. Rotwell lounged in an armchair across from him.

"Ms. Cooney is with my lawyer," Rotwell announced. He spread his hands. "We need to move right along. Lucky I happened to be here when you called, since we must talk, what what?" he said, and laughed. "I popped back to get something she needed."

"Her purse," Fred volunteered.

Rotwell's eyes skipped from Fred's to the Vuitton handbag that stood on the little where-shall-we-stick-this? table next to the door. They skipped back to Fred's again with renewed candor.

"Exactly," Rotwell said. "Now, Fred. I have not heard from Mr. Reed. Your message this morning confused me. I waited for some time. Normally I am a patient man." He laughed. "But I am recently bereaved, ha! ha! and I am also under considerable pressure. Business at home, ha! ha!...and then this little matter as well. I'll not ask what you want with Isabel Cooney—"

"Need help researching a Constable painting we bought at that blasted sale you're trying to turn inside out," Fred said. "Which I claim is fake, though Clay...but listen, Rotwell, what I wanted to say this morning, I'll tell you now. Clay Reed won't play ball."

"He has not had the courtesy even to telephone to discuss my offer," Rotwell said. "There has been no message. Nothing."

Fred said, "I propose an alternate plan. Clayton Reed, once his mind's made up, won't move, especially if he thinks he's being pushed."

"What duress is there?" Rotwell demanded.

"Being a rich man, he regards the offer of large amounts of money as duress. Again, he's funny that way. Whereas I—well, I can take that in my stride." Fred rubbed his face and listened to the whiskers crackle against his fingers.

"You're going after a settlement, of course," Fred went on. "I mean, down in Westport. You start by letting the little widow find out how much trouble you can cause. First they'll dig up the body—when's that happening?—then, when they find nothing—"

Rotwell interrupted, "I'd offer you a drink, but I don't see that you are worth the time." He glanced at Fred's pants. His own were cut from some dark-brown fabric that had been born with an excellent crease.

"Mr. Reed's playing coy," Fred said. "But I can help. Put it this way: *maybe.* I am considering a career change."

Chapter 27

Rotwell studied Fred's honest countenance. "You are willing to work for me?"

Fred shrugged. "For about two minutes. I can tell you where Reed's holed up with the drawings you want, the ones your mother wished you to have."

"My mother? Ah, yes. Ha! ha!" Rotwell remembered.

"If you know where he is, you can serve paper on him," Fred said. "Or you can try something more direct. Which is the route I'd recommend. But why you want that stuff—"

"So it's true that he has the collection," Rotwell said. He chuckled, shaking his head of golden curls with the pleasure of how easy this was all going to be after all, for everyone. "Do you happen to know a Mr. John Columbo?"

"He's one of the small fry around," Fred admitted. "Why?"

Rotwell checked his watch and said, "One hears things. How much do you want?"

"For what, exactly?" Fred asked.

"To take me to Clayton Reed and disappear."

"You have a figure in mind?"

Rotwell stood, the muscles jumping in his arms and face. "Don't play games with me," he said, and laughed.

"We'll work something out," Fred said, standing himself. "I'll walk with you to Parker Stillton's office. We'll both take Cooney's bag." He chose a blow to the side of Rotwell's neck that should have dropped him, but he'd misjudged the man's bulk of muscle and erred on the side of not making the blow fatal. Rotwell lurched smoothly into silent action, sliding and pounding with an easy grace even as he dodged furniture, as if he had often fought in the stately homes of his native isle. The two men slammed each other in the eerie, carpeted, silent calm of white elegance done up with vines and roses.

The match was an uneven one. Bobby Rotwell fought with the desire to kill, whereas Fred's intent was more to interrupt. But neither of them wanted company. DO NOT DISTURB, Fred's left fist sang into Rotwell's solar plexus, while Rotwell's jab toward the jugular cautioned, DIE BUT DON'T BLEED. After four minutes they found themselves facing each other from opposite sides of the sofa.

Bobby Rotwell breathed smoothly, a glad light in his eye, before he chuckled. "Took me by surprise," he said. "Suppose we say two hundred thousand?"

"Dollars or pounds?" Fred asked. He was drenched with sweat. Rotwell looked as dry as the Queen Mother's scrapbooks.

"This is America," Rotwell said, chuckling again. "Dollars should do it, don't you think? Let's go to my room." He flexed his arms, looked sideways, and offered his friendly hand, in readiness for the circus toss that lets its victim wonder, for as long as a half-second, sometimes, What hit me? before the kick in the side of the head answers that other age-old question, What is the meaning of life?

Fred took the opportunity to use the force he should have in the first place, and Rotwell lay down snoring.

"All right, Isabel," Fred announced loudly. "The movie's over." He kept his attention on the grounded man, working quickly, taking off the shoes from Boodle's or Booth's or Blow's of Piccadilly and appropriating the laces to tie Rotwell's thumbs together behind his back. The tan socks patterned with clocks he stuffed into Rotwell's mouth before looking around for something to secure them with.

"You got a stocking, Isabel?" he called. "Will you stop fooling around, or—jeekers! Is there a door to the corridor from the bedroom?"

The first door he tried gave onto a luxurious empty bathroom, fragrant with reassurance that washing, for the elect, was a matter of virtue rather than of necessity. Aside from moral uplift, nothing was there for Fred. The bedroom, however, offered a large, half-naked woman, gagged and plunging with pinioned anger on a bed so well engineered that it refused even to squeak.

"Be right with you," Fred promised her as he yanked the belt from the dark-blue skirt that lay on the floor. He used it to finish the gagging job on Rotwell, then took the man's own belt and bound his ankles with it. "You'll be all right for a minute," Fred told the sleeping man, and ran back into the bedroom.

Isabel Cooney had been tied by her wrists to the headboard of the unmade bed and stripped from the waist down. Her lower nakedness offset the neat white blouse and blue suit jacket she still wore on top. Her red hair was a mess against white pillows, around a face ugly with alarm, straining against the suffocating gag. Fred flipped the sheet quickly over her legs.

"Rotwell's out of it," Fred said. The woman's face was bruised. Rotwell had used a stocking to keep her from crying out, and Fred now started to work on it, trying to distinguish the nylon from her thick hair. "I hope we can talk, unless you're injured," Fred said. "Rotwell is big trouble, as you now understand. You've been wanting to scream, I know, and you'll be able to in a jiffy, but if you don't mind waiting, I'd appreciate it."

He'd got the gag off by now, and the woman thrashed her head back and forth, gulping the cool recirculated air that the Royal Court Hotel provided for its guests.

"About Alexander Small...," Fred said, making a feint toward her bound left wrist. Isabel Cooney went rigid.

"Where *is* Alex?" she mourned, like a sailor's wife on shore during an awful storm.

"I'm going to untie you," Fred said. "At the same time, may I ask you a favor? Talk quietly with me until we both agree on the next step, OK? Is that fair?"

Isabel Cooney nodded her head, unwilling to trust her voice again. Fred got her left hand free after unknotting more stocking, the kind that adheres on its own to a woman's upper leg, like a randy dog. He moved around the bed to the other side and started to work on her right. The bedroom's decor was exactly the same as the sitting room's, except with beds in place of chairs and sofa. The woman used her freed left hand to worry the sheets that covered her to the waist.

"It is not generally known," Fred said as he finished untying her, "but Mr. Small is dead."

Isabel Cooney covered her face with both hands and began to sob, shaking. Fred found a chair and sat at the window, looking out at the Public Garden past white drapes decorated with the afterglow of Laura Ashley. Next to him the bed moaned with tormented disappointment at the fallacy of hope.

"Lord Bobby Junior said Alex would meet me here," Cooney mourned.

Fred said, "I saw Small's body. I believe Bobby Rotwell killed him. Small was dead by last Wednesday, if that means anything to you. Wait a minute." He unplugged the phone and carried it with him into the sitting room, where Bobby Rotwell was beginning to stir furiously. He'd flipped himself onto his back. Fred picked up the couch and laid it across Rotwell's head and upper body; it was a heavy, well-made reproduction, upholstered in white brocade or chintz or something.

Isabel Cooney was still sitting up as Fred had left her, her head in her hands. She said, "I want to wash. My hair...I want a lawyer."

"I bet you do. But I'm not law. Help me with some questions. You've had a shock, and it's just the first in what's going to be a series. I'm calling room service. Don't wash. What do you want? Tea? Gin? Soda?"

"I don't want anything," she groaned. "He was going to leave his wife and everything."

"Rotwell is married?" Fred stopped in the doorway.

"Small, you fool!" She had slid to the side of the bed and stood up now, bent for her skirt, and stepped into it, tucking her blouse in with vicious despair. Fred waited until she was ready to come with him into the sitting room, where she stood looking down on a pair of athletic legs, in bare feet and brown trousers that turned at their waist into a small sofa.

Fred said, "I'm going to patent that. It beats a mermaid or a centaur: a self-moving sofa."

"Turn your back, please," Isabel Cooney demanded. Fred, though taken aback, gallantly did as she asked. Hearing her grunt with sudden effort, he turned back to see the sofa almost hurled upright with the violent thrashing of Rotwell's legs.

"Once more," Isabel Cooney pleaded.

Fred told her, "Sit down," and called room service.

"Next we call Parker Stillton," Fred said. "Yes, he's Rotwell's lawyer, but he'll advise you. He'll tell you to get yourself a different lawyer, and what *that* lawyer will say is that you should make a deal with the district attorney's office, one that will help them get this joker Rotwell sewn up. I don't mean to be unsympathetic. Did he rape you?"

She shook her head and trembled, opened her mouth but said nothing, then: "There's rape and there's rape. He was having fun, seeing how long he could pinch my nose closed while I watched... while I watched his..."

"They'll want to hear about that," Fred said. "I don't know how much they'll care about the conspiracy to defraud that you were part of, since it didn't work."

"Alex told me, 'Don't worry. It's fixed. Don't bother me. Everything's under control.' So I believed that that man, that whoever he was—Hricsó—was part of Bobby's program."

"Good. That's the kind of thing they'll be asking you," Fred commended her. "So you see, your interests and Rotwell's may have parted company."

"'Parted company'!" she exclaimed. "Is that what he was doing? Parting company? That bastard's English version of safe sex— Jesus—knocked out and strangled and forced...Who are you? Why are you here?"

"That'll be room service," Fred said at the knock. "They're quick. That's why I ordered cold food. Hold it a moment." He called at the door, "Leave it."

He brought in the tray and set it on the table where he could reach it from the sofa, on which he now sat down heavily, getting a muffled response from Bobby Rotwell below.

"I got coffee, soda, or scotch," he offered, picking up his fat ham sandwich and taking a bite.

"I did nothing," Isabel Cooney tried. "You're blaming the victim, saying I need a lawyer."

Fred swallowed, took another large bite, and swallowed it before pointing out, "All of you, even your suit and your Louis Vuitton handbag, was in Alexander Small's bedroom, six-eleven, when I stopped by last Tuesday. Other conspiracy theories are equally feasible, such as the conspiracy to murder an English art dealer who fucked up a sweet inside deal." He had another bite of his sandwich and poured coffee. Isabel Cooney put scotch into a glass.

Fred called Parker Stillton's office. "Fred Taylor," he told the attorney. "I am calling for Mr. Rotwell, who is not able to come to the phone. You represent him?"

"I have that honor and pleasure," Parker Stillton affirmed. "You reached Isabel Cooney? Clay Reed said he wanted some information on that Constable he bought." Parker Stillton sent a guffaw across the line. "Snookered!" he shouted. "It's rich. It's really rich! He thought he could snooker me, and Clay himself gets snookered. I love it!"

Fred took another bite of sandwich and chewed it while Parker Stillton enjoyed the joke. When both Parker and the sandwich were finished, he said, "Your client Rotwell wants to turn himself in for the murder of a Mr. Alexander Small and the attempted murders of Marek Hricsó and Isabel Cooney. Cooney is here with me now, and she'll testify against him. Rotwell is restrained but still dangerous. He may be of unsound mind."

Stillton's end of the conversation was a vacuum of stunned disbelief. The sofa tried to heave underneath Fred, Rotwell's legs floundering angrily.

Isabel Cooney, her fists clenched, stared at the man's bare feet and looked toward her handbag. "Not murder—some perverted rape, I guess," she whispered. "He made me watch his thing while I couldn't breathe."

"You're thinking cigarette lighter, and I don't blame you," Fred whispered back to her. "The problem is, if it looks like the man's been tortured, the whole thing'll take forever."

"Tell Lord Bobby to say nothing," Stillton ordered. "You're talking nonsense, but there's no reason he should implicate himself further. Where are you? I'll be right there." Fred told him. "Give me half an hour," the attorney amended.

Fred went to the chair over which Rotwell had draped his coat and took out the man's wallet, from which he slid a hotel room's electronic key card. "You know what room he's in?" he asked Isabel Cooney.

"Six-oh-two."

"I can't let you out of my sight, I'm afraid. Put on some shoes and come with me. I want to check something."

—⟨⟩—

Rotwell had taken only a single room for himself, not a suite, and it overlooked merely Commonwealth Avenue, not the Public Garden. "Don't touch anything," Fred reminded the curator turned museum director pro tem. "I just wondered how he was planning to deal with the body—ah, I see." He gestured toward the huge green canvas duffel bag on the bed, out of whose open zipper blue plastic sheeting protruded as from a wound. Isabel Cooney began to retch, and Fred led her quickly into the hall, directing her attention to a curly gilded desk on which sat a convenient geranium. The woman shuddered and fertilized the plant with scotch and terror.

"Oh, Jesus," she said. "Oh, Christ! I didn't believe it. I thought it was all sick talk. He was going to…going to…and carry me out afterward in that bag."

"Let's be there when Parker Stillton arrives," Fred said.

Chapter 28

Rotwell's face had reached the purple that decorators call aubergine by the time Fred lifted the sofa off him. He began to sputter around the gag until he remembered that this action threatened his nasal passages. "It certainly gives you a new perspective on the breathing process," Fred observed. "You're going to have nightmares about that, Ms. Cooney." He sat on the sofa again, a few feet from the prone Englishman. "The only further revenge I can let you take is to testify against this guy."

Cooney poured herself another scotch and sat in a small armchair at some remove. She'd start to reorganize her whole life and all her plans and motives now, very speedily, and disappear into self-justification and its consequence, self-pity, unless Fred could keep her attention.

"As long as we have a moment," Fred said, "and disregarding any arrangements you made with Small and Rotwell to divide the Turner score—"

"Divide the collection!" Cooney exclaimed. "I'd never allow such a thing. That would be a crime! Rotwell intended to donate it to his nation! The British nation!"

"What?"

"The works belong in England. Bobby has all the money he wants, from his mother's land and the stately home in Norfolk and all that garbage. But he wanted to be Lord Humpty-hump, and you can't get that these days without building a hospital or inventing clean air or giving the queen and Parliament such a fabulous payoff that they all fall on their faces and worship you as Lord Bacon and Eggs, Baron of Kill-Anyone-in-the-Way."

Fred stared at the purple face in its corona of curls: the King of the Golden River waiting for someone to finish the job and pull the chain. Fred shook his head. "I don't believe it. He was lying to you. If you have to buy glory, how is it glory? Would you *buy* the Congressional Medal of Honor? Once you have it, do you put Tabasco on it and swallow it like an oyster? No, it was something else."

"Will I be arrested?" Cooney asked.

Fred said, "I saved your life. I want to know where, and how, Lord Hanford got that Turner collection. There's the door."

Parker Stillton came in sweating profusely into a seersucker suit of blue and white stripes. He looked the room over, nodded to both Fred and Isabel Cooney, and then stared down on his client. Having learned from the lawyer's manual that verticality commands at least temporary respect, especially for those who are endowed by their Creator with better-than-average height, he stood in the center of the sitting room, streaming sweat, and complained, "My client cannot speak."

Fred said, "Sit down. Ms. Cooney, are they going to find Rotwell's sperm? On you, or in you? That's important."

Parker Stillton collapsed into a chair, staring. "This is not my kind of law," he faltered. "I specialize in charitable—"

"On one of the pillows," Isabel Cooney said. "Up near my head. And"—she gagged—"in my hair. I'm not sure. I kept blacking out."

Fred told Parker Stillton, "I have to make a speech. Before I start, Parker, you be thinking about what kind of lawyer Ms. Cooney wants. She needs guidance in both roles: victim and criminal. This other guy is your business, but he's going to stay where he is until he's hauled out of here by the—"

"You said he wanted to turn himself in," Parker Stillton objected. "How do *I* know what he wants?"

"It's my guess that's how it's going to work out: either he volunteers or he's drafted kind of thing. Now, my speech. Make yourself comfortable. Take off your coat." Parker gazed with longing at the scotch, abstained, and took off his suit jacket.

"Bobby Rotwell has a history of murdering people for fun and profit. The recent incidents are all I'll go into on that score, and what I really care about is completely beside that point anyway. I want you to talk to your Capstan Club friend what'shisname, Spar Ballard, and get him to call off this exhumation scam of—don't talk, Parker. There's nothing to argue about.

"You both know that Rotwell was cut off and cut out of the will by his father, after his mother...died. Then Lord Hanford remarried and came to live in this country—"

"Came to live in this country and *then* married Jane," Isabel Cooney corrected.

"Whatever," Fred said. "Let me finish. One particular item from Hanford's estate that went into the auction was not publicly identified as being of any value. But it had a considerable value, as Rotwell knew, and Isabel Cooney, and also a dealer from London named Alexander Small, who was supposed to buy this lot cheaply for the group. Cooney couldn't put up her hand to buy since that would be seen as a conflict of interest, and thanks to a restraining order, Rotwell couldn't show his face in Bristol County around his stepmother—a story there, I wonder, that nobody needs to know right now?"

Rotwell's eyes followed the narrative with sullen belligerence.

"The value of what these people wanted to buy was many millions of dollars, and they needed to buy it in open competition so that later, if they were challenged, Small could say, 'Everyone at that sale had the same chance. Everyone saw exactly what I saw. I was just smarter than they were.'

"Well, Parker, Small screwed up."

"The idiot took a taxi to Westport, Maine," Isabel Cooney said. "*M-E*, not *M-A*. Tiny difference." She poured scotch.

Fred said, "Don't drink that. I want you credible, and you want you smart." He took the glass out of her hand. "So someone else bought what the Rotwell group wanted," Fred continued. "After the sale was done and they'd compared notes, once they'd discovered they'd snookered *themselves*, only then did Bobby Rotwell start pretending he had a case and a reason to upset the will. You know yourself, as a man who gets paid by the hour—or are you in it for a percentage?—that there's no merit to Rotwell's claim. He was hoping to settle, and you've already talked together about what he would settle *for*.

"The problem is, Parker," Fred concluded, "your meal ticket is a sadistic rapist-killer."

"Is this true?" Parker asked Isabel Cooney. "Any of it? And I ask you this in my supervisory role as trustee of your employer, the Runnymede House Museum."

"The man is a sadistic rapist," Cooney affirmed. "As for the rest…"

"Small's body was found by wild dogs between here and Westport," Fred said. "Sorry, Ms. Cooney. That's brutal. It's like having your husband dug up to…Parker, won't you get a tax break of around forty thousand as long as last Sunday's sale remains unchallenged? Or if the challenge is withdrawn?"

Parker nodded his head wisely. "My client will need to consult, as well, with a criminal lawyer," he said. He studied the situation and added, "No. Not *as well—instead*. My first allegiance is to the board on which I serve, that of the Runnymede House Museum. To continue to represent this man, under the circumstances, might be seen as constituting a conflict of interest. Lord Bobby Junior—I mean, Mr. Rotwell—I herewith advise you to continue your present course, standing mute pending further counsel by your new attorney. Furthermore, I advise that you immediately withdraw your challenge to Lord Hanford's will. With your permission I will start the ball rolling. Will you face the police alone, or shall I find you an attorney?"

Rotwell nodded his head and spluttered around the gag. Parker Stillton coughed. "Fred," he said. "And Isabel—may I?—this is a delicate matter, but I would like to confirm your disinterested witness of Mr. Rotwell's assent to my propositions."

"We saw it," Fred said. "Ms. Cooney?"

"Affirmative," Isabel Cooney declared.

Parker Stillton rose and started for the bedroom. "Not in there," Fred ordered. "It's a crime scene. If you want to talk confidentially, use the phone on the desk in here. We won't listen; we're family."

Parker Stillton, in the green of the big window, stood mumbling into the telephone there.

"When he's finished I want to call my boyfriend," Isabel Cooney said. "After what I've been through, I'm going to need tons of support."

Fred asked her, "Where did Lord Hanford get the Turner drawings?"

"Alex knew all about that. Here's why none of this is fair: it was Alex who traced them in the first place. It took him years. It was his big find! Alex Small told Lord Hanford about them and got a whopping commission that he wasted on some fake Alma-Tademas, back when Alma-Tadema was big, after Lord Hanford got the collection. I mean that's when Alex got his commission, or finder's fee, or whatever they call it; we curators—"

"How did you come into the picture?" Fred interrupted.

"Alex got me the job with Bobbito—I mean, Lord Hanford—and told me to keep my eye on the collection."

Parker Stillton crossed the room and stood over Bobby Rotwell. "Ishmael Bedford has agreed to represent you," he said.

"Go on," Fred told Isabel Cooney.

"Will they arrest me?"

"They'll talk to you for a long time, but they probably won't take you into custody. Parker, you're lining up someone for Ms. Cooney?" Stillton nodded his head and went back to mumble into the phone again.

"Go on," Fred pressed. "Alex got you the job as Hanford's curator and told you to keep your eye on the drawings. Why? They're an amazing find! Why in the devil didn't you publish them, frame them, exhibit them? Instead of all those William Holman Hunts and *Stags at Bay* he had? Keep your eyes open? What in the hell for?"

"She didn't have a clue what they were."

Parker Stillton called from his station at the desk, "Isabel, I have Margo Parker on the line. Will you take it?"

"One moment," Fred demanded.

"'One moment,' hell!" Isabel Cooney said, getting up fast and making for the telephone. "We're talking rape and attempted murder. We're talking *ME!*"

Parker Stillton wandered across the white carpet and stood by his former client's head. "At least this way he can't say anything that can be used against him," he remarked.

"There's nothing I want to hear him say at all," Fred agreed.

"I have shares in the Royal Court chain," Parker said. "A few of us do. They are not publicly offered."

Fred nodded. "When the story gets out, it should do wonders for their value: Alexander Small beaten to death, strangled, raped—

whatever Rotwell did to him—and then wrapped up in a blue tarpaulin and dragged out in a duffel bag. People are going to flock in when they read all about the class of guest you cater to."

Parker said hastily, "I'll sell my shares immediately. Isabel! I need the phone urgently!"

Isabel Cooney had finished her call and disconnected and was now dialing someone else. She fought Parker Stillton off until she could complete a frantic call to Osbert, Heap, Fine, P.C.

"He's rushing over," she told Fred. "My boyfriend. Now, whatever I may have said about Alex, when I was in shock—"

"Go on, Isabel. You were saying, 'She didn't have a clue what she had'—who didn't? *Who* didn't have a clue?"

"Jane. The wife, Lady Jane. Why in the hell do you think Bobby Hanford married her? He was still trying to get her to give them to him when he died. She wouldn't. They embarrassed her. And then I told her, look, don't be shy. Let's put those dirty drawings in the sale and get some good out of them."

⸺∙⸺

Cooney's lawyer arrived first, followed shortly afterward by six uniforms in the company of Rotwell's lawyer. Fred helped until it was clear to everyone that he was on his, her, or their side. Then he slipped out and sidled down the corridor to the stairs.

Mrs. Wen, the concierge, had been replaced at the desk by a portly, elderly man with bright-white hair straight out of the bag. He was looking with dramatic disapproval at John Columbo's yellow leather pants.

"He told me four-fifteen," Columbo insisted.

"His telephone does not answer," Mr. Roody said firmly, in the same sad tone adopted by the mortician when the corpse sits up at the wake.

"He moved up to eight-twelve, John," Fred whispered into Columbo's ear. The picker jerked, startled. "It's OK," Fred assured him. "Go on up. You may have missed a memorable one-on-one, but Rotwell will see you, though I can't promise he'll notice you. I'm on my way to deal with the Clayton aspect now."

Chapter 29

After legging it to Park Street at a pace designed to resemble exercise rather than escape, Fred called Mass. General and demanded Marek's room. When, after many rings, an irritated nurse answered, Fred asked, "There's been a woman, Lakshmi Thomas, visiting?"

"She left. Tell you the truth, she was asked to leave."

"Mr. Hricsó's worse?"

"We're not allowed to say, but—no, we are better. We're moving upstairs tomorrow, aren't we Mr. Harxo?" A faint, halting, masculine voice responded at her end.

———

Fred was about to descend into the subway when he recalled Molly's car. Where had he left it? Remembering, he was obliged to trundle back to Newbury Street and retrieve it from the parking lot.

The afternoon burned toward evening as the day's traffic crawled out of Boston. If Marek was talking, and if he was making sense, Fred should be off the wanted list and thus free to stop by Mountjoy Street. However, if some electronic link existed between the forces of law and order at the Royal Court Hotel, suite 812, and the rest of the Boston force, someone, right about now, would be wanting to ask Fred where he was, and why, and where he'd been.

There's nothing at Clay's I need, Fred concluded. I could stop at the nearest library or neighborhood bookstore or museum and find out what I know I'm going to learn as soon as I get a chance to do some work on my own: the painting by Turner that Roberto has had all week was done at Petworth House. I *know* it, and why shouldn't something I know this well turn out to be true?

He hadn't seen much of Molly and the kids for days, and he'd be swept up tomorrow doing whatever he'd have to do to get the district attorney of Suffolk County to leave him alone. Then there'd be the Bristol County authorities next, wondering why he had failed to mention that he knew the identity of the dead John Doe the dogs had been at. But Bristol County's D.A. was Spar Ballard, and Spar was family. Fred would make it through.

Then he'd have to pick up his car at the Silver Spur. Maybe Molly would drive down there with him—except with her mom coming home the next day, she'd be spending all day Saturday dipping Prince Charles in bleach and rolling him across the worst parts of the carpet.

<hr />

A hot Friday night in Harvard Square allowed no place to park near Wombswell Croft. When he finally found a space down by the river, Fred had seven blocks to walk, and therefore time to start letting loose ends unravel and worry at him. He took his time and did not reach Rush Street until almost seven. Prince Charles was out front on his leash, looking sad, tied to the sign-post. An ominous sound of vacuuming came from within.

"Ho, Molly!" Fred shouted, marching inside. "Burn your apron. I'm taking everyone out to dinner."

Molly turned off the machine and called from upstairs, "'Everyone' is just me. My sister Ophelia said, 'Hell, if Fred won't do it, I'll take the kids fishing. Let them come for the weekend.'"

She appeared at the top of the stairs, wearing only a pair of tan shorts and looking frazzled, delicious, and dangerous. "Can you do the kitchen and the half-bathroom downstairs?"

"You look very nice."

"*Now* you talk," Molly said. "Listen, Lakshmi will be here with something to eat in about an hour, and Mom's coming home tomorrow."

"I thought you said Sunday?"

"I did. The goddamned charter got changed. So the kids are spending the night with Ophelia. Now, don't bother me."

Fred sat in the living room and interviewed voice-activated computers until he got the number for Clayton's New Haven hotel. Clay was in 716, a suite. "Yes?" he admitted when he picked up the phone.

"It's Fred. We are moving along."

"I am expected for sherry, Fred. I do not wish to seem brusque, but—"

"Right. I'll run through it quickly, then. First, I'll bet you three dollars that the big Turner painting you own was done at Petworth House. The Wyndham family—well, Lakshmi has a new conspiracy theory that the drawings passed down through them somehow. Lord Leconfield—or is it Lord Egremont?—the present owner—"

Clay interrupted, "Gad, Fred, don't speak so cavalierly. Must you allow that young woman to spread such rumors? I declare, she has become a *fountain* of fiction! Max Egremont is above reproach: a trustee of both the Wallace Collection, as was his father before him, and the British Museum! I cannot say he is my friend, not as yet, but he moves in circles into which I shortly expect…but enough! Let us not carelessly toss away the opportunity, should it arise, by casting unwarranted aspersions."

"Gotcha," said Fred. "Well, on to more mundane affairs. I had Rotwell arrested, but not until after I'd made his attorney, your cousin Parker Stillton, call off the bogus challenge to the will."

"Yes? Yes?" Clay prompted. "Excellent, Fred. You will fill out the details later, as needed. I am relieved beyond description. So my ownership is unclouded, beyond the question of whether their import was legal in the first place. There are loose ends, but this will do for now. Excellent work. I expected no less. Is there more?"

Fred said, "I'm confused, even buffaloed. According to Isabel Cooney—I was able to get her attention for a few minutes this afternoon—the Turners didn't belong to Lord Hanford at all. Not ever. They belonged to his *wife*. If Cooney's to be believed, Lord Hanford married her in order to get hold of them. He never told her what she had."

"Good God," Clay said. "They belonged to the widow all along! Even before she was a widow! Even before she was married! We have been barking up the wrong tree. Do I hear a dog?"

"It's outside," Fred assured him. "This is a secure phone."

"I have no reason to distrust any service provided by the Royal Court chain. As it happens, though they are not publicly offered, Fred, I own shares...."

"Parker Stillton is selling his," Fred said. "Because of this scandal in the Boston branch, which he thinks will depreciate—"

"The man's a cretin," Clay interrupted testily. "Does he not recognize that nobility and scandal are inseparable? Nobility is already a scandal. It's why we had our revolution. Fred, now that we have learned that the provenance of the Turners descends through the line of the widow—will that settle the issue of import, I wonder?—would it be too much to ask you to drive to Westport again this evening...?"

"Yes," Fred said.

"My point is, Fred, you have already established such a fine rapport with Lady Hanford."

Fred said, "When you speak to her, tell her you want her to have your Constable. I left it with her. She has been royally cheated. She likes the picture. Tell her it's a token, a tribute, a reward— you'll think of something. I know you have to run. Whatever you're in New Haven for is of such blistering importance—what is it, a wedding? I really don't care. I've got business of my own, Clay. Pressing business. Miss Thomas will call you later. For the rest, we can take our time—or at least *I* can."

———

Lakshmi showed up dressed in seventeen narrow red and white stripes, with a bucket of chicken strapped to her briefcase. "I've got your villain, Fred," she shouted, locking her bike to the post where Prince Charles's ecstasy was quickly replaced by despair as the chicken bounced out of his ken and up the porch steps.

"Marek's better," Fred said.

"Yes. Sure. Those bastards stole or threw away my Harvard library books, and I'm responsible. They weren't even supposed to circulate. I raised holy hell, but—"

"Sorry," Fred told her. "I took them. I'd have left you a—"

"You son of a bitch," Lakshmi said. "I'll get you. I was going to have to go crawling to Mr. Rudenstine, who's so busy....Marek asked me to open up the shop for him, but I've got all this work for Mr. Reed, and my thesis to work on. I don't know."

"So he's talking," Fred said.

"Yes, sure; in fact, they can't make him stop. He's been trying to tell you he's sorry he couldn't hold out. Fred, he's really sorry. He did his best, I know."

"And he named Rotwell?"

"On tape and on paper and signed. Where's Molly?" She opened the screen door and yelled, "Molly! Come down here!"

The chicken smelled like just what the doctor ordered (everyone not to have). Fred got out paper plates and beer and ice water, and they set themselves up on the porch steps, the only people on all of Rush Street who understood how to make proper use of a stoop on a hot night.

"Everything but fireflies," Fred said.

Although Molly had remembered to put on a shirt, she was almost as close to nude as Lakshmi was. She chose a chicken thigh out of the tub and licked her fingers.

"I told you I had your villain," Lakshmi reminded Fred, breaking a plastic fork into the potato salad. "You're not interested?"

"I thought you meant Bobby Rotwell," Fred said.

"Oh, no. I'm talking about John Ruskin. I have him dead to rights. It was John Ruskin all along," she said around a mouthful of the Colonel's corn bread. "I can't wait to tell Mr. Reed. See, all those dirty pictures did belong to the British government. They were in the Turner Bequest, and I can prove it. I found out that in eighteen sixty-one, ten years after Turner died, Parliament's House of Lords got antsy about the Turner Bequest and whether it was being handled properly. Also, someone had heard rumors about a batch of obscene pictures being part of it, so the Lords huffily called Lord Eastlake up on the carpet. He confessed that, well, yes, there had been some quote *reserved parcels which he himself did not look into: things fastened up and labeled by the Executors 'not fit for general inspection' or words to that effect. We did not open them so that I cannot speak to them from my own observation,* Eastlake claimed.

"So Lord Eastlake is on record as saying this in the House of Lords. But then you go on in time, and someone else says this, and Rossetti says that, and the story never really dies, or gets finished, and then years later Frank Harris—you know his *My Life and Loves*? Wait a minute, this I have to read you."

Lakshmi wiped her hands on a napkin and pulled the book from her briefcase. "Listen to this. According to Harris, Ruskin told him that while he was cataloging the Turner Bequest, *one day (I think it was in 'fifty-seven) 'I came across a portfolio filled with painting after painting of Turner's of the most shameful sort—the pudenda of women—utterly inexcusable and to me inexplicable. I went to work to find out all about it and I ascertained that my hero used to leave his house…and go down to Wapping on Friday afternoon and live there until Monday morning with the sailors' women, painting them in every posture of abandonment. What a life! And what a burden it cast upon me! What was I to do?*

"*'For weeks I was in doubt and miserable, though time and again I put myself in tune with the highest, till suddenly it flashed upon me that perhaps I had been selected as the one man capable of coming in this matter to a great decision. I took the hundreds of scrofulous sketches and paintings and burnt them where they were, burnt all of them. Don't you think I did right? I am proud of it, proud—' and,* Harris said, *his lower lip went up over the upper with a curious effect of most obstinate resolution.*"

"God, what a crime," Molly said. "Except—but he didn't destroy them at all. Clay has them. These are the very works in Clay's collection!"

"Yeah, but remember, this is Frank Harris talking," Fred pointed out. "Frank Harris was not a notoriously dependable witness."

"Poor old Turner," Molly said. "After a long hard week strapped to his easel, doing sunsets and ships, he had to go down to the docks to unwind. It sometimes occurs to me that a man can get so caught up in his professional work that he forgets his part in the business of procreation, and all that that entails."

"Ha! But there's more," Lakshmi proclaimed, a smile of triumph lighting her face. A couple passing down the middle of Rush Street, heading for Harvard Square, looked over at her and away again, quickly minding their business. Lakshmi pulled from her briefcase a final sheet of paper. "OK, listen, we're going to get enough on John Ruskin to convict him. Harris is corroborated—but it gets more complicated. In nineteen seventy-five, a man named Andrew Wilton found a letter in the library of the National Gallery, written by Ruskin himself to R. N. Wornum."

"Who's R. N. Wornum?" Fred asked. A langorous sense of *who cares?* was drifting up Rush Street from the river, aided and abetted by the warm evening, the beer, and the letdown after a fitful afternoon.

"Fred doesn't remember names," Molly confided to Lakshmi. "It's one of his things: he travels light. Ralph Wornum, Fred, was the keeper, or curator, of the National Gallery in London when Lord Eastlake was the director. So, Lakshmi, what did this letter say?"

Lakshmi stood under the porch light, most of her bronze skin shining a welcoming defiance at the bugs, looking—except for the seventeen stripes—like a Victorian Truth defying Cupid.

"Ruskin to Wornum, then, dated May third, eighteen sixty-two," she read. *"As the authorities have not thought it proper to register the reserved parcel of Turner's sketchbooks, and have given me no direction about them, and as the grossly obscene drawings contained in them could not be lawfully in one's possession, I am satisfied that you had no other course than to burn them, both for the sake of Turner's reputation (they having been assuredly drawn under a certain condition of insanity) and for your own peace. And I am glad to be able to bear witness to their destruction, and I hereby declare that the parcel of them was undone by me, and all the obscene drawings it contained burnt in my presence in the month of December eighteen fifty-eight. Signed, John Ruskin."*

"So, great. We have everything we need to prove to the world that what Clayton bought does not exist," Fred said. "Will you call him, Lakshmi, or shall I?"

Molly said, "No. The letter is a lie. It's like any politician manufacturing evidence after the fact. Ruskin and Wornum were bewildered, or else they were covering their own or each other's asses. Do you know, at the Victoria and Albert Museum, where they have a full-sized replica of Michelangelo's *David*, they still keep a big old plaster fig leaf in a box, to hook over the hero's plaster wibble-wobbles should the queen happen by? Suppose Ruskin or Wornum, or the pair of them, walked off with that collection of drawings? *Somebody* saved it, and whoever that somebody was, he was a hero. In its day, such erotica, according to Ruskin's own words, could not *lawfully* be in the possession of anyone, not even the queen! So to save it, someone committed a crime. Someone took a huge risk."

"Yes, 'someone,'" Fred agreed. "But who? And how? There's one more piece of chicken, the wing, which happens to be my favorite part. Does anyone want it?"

"I do," Lakshmi said. "It makes you wonder, doesn't it, how, in those days, they managed to get the human race perpetuated?"

"I frequently wonder, even now," Molly said. "People get so distracted."

"So I thought to myself, Maybe it's Wornum," Lakshmi said, between expert lateral bites at the crisp skin. "These two men in front of a bonfire in the National Gallery: either one could have fooled the other. Or someone else could have fooled them. Neither one would have dared to be seen looking at what they were burning. But you know, they weren't blind. They did *see* each other, all these people. They got turned on, like the rest of us. They were human; they were just funny about it. I mean, here's someone talking about Wornum as a young man—you know me, I pick up much too much flotsam and jetsam—when he *was writing articles for the Society for the Diffusion of Useful Knowledge, and his editor, Professor George Long, the well-known classical scholar, had a young and statuesque*—read: She was built!—*American stepdaughter, the very image of Clytie* (that's one of those Greek Victorian naked marble women—one of the muses, maybe), *but more amiable; and this Miss Selden became Mrs. Wornum.* I mean they could see and feel and touch and all the rest of it, most of them—except for that pervert Ruskin—but they just *had* to pin fig leaves on everything. Ralph Wornum, said his friend William Scott, *was a Hercules in muscular development, and he married one of the most perfectly formed and beautiful women in London.*"

"Kathy Selden," Molly said.

"What?" Fred and Lakshmi asked together.

"Why don't you look around and ask around and find out what happened to Wornum's American wife, and her siblings and cousins back home?" Molly suggested. "Pay attention to the women for a change. Start by asking your young widow in Westport. She was Jane *Selden*, remember? Selden. The same as Wornum's wife. Same name. Same family. She was Jane Selden until she was swallowed up by Lady Hanford."

Chapter 30

Molly went upstairs to execute rough censorship on the children's bedrooms while Fred and Lakshmi dragged the telephone out onto the porch. Prince Charles complained from the outpost of his little empire that he had been many long, dull, hard years waiting on his leash. Lakshmi had been blathering on about Victorian lit, until it seemed to Fred almost time to send her to the store for something.

"Then I thought," Lakshmi continued, inspired by the light of discovery, "what if I did my thesis just on Turner's poetry? Any work you do on a woman, it keeps getting shoved into Women's Studies, and people forget it's literature, whereas a man, however bad his stuff is, they always keep him in the camp of Art. There are bushels of Turner's poetry, and nobody will care that it's no good. He tacked scraps of his own verse to his picture frames when he hung his great works at the Royal Academy shows for people to grovel in front of. Listen to this—it's from his 'Fallacies of Hope,' but he stuck it on a painting he called *The Fountain of Fallacy*, in eighteen thirty-nine: *Its rainbow-dew diffused fell in each anxious lip/Working wild fantasy, imagining:/First, Science in the immeasurable abyss of thought/Measured her orbits slumbering....*

"You gotta ask yourself, now, given all we know about his dirty pictures, what are these orbits, really, that the old boy wants to measure while the lady slumbers? But my problem is, I'd go crazy. If all you're going to prove is that the poet keeps thinking about tail, it makes for a real slow read. Besides, these poems of his turn out to be as vague as they are awful. It's the trouble with English lit. So I guess I'll stick to Lady Eastlake. With her at least you get good stories—about *people*. And maybe in ten thousand years folks will take her out of Women's Studies and put her in with the humans."

"About time to call Clay," Fred said. "Why don't you get that going and put me on when you're done?"

Fred sat on the top step, looking into the dusk of Rush Street and smelling the hints of river and earth and sky filtering past the declaration of civilization. Molly's militant cleaning rattled the house. Lakshmi started to argue with operators.

"He's in the Duke of York Room," she told Fred sotto voce. "It's a secret meeting of hush-hush bigwigs from Yale.

"Yes," she said sharply into the phone. "It's an absolute emergency. I am Mr. Reed's personal confidential assistant. Mr. Reed instructed me to telephone him at this time. I don't care if he's with the Duke of Earl, interrupt them!" She turned back to Fred. "You gotta be rough with these people," she informed him. "If there's anything worse than the upper class, it's the jokers who block for them. It's OK. They're getting him."

Fred let his gaze and attention dawdle in the pleasant wash of evening. From the music and speed of Lakshmi's words, he could easily infer the progression of irritations and emotions on the far, and wonderfully invisible, end of the conversation. Inside, the house crashed its own accompaniment, responding to the ministrations of a Molly whose energies had been revived by chicken and potato salad and her own version of the fear of womankind.

"Well, yes, yes, I suppose I could," Lakshmi said into the phone. She waited for the buzz on the far side. "Yes, sure," she said. "And I can bring down Finberg's inventory as well, since that proves the Venice group. Yes?" She raised her eyebrows desperately at Fred, who nodded confirmation. The books were inside. For all her panic, Molly would not have tossed them, would she?

"But that's very sweet of you," Lakshmi exclaimed. "I'd love to."

Clay's deliberate buzzing continued for another five minutes, interrupted only by syllables of encouragement from Lakshmi, until she finished, "See you tomorrow, then. Sure, here he is."

"Will you give Miss Thomas what she needs to buy her ticket to New Haven?" Clay asked Fred. "She has agreed to bring me the fruits of her research, and to write the preliminary summary report for the acquisitions committee, while she is on the train. I understand from her that she will use a thing she calls a laptop. This sounds indiscreet. She is a liberated young female person. Do you know what a laptop is? Is it decent?"

"Just a computer," Fred assured him. "But Clay, what's going on?"

"It is my intention to present my collection of Turner drawings and sketches to the Center for British Art at Yale University. The matter is even now under negotiation."

"I'm flabbergasted," Fred said. "That's a huge gift. But listen, Clay, there's going to be trouble if you go public with the collection. There's no possible doubt that however it was accomplished, and whenever, the whole thing was stolen from Her British Majesty's government. Times have changed. They're going to want them back. They'll put up a ruckus."

Lakshmi's face fell. She'd been packing her papers back into her briefcase, sitting next to Fred and listening. Clay tutted and paused, annoyed, amused, or distraught—who could tell without seeing his face? When he spoke, it was clearly for more ears than Fred's alone.

"I have not failed to take this eventuality into account," he said. "Our claim—Yale University's claim—shall be that the British Empire, in its limited prudery, and represented by imbeciles, forfeited its ownership of this parcel of works by its greatest master until Francis Bacon. Nonetheless, I recognize that there may be prolonged discussion. The matter shall soon be out of my hands. Even so, my confidence is serene. In any contest between my alma mater and the United Kingdom, why need we doubt the outcome?"

"You haven't mentioned the...the wrapper...that the drawings came in," Fred said.

Clay chuckled. "I have not, and I shall not," he announced. "Good God, I have not lost my sense of priorities entirely! Once the university has prevailed in any struggle that may develop, my personal right and title to that object will be, coincidentally, cemented to the satisfaction of the world. And Fred, pursuant to your excellent suggestion—I have had a moment free this afternoon to pursue my own research here—I shall give the object in question the title *Interior at Petworth*. Yes, Lord Gmfrdg?" He had covered the mouthpiece. "Fred, I must ring off. A small group of connoisseurs has gathered here to examine...you will excuse me?"

"I'm staying in New Haven tomorrow night, and then the night after," Lakshmi said, delighted. "As Mr. Reed's guest, in the Royal Court Hotel! He's booked me a room! Then he asked, would I mind very much—and did I have suitable clothing—standing beside him at some kind of tea thing they're having on Sunday."

"Probably dropping crates of tea into New Haven Harbor," Fred said. "You'll want your overalls."

Lakshmi didn't hear this last. "You don't suppose…," she faltered. "You don't suppose…Mr. Reed is the most unique, strangest person I ever met except for my Aunt Chieftain. Do you think…?"

"I'll get you those books," Fred said from the screen door.

"Then there's something else I'm not supposed to tell you," Lakshmi teased.

"OK," Fred said.

"He's invited me to attend the convocation next October when they give him his doctorate in the fine arts, *honoris causa*. He's to be some honorary curator or trustee thing, too, of the British art center. Don't tell him I told you. They're making up the fall list this weekend, the committee is. It's why we had to rush to do the research, so he could give them the drawings in time, and they'd elect, appoint him, vote—whatever it is they do. Nobody's supposed to know, especially you."

"Your secret is safe with me," Fred promised.

As he saw her off, Fred untied Prince Charles's leash and stood holding it until Lakshmi's stripes were out of sight. Then he called up to Molly, "What about this dog?"

Molly raised the screen in the window of what had been Terry's room, over the porch roof.

"I can run him down to the river and let him swim," Fred offered. "But that might make him worse."

"Fred, there's a bunch of boxes filled with very odd stuff in the basement. Do you know anything about them?"

"Oops!" said Fred. "That's some loose ends."

"Speaking of loose ends," Molly said, "and speaking also as one who is about to take a much-deserved shower—Fred, you look very silly holding that tiny dog on a string—did you ever get around to reading the message I gave you?"

"What message?"

"Yesterday. Lakshmi hates Turner's poems, but I happened to find one I liked. You never even looked at it. You stuck it in your damned shirt pocket."

"I did?" Fred reached for it and found the Xerox paper, which had crackled once but whose crackling days were now long gone. As he started to unfold it one-handed—the other hand now being occupied by Prince Charles—Molly called, "Read it aloud, Fred, why don't you? I want all of Rush Street to hear."

"It looks like a song," Fred objected.

"Then sing it. I can take a little serenading."

What he lacked in talent, Fred did his best to make up for with gusto, adapting what might pass for the tune of the national anthem of Kashmir:

> *By thy lips' quivering motion I ween*
> *To the center where love lies between*
> *A passport to bliss is thy will*
> *Yet I prithee dear Molly be still.*

> *By thy Eyes which half closed in delight*
> *That so languishly turn from the light*
> *With kisses I'll hide them I will*
> *So I prithee dear Molly be still....*

"But I don't *want* you to be still," Fred interrupted himself.

"Sing on. There's another verse," Molly demanded.

Into the cool silence of Rush Street, Fred went on singing, accompanied only by the howling of a very worried Prince Charles.

> *By the touch of thy lips and the rove of my hand*
> *By the critical moment no maid can withstand*
> *Then a bird in the bush is worth two in the hand*
> *Oh Molly dear Molly I will.*

"OK," Molly agreed. "Give me half an hour. That should be time enough for you to finish up Mom's kitchen."

Afterword

Erotic art remains the dirty little secret of art production and con-sumption.[1] We can see from the scale and variety of pornographic web sites today that there is a virtually unlimited (dare one say insatiable?) demand for clandestine, yet available, erotic material in every medium, even for the newest, electronic forms, and this truth can be confirmed for each preceding technology. Think of all the "hard-core" film loops available only through mail order as well as more "soft-core" adult movies, whose viewing sites may range from "peep shows" to more public X-rated movie houses. One film scholar, Linda Williams, has even devoted a major study to defining the variety and forms of pornographic films as a dis-creet (pun intended) genre of its own.[2] Indeed, it is arguable that one of the few human constants across cultures for visual imagery is sexual: scholars who have almost no other access to the reli-gious or cultural meaning of ancient cave paintings and carvings do agree that many of them have sexual meaning. Some of the earliest stone figures from prehistoric Europe depict buxom female figures with explicit genitalia.

Of course, cultures vary in what eroticism they determine to be permitted for display as well as what they find stimulating or forbidden. As one character famously put this dictum in the play *Teahouse of the August Moon*, "pornography is a question of geography." We are all familiar with the debates on censorship and the limits of sexual explicitness in the public domain here in America, from the famous trial of James Joyce's *Ulysses* to all of the local squabbles that have rendered "banned in Boston" a badge of honor. Certainly the cultural variety of explicitness in the visual arts ranges widely in other parts of the world, for example in Asia from the celebrated erotic couplings on medieval Hindu temples in India to the "floating world" (*ukiyo-e*) colored woodblock prints of Edo Japan's urban night life in the early nineteenth century.

European art really began its flirtation with the erotic during the Italian Renaissance, when the revival of interest in Roman antiquities and pagan mythology stimulated an innovative fascination with the nude human body. Celebrated leading painters, such as Michelangelo, Correggio, and Titian, provided charged erotic images of the "loves of the gods" for their sophisticated and princely patrons. At the same time the rise of a new, inexpensive medium of printmaking further facilitated the production of private, often more sexually explicit material, previously the exclusive and costly prerogative of those princely palace bedchambers.[3] Indeed the first major case of censorship was a papal ban on the distribution of hard-core images of intercourse, *I modi* ("The Positions"), engraved by Raphael's designated printmaker, Marcantonio Raimondi, after designs by his major disciple, Giulio Romano, a noted painter of the erotic for the court of Mantua. And homosexual imagery did not lag far behind, with the myth of youthful Ganymede abducted by a lustful Jupiter providing the principal prototype.[4]

We associate both bawdiness and sexual explicitness with the fashions and artwork of eighteenth-century France and England (as well as with the rise of early novels, where such figures as Defoe's *Moll Flanders* or Cleland's *Fanny Hill*, not to mention Fielding's *Tom Jones* or Laclos' *Les Liaisons Dangereuses*, set a tone of permissive yet socially structured erotic behavior). But the nineteenth century, the epoch of J.M.W. Turner (1775-1851), is more closely associated with the rise of Victorian mores and the driving of explicit sexuality underground.[5] During the course of the nineteenth century, visualized sexuality usually assumed the mantle of exotic Orientalism (harems and slave auctions in the Levant) or respectable mythology; otherwise it remained the covert and private domain of individual prints or drawings, such as the brothel imagery of Degas or Toulouse-Lautrec, or else shifted to the clandestine offerings in the newest mass-produced medium: photography.

Turner himself is best known for his landscape art and his mastery of both oils and watercolors as expressive media. The artist's official position as of 1807 was Professor of Perspective at the Royal Academy in London (a member since 1799), so his training largely consisted of human figure painting, and his surroundings fully encouraged an awareness of Old Master pictorial traditions. These conditions render the circumstances of Nicholas Kilmer's boldly imagined stash of secret Turners eminently plausible, though there is no hard evidence for them in the official corpus of the artist's works (compiled by Andrew Wilton) to suggest that such a cache existed or exists. Yet in Turner's era and with his own elevated public standing and prominence, we could well understand that such visual experiments, if undertaken, would necessarily remain secret and hidden.

Wilton describes the artist's private life as "destined to be secret, and largely surreptitious."[6] The artist never married, though he is known to have had an intimate relationship with a young widow, Sarah Danby, who bore him two girls; the artist maintained his small family in London during much of his early successes at the Academy, until the end of the 1820s. Wilton does offer the tantalizing note that "there are pages in his sketchbooks rough scribbles of nude figures which offer evidence enough that he was prone to erotic fantasies." [7]

An early biographer, Walter Thornbury (1862) reported that the artist frequented the brothels of portside Wapping and there made drawings of prostitutes like Degas and Toulouse-Lautrec, but there is no corroboration for this claim. The artist's acolyte and promoter, John Ruskin (1819-1900), a major writer, critic, and artist but also a noted prude[8] does indeed attest that a parcel of sketchbooks containing "grossly obscene drawings" (not that Ruskin's threshold for obscenity was very high) was burned in his presence from the Turner bequest to the National Gallery in December 1858.[9] The contents of that parcel remain unknown.

From such small seeds grow the literary fruits of imagination, and Nicholas Kilmer has managed to extrapolate a plausible, if secreted Turner artistic past, a seamy underbelly which pops up bumptiously and threateningly into the light of the fictional present. However, if there is a presiding spirit over this intriguing and learned yarn, it is Lakshmi, the name of the mythological equivalent of Venus in India, born from the churning of the sea and associated with the ideals of love and beauty. Those of us who are art historians as well as mystery buffs can delight in this recreation, using the mystery of art to make the art of mystery.

Larry Silver,
Farquhar Professor of History of Art
University of Pennsylvania
Summer, 2000

1. Surprisingly few serious studies of erotic art have been attempted. A useful pictorial survey is Edward Lucie-Smith, *Sexuality in Western Art* (London: Thames and Hudson, 1991)

2. Linda Williams, *Hard Core* (Berkeley: U. of California Press, 1999)

3. Bette Talvacchia, *Taking Positions. On the Erotic in Renaissance Culture* (Princeton: Princeton University Press, 1999)

4. James Saslow, *Ganymede in the Renaissance: Homosexuality in Art and Society* (New Haven: Yale University Press, 1986); Leonard Barkan, *Transuming Passion. Ganymede and the Erotics of Humanism* (Stanford: Stanford University Press, 1991)

5. For studies of Turner, the principal names to know are Andrew Wilton, especially his *J.M.W. Turner. His Art and Life* (Secaucus: Poplar, 1979), and Andrew Gage, especially his *J.M.W. Turner. A Wonderful Range of Mind* (New Haven: Yale U. Press, 1987); more briefly, now see Sam Smiles, *J.M.W. Turner* (Princeton: Princeton U. Press, 2000).

6. Wilton, *Art and Life*, 17.

7. Wilton, *Art and Life*, 16.

8. Ruskin wooed and married a young woman, Effie Gray, who sued him for annulment six years later, because he failed to consummate their marriage, This compromising fact is noted by Kilmer, with characteristically good research, through the scornful voice of Lakshmi Chapter 24.

9. Letter from Ruskin to R.N. Wornum, dated May 3, 1862, now in the National Gallery Library; cited by Wilton, *Art and Life*, 17, n. 36. For Ruskin's biography, Wolfgang Kemp, *The Desire of my Eyes. The Life and Work of John Ruskin* (New York: Noonday, 1990), esp. 137-40.

To receive a free catalog of other Poisoned Pen Press titles, please contact us in one of the following ways:

Phone: 1-800-421-3976
Facsimile: 1-480-949-1707
Email: info@poisonedpenpress.com
Website: www.poisonedpenpress.com

Poisoned Pen Press
6962 E. First Ave. Ste 103
Scottsdale, AZ 85251